Praise for the
New York Times bes

RACH
VINCENT

'I iked the character and loved the action. I look
f rward to reading the next book in the series.'
Charlaine Harris

Vincent is a welcome addition to the genre!'
Kelley Armstrong

'C npelling and edgy, dark and evocative, *Stray* is a
nust read! I loved it from beginning to end.'
Gena Showalter

'I iad trouble putting this book down. Every time
said I was going to read just one more chapter,
I'd find myself three chapters later.'
Bitten by Books on *Stray*

' ent continues to impress with the freshness of her
oroach and voice. Action and intrigue abound.'
RT Book Reviews

Find out more about Rachel Vincent by visiting
mirabooks.co.uk/rachelvincent
and read Rachel's blog at urbanfantasy.blogspot.com

Also available from **Rachel Vincent**

THE STARS
NEVER
RISE

RACHEL
VINCENT

MIRA Ink is a registered trademark of Harlequin Enterprises Limited, used under licence.

Published in Great Britain 2015
MIRA Ink, an imprint of Harlequin (UK) Limited,
Eton House, 18-24 Paradise Road,
Richmond, Surrey, TW9 1SR

© 2015 Rachel Vincent

Jacket art © 2015 Mark Swan/kid-ethic.com

ISBN: 978-1-848-45383-8
eBook ISBN: 978-1-474-02845-5

47-0615

Harlequin (UK) Limited's policy is to use papers that are natural, renewable and recyclable products and made from wood grown in sustainable forests. The logging and manufacturing processes conform to the legal environmental regulations of the country of origin.

Printed and bound by
CPI Group (UK) Ltd, Croydon, CR0 4YY

Rachel Vincent is the *New York Times* bestselling author of many books for adults and for teens, including the Shifters, Unbound, and Soul Screamer series. A resident of Oklahoma, she has two teenagers, two cats and a BA in English, each of which contributes in some way to every book she writes. When she's not working, Rachel can be found curled up with a book or watching movies and playing video games with her husband.

Visit Rachel online at
rachelvincent.com
Follow Rachel Vincent on

To my husband,
who helped me brainstorm this project
in various versions for two full years
before I even told my agent about it.
Thanks for all the plotting sessions,
for the sketches you drew of my concepts
and for your endless patience.
You're the best.
No, really.

ONE

There's never a good time of day to cross town with a bag full of stolen goods, but of all the possibilities, five a.m. was the hour best suited to that particular sin.

Five a.m. and I were well acquainted.

"Nina, hurry!" Marta whispered, glancing over my shoulder at the cold, dark backyard, but she probably couldn't see much of the neat lawn beyond the rectangle of light shining through the open screen door. "Mrs. Turner's already up." She wiped flour from one hand with a rag, then flipped the lock and pushed the door open slowly so it wouldn't squeal and give us away.

"Sorry. Mr. Howard locked his back gate, so I had to go the long way." My teeth still chattering, I stepped into the Turners' warm kitchen and handed Marta the garment bag I'd carried folded over my right arm. The plastic was freezing from my predawn trek. Marta would have to hang the uniforms near a heater vent, or Sarah Turner would figure out that her school clothes hadn't spent the night in her warm house, and I'd be out of a job. Again.

I couldn't afford to lose this one.

Marta set her rag on the butcher-block kitchen island, where she'd been cutting out homemade biscuits, then hooked the hangers—I'd bundled them just like the dry cleaner would have—over the door to a formal dining room half the size of my house. I'd been in there once. The Turners' cloth napkins probably cost more than my whole wardrobe.

Mr. Turner owned the factory that made the Church cassocks—official robes—for most of the region. I found that ironic, considering the illicit work I was doing on his daughter's clothes, but I refused to feel guilty. The Turners' monthly tithe would feed my whole family for a year.

"They're all here?" Marta unzipped the garment bag to inspect my work.

"Same as always. Five blouses, five pairs of slacks, all starched and pressed. That raspberry stain came out too." I picked up the sleeve of the first blouse to show her the bright white cuff, and when she bent to study the material, I took a can of beef stew from the shelf at my back and slid it into the pocket of my oversized jacket.

"Good. Here's next week's batch." Marta straightened and gestured to a bulging brown paper bag sitting on the tile countertop. "Sarah cut herself and bled on one of them. . . ." She opened the bag and lifted the stained tail of a blouse at the top of the pile. "I told her blood won't come out of white cotton, so she's already replaced it, which means you're welcome to keep this one. The stain'll never show with it tucked in."

"Thanks." I mentally added the secondhand blouse to the small collection of school uniforms my sister and I actually owned.

Marta rolled down the top of the bag and shoved it at me, and when she turned to open a drawer beneath the counter, I slid another can of stew into my other pocket. My coat hung evenly now, and the weight of real food was reassuring.

"And here's your cash." She pressed a five and a ten from the drawer into my hand, then ushered me out the back door.

I grinned in spite of the cold as I jogged down the steps, then onto the Turners' manicured back lawn, running my thumb over the sacred flames printed in the center of the worn, faded bills. That fifteen dollars put me within ten of paying this month's electric bill, which wasn't due for another week and might actually be paid on time, thanks to my arrangement with Marta.

Every week, Mrs. Turner gave her housekeeper twenty

3

dollars to have Sarah's school uniforms cleaned and pressed. Every Monday, Marta kept five of those dollars for herself and gave the rest to me, along with that week's dirty clothes. Sarah had two full sets of school clothes. As long as she got five clean uniforms every Monday morning, Marta didn't care what my sister and I did with them until then. So we laundered them on Monday afternoon, wore them throughout the week to supplement our own hand-me-down, piecemeal collection of school clothes, then laundered them again over the weekend in time to deliver them fresh and clean on Monday morning.

Marta got a little pocket money. Sarah got clean uniforms. My sister and I got cash we desperately needed, as well as the use of clothes nice enough to keep the sisters from investigating our home life.

So what if deception was a sin? You can't get convicted if you don't get caught.

Shivering again, I crept around square hedges, careful not to step on the layer of white rocks in the empty flower bed, then into the yard next door. The Turners' house was only three-quarters of a mile from mine, but at 5:50 in the morning, with the temperature near freezing, that felt like the longest three-quarters of a mile in the world. Especially considering that from Sarah's backyard, closer to the center of town, the town wall wasn't even visible.

From *my* backyard, that hulking, razor-wire-topped steel wall was the primary landmark.

I cut through several backyards and a small alley on

the way home, and to avoid Mr. Howard's locked gate, I had to detour onto Third Street, where most of the store windows were still dark, the parking lots empty. The exception was the Grab-n-Go, which stayed open twenty-four hours a day. As I skirted the brightly lit parking lot and gas pumps, I glanced through the glass wall of the store at the huge wall-mounted television dutifully broadcasting the news, as required by the Church during all business hours. In the interest of public awareness, of course.

Willful ignorance was a sin.

The Grab-n-Go was playing the national news feed. The only other choice was the local news, which repeated on a much shorter, more annoying loop. Still, I kind of felt sorry for the night clerk, sentenced to listen to the same headlines repeated hour after hour, with few customers to break the monotony.

I couldn't actually hear the newscaster, in her purple Church cassock with the broad, gold-embroidered cuffs, but I could tell what she was saying because in the absence of actual breaking news, newscasters all said the same things. Tithes are up. Reports of demonic possession are at an all-time low. Our citizens are safe inside their steel cages—I mean, *walls*. The battle still rages overseas and degenerates still roam the badlands, but the Church is vigilant, both at home and abroad, for your safety.

It had been more than a century since the Unified Church and its army of exorcists wiped the bulk of the great demon horde from the face of the earth—the face of America, anyway—yet the headlines never changed.

I stuck to the shadows, walking along the windowless side of the convenience store. Old posters tacked to the brick wall read "Put your talents to work for your country—consider serving the Church!" and "Report suspicions of possession—the Church needs your eyes and ears!" and "Tithe generously! Every dime makes a difference!"

That last one was especially funny. As if tithing were optional. My mom owed several thousand in overdue tithes, from back when she was still working, and if the Church came looking for it, we were screwed.

Behind the store, I rolled the top of the bag tighter to protect the clothes inside, then tossed my bundle over the six-foot chain-link fence stretched across the width of the alley, shielding the Grab-n-Go's industrial trash bin from casual dumping by the adjoining neighborhood. *My* neighborhood.

The bag landed with the crunch of gravel and the crinkle of thick paper. I had the toe of one sneaker wedged into the chain-link, my fingers already curled around cold metal, when I heard a rustle from the deep shadows at the other end of the alley. I froze, listening. Something scraped concrete in the darkness.

I let go of the fence and took a step back, my heart thudding in my ears.

6

Dog. But it'd have to be a big one.

Bum. But there weren't many of those anymore—the Church had been taking them off the street and conscripting them into service for more than a decade.

Psycho. There were still plenty of those, and my mom seemed to know them all. But not-quite six in the morning was early, even for most psychos.

Something shuffled closer on the other side of the fence, and I saw movement in the shadows. My fists clenched and unclenched. My pulse whooshed in my ears, and I regretted throwing Sarah's clothes over the fence. I regretted not taking the even longer way home, through the park. I regretted having a mother who couldn't shake off chemical oblivion in order to feed and clothe her children.

The thing shuffled forward again, and two pinpoints of light appeared in the darkness, bright and steady. Then they disappeared. Then reappeared.

Something was blinking. Watching me.

Shit! I glanced at the paper bag through the fence, clearly visible in the moonlight, just feet from deep shadows cast by the building. Deep shadows hiding . . . a dog.

It's just a dog. . . . It had to be. People's eyes don't shine in the dark.

You know whose eyes do *shine in the dark, Nina? Degenerates'*.

My pulse spiked. There hadn't been a confirmed possession in New Temperance in years, and the last time a degenerate made it over the town wall, I was in the first grade.

It's a dog.

No stray dog was going to scare me away from a bag of uniforms that cost more than I could make in six months of washing and pressing them. That wouldn't just be the end of *my* work for the Turners, it would be the end of Marta's work for the Turners and the beginning of my conviction for the sin of stealing. Or falsehood. Or whatever they decided to call borrowing and laundering someone else's clothes under false pretenses.

I stepped up to the chain-link, mentally berating myself for being such a coward. I was halfway up the fence when the shuffling started again, an uneven gait, as if the dog—or the shiny-eyed psycho?—was injured and dragging one foot. I could hear it breathing now, a rasping, whistling sound, not unlike my own ragged intake of air. I was breathing too fast.

My hands clenched the fence, and metal dug into my fingers. I froze, caught between fear and determination. Injured dogs don't approach strangers unless they're sick or hungry. It couldn't get through the fence. But I *needed* those clothes!

One more shuffle-scrape on concrete and a shape appeared out of the shadows. My throat closed around a cry of terror.

Part human, part monster, the creature squatted, a

tangle of knees and elbows, stringy muscles shifting beneath grayish skin. The limbs were too long and too thin, the angles too sharp. The eyes were too small, but they shone with colorless light that seemed to see deep inside me, as if it were looking for something I wasn't even sure I had.

Degenerate.

It wasn't possible. I'd seen them on the news, but never in person. Never this close. Never in New Temperance . . .

It was bald, with cheekbones so sharp they should have sliced through skin, and ears pointy on both the tops and the lobes. And—most disturbing of all—it was female. Sagging, grayish breasts swung beneath torn scraps of cloth that were once a dress. Or maybe a bathrobe.

The monster roared, and its mouth opened too wide, its jaws unhinging with a gristly pop I could hardly hear over the horrific screech that made my ears ring and my eyes swim in tears. It watched me, and I stared back, frozen in terror.

Run!

No, don't run. Back away slowly. . . . Maybe degenerates were like dogs, and if I ran, it would chase me.

I pulled my right shoe from the fence and slowly, carefully lowered myself, without looking away from the monster. It shuffled closer in its eerily agile squat, and I fumbled for a blind foothold in the metal as I sucked in air and spat it out too quickly to really be considered breathing.

The degenerate was six feet from the fence when I reached the ground and began slowly backing away, the uniforms forgotten. My hands were open, my legs bent, ready to run.

The monster squatted lower, impossibly low, and tensed all over, watching me like a cat about to pounce. Then it sprang at me in one powerful, evil-frog leap.

I screamed and backpedaled. The monster crashed into the chain-link fence. The metal clanked and shook, but held. The demon crashed to the ground, her nose smashed and bleeding, yet she still eyed me with hunger like I'd never seen before. She was up in an instant, pacing on her side of the fence on filthy hands and feet, her knees sticking up at odd angles. She stared through the metal diamonds at me with bright, colorless eyes, and I backed up until I hit the trash bin.

A low, rattling keening began deep in her throat when I started edging around the large bin, my palms flat against the cold, flaking metal at my back. The degenerate blinked at me, then glanced at the top of the fence in a bizarre, jerky movement. I realized what she intended an instant before she squatted, then leapt straight into the air.

Metal squealed when her knobby fingers caught in the top of the chain-link and her bare, filthy toes scrambled for purchase lower on the fence. For a moment, she balanced there like a monstrous cat on a wall.

My heart racing, I backed away quickly, afraid to let

her out of my sight. She leapt again. I heard a visceral snap when she landed on the concrete just yards from me, her deformed right foot bent at a horrible angle. She lurched for me, in spite of the broken bone, and I screeched, scrambling backward.

The demon lunged again, clawlike fingers grasping at my sleeve. I kicked her hand away, but she was there again, and again I retreated until I hit the trash bin and realized I'd gotten turned around in the dark, and in my own fear. I was trapped between the demon and the fence.

She lurched forward and grabbed my ankle. The earth slipped out from under me, and my head cracked against the industrial bin. My ears rang with the clang of metal, and I hit the ground hard enough to bruise my tailbone. My head swam. Fear burned like fire in my veins.

The degenerate loomed over me in her creepy half crouch, rank breath rolling over my face as she leaned closer, her mouth open, gaping, ready for a bite.

"Over here!" someone shouted, and the degenerate twisted toward the fence, snarling, drool dripping from her rotting teeth and down her chin. Over her bony shoulder, I saw a shadowy form beyond the chain-link. A boy—or a man?—in dark clothes, his pale face half hidden by a hood.

She snarled at him again, one clawed hand still tight around my ankle, and I saw my chance. I kicked her in the chest with my free foot, and she fell backward, claws shredding the hem of my jeans.

"You don't want her. Come get *me*!" Metal clinked and rattled, and I realized the boy was climbing the fence. And he was *fast*.

I crawled away, trying to get to my feet, but she grabbed my ankle and gave it a brutal tug. I fell flat on my stomach, then rolled over as she pulled and I kicked. My foot slammed into her belly, and her shoulder, and her neck, but she kept pulling until she was all I could see and hear and smell.

Concrete scraped my bare back when my coat and shirt rode up beneath me. I threw my hands up and my palms slammed into the degenerate's collarbones. I pushed, holding her off me with terror-fueled strength. The chain-link fence rattled and squealed on my right. The beast snarled over me, deformed jaws snapping inches from my nose as my arms began to give, my elbows bending beneath the strain of her inhuman strength.

"Hey!" the boy shouted, and a thud told me he'd landed on my side of the fence, just feet away. His arm blurred through the shadows, and the degenerate snarled as it was hauled off me.

I scrambled backward, and the seat of my jeans dragged on the ground until my spine hit the trash bin again. My hands shook. My back burned, the flesh scraped raw by the concrete.

A bright flash of light half blinded me, and when my vision returned a second later, I could see only shadows in dark relief against the even darker alley. One of those shadows stood over the other, malformed shape, his hand against her bony sternum, both glowing with the last of that strange light.

What the hell . . . ?

An exorcist.

An exorcist in a *hoodie*. Where were his long black cassock, his cross, and his holy water? Where were his formal silence and grave demeanor?

As I watched, stunned, that light faded, and slowly, slowly, the rest of the alley came into focus.

The boy stood and wiped his hands on his pants, his hood still hiding half his face. The degenerate lay unmoving on the ground, no less gruesome in death than she'd been in life, and now that the violent flash had receded from my vision, I realized the alley was growing lighter. The sun was rising.

I pushed myself to my feet while the boy watched me with eyes I couldn't see in the shadow of his hood. "I . . . I . . . ," I stammered, but nothing intelligent followed.

"Holy hellfire!"

We turned to see the Grab-n-Go night clerk standing at the end of the alley, backlit by the parking lot lights, staring at us both. In the distance, a siren wailed, and I realized three things at once.

One: The clerk had reported the disturbance, and the Church was on its way.

Two: He hadn't realized this was more than a scuffle in an alley until he saw the dead degenerate.

Three: I was still in possession of borrowed/stolen clothes, and since I was the victim of the first degenerate attack in New Temperance in the last decade, the Church would want to talk to my mom.

I couldn't let that happen.

"Is that . . . ?" the night clerk stared at the degenerate, taking in her elongated limbs and deformed jaw. His gaze rose to my face and he squinted into the shadows. He couldn't see me clearly but was obviously too scared to come any closer. His focus shifted to the boy standing over the degenerate, and his eyes narrowed even more. "Are you . . . ?"

"Run." The boy didn't shout. He didn't make any threatening gestures. He just gave an order in a firm voice lent authority by the fact that he was standing over the corpse of a degenerate.

The clerk blinked. Then he turned and fled.

"You okay?" The boy shoved his hands into the pockets of his black hoodie. And he *was* a boy. My age. Maybe a little older. I still couldn't see his eyes, but I could see his cheek. It was smooth and unscarred. No Church brand. No sacred flames.

What kind of exorcist has smooth cheeks and wears a hoodie?

"That's a degenerate," I said, and it only vaguely occurred to me that I was stating the obvious. *I was just attacked by a demon.* I couldn't quite wrap my head around it. How had it gotten into town?

"Yeah. Is there any way I can convince you to maybe . . . not tell anyone what I did?"

I frowned. Why wouldn't he want credit for killing a degenerate? How could he be an exorcist—obviously trained by the Church—yet bear no brand and wear no cassock?

"Please. Just . . . don't mention me in your statement, okay?" He glanced to the east, and shadows receded from his jaw, which was square and kind of stubbly. The sirens were getting louder. I could see the flash of their lights in the distance, and the sky seemed to get lighter with every second.

I had to go.

"Not a problem." I grabbed the chain-link and started hauling myself up the fence. I could *not* afford a home visit from the Church. Fortunately, the night clerk—Billy, the manager's nephew—hadn't recognized me. "I'm not making a statement."

"You're not?"

I could hear the question in his voice, but I couldn't see his face because I was already halfway up the fence.

"Thanks for that." I let go of the chain-link with one hand to gesture at the degenerate below. Then I climbed faster and threw one leg over the top.

"Wait!" he said as I lowered myself from link to link on the other side of the fence. "Who are you?"

"Who am *I*?" The rogue teenage exorcist wanted to know who *I* was? "Who are *you*?"

"I'm . . . just trying to help. Why was it following you?"

Following me? The goose bumps on my arms had nothing to do with the predawn cold.

"I guess my soul smelled yummy." Or, more likely, I would have been a meal of convenience—few people were out and about so early in the morning.

Two feet from the ground, I let go of the fence and dropped onto the concrete. When I stood, I found him watching me, both hands curled around the chain-link between us.

The sirens were wailing now, and the sun was almost up. I needed to go. But first, I had to see . . .

I stuck my hand through the fence—it barely fit— and reached for his hood. He let go of the chain-link and stepped back, startled. Then he came closer again. I pushed the hood off his head, and my gaze caught on thick brown waves as my fingers brushed them.

Then I saw his eyes. Deep green, with a dark ring around the outside and paler flecks throughout. For just a second, I stared at them. I'd never seen eyes like that. They were beautiful.

Then the wail of the siren sliced through my thoughts with a new and intrusive volume as the wall of the alley was painted with strobes of red and blue. The Church had arrived.

"Gotta go." I pulled my arm through the fence too fast, and metal scraped the length of my thumb.

"Wait! We need to talk."

"Sorry. No time. Thanks again for . . . you know. The demon slaying." I bent to grab the bag of clothes. Then I ran.

At the mouth of the alley, I looked back, but the boy was gone.

The Grab-n-Go parking lot was alive with flashing lights and crawling with cops in ankle-length navy Church cassocks and stiff-brimmed hats. Billy, the night clerk, stood in the middle of the chaos, gesturing emphatically toward the alley while three different officers tried to take his statement. A second later, two of the three pocketed their notebooks and headed into the alley, slicing through the last of the predawn shadows with bright beams from their flashlights.

One squatted next to the dead degenerate while the other aimed his flashlight down the alley. I ducked around the corner in time to avoid the beam, and for a moment I just stood there, clutching the paper bag to my chest, trying to wrap my mind around everything that had just happened.

A degenerate in New Temperance.

A rogue exorcist with beautiful green eyes.

A parking lot full of cops.

And they were all looking for me.

TWO

Dawn had officially arrived by the time I crossed my crcked patio and stepped into the kitchen, though the sun had yet to rise over the east side of the town wall. My heart was still pounding. A siren wailed from several blocks away. When I closed my eyes, I saw the monster looming over me, snapping inhuman jaws inches from my nose. I shut the back door softly, then dropped the bulging paper bag next to a duffel full of our own dirty laundry.

The clerk couldn't identify me. The rogue exorcist didn't know my name. The Church would *not* come knocking.

I repeated it silently but still had trouble believing it.

The clock over the stove read 6:14. School started in an hour and a quarter.

On my way through the kitchen, I noticed my mom's purse on the table. I wasn't sure whether to be relieved or pissed off that she'd returned home while I was fighting a degenerate in the alley behind the Grab-n-Go. I glanced into the living room, empty except for the scarred coffee table, worn sofa, and two mismatched armchairs. For the first time in weeks, she hadn't passed out on the couch.

In the short, narrow hallway, I pushed her door open slowly to keep it from creaking, then sighed with relief. She'd made it to the bed this time. Mostly. Her arm and her bare right leg hung off the mattress. Her left leg was bare too, of course, but somehow she'd gotten her pants off without removing that one shoe.

Her legs were getting thinner—too thin—and so was her hair. Her kneecaps stood out like bony mesas growing beneath her skin, and her eyebrows were practically nonexistent. She'd been drawing them on for most of the past year, until she'd given up makeup entirely a few weeks ago. She didn't go out during the day, anyway; she "worked" all night now, then stumbled home at dawn.

There was a spot of blood on her pillow, and more of it crusted on her upper lip. Another nosebleed. She was killing herself. Slowly. Painfully, from the looks of it.

"One more year, Mom," I whispered as I pulled her door shut softly. "I just need one more year from you."

In the room I shared with Melanie, our radio alarm had already gone off, and as usual, my little sister hadn't noticed. I swear, a demon horde could march right through our house and she'd sleep through the whole thing.

". . . and I, for one, am looking forward to a little sun!" the DJ said as I dropped my oversized coat on the floor. It thumped against the carpet, which is when I remembered the pilfered cans of stew I'd meant to leave in the kitchen. "In other news, Church officials in New Temperance are expected to announce their choice for headmaster of the New Temperance Day School today, a job vacated just last month when Brother Phillip Reynolds accepted a position in Solace. . . ."

I listened for a couple of minutes, waiting to see if they'd announce a degenerate attack in New Temperance and the mysterious boy and girl spotted in the alley. When that didn't happen, I poked the alarm button, relieved that I hadn't yet made the news, and the DJ's voice faded into blessed silence.

That alarm radio was the only thing on my scratched, scuffed nightstand. It was the last thing I saw before I fell asleep and the first thing I saw every morning. The clock divided my days into strict segments devoted to sleep, school, homework, housework, and real work. I had little time for anything else.

My sister's nightstand was covered in books. Not textbooks or the Church-approved histories and biographies available in the school library. Mellie had old, thick hardcover volumes, some with nothing but black-and-white print stories, others with brightly colored strip illustrations of people with ridiculous powers, speaking in dialogue bubbles over the characters' heads. She borrowed them from Adam Yung's dad, who had a secret collection of prewar stuff in his basement.

The Church hadn't officially outlawed secular fiction, but they had a way of making things like that unavailable to the general public. Right after the war against the Unclean, they'd recycled entire public library collections to reuse the materials. And after they'd brought down all cellular transmission towers—to keep demons from communicating with one another en masse—people had no use for their portable phones and communication devices, so there were recycling drives for those too.

Collections like Mr. Yung's were rare. When we were kids, I'd read his stories with Melanie, curled up in our bed, dreaming of eras and technologies that were long past by the time we were born.

Then I grew up and realized that was all those stories ever were. Dreams. I lived in the real world, where Mellie was only a part-time citizen.

"Time to get up, Mel." Standing, I gave my sister's shoulder a shove. She groaned, and I grabbed the towel hanging over the footboard of the bed, then trudged into the hall.

My shower was cold—the pilot light on the hot water heater had gone out again—and we were out of soap, so

I had to use shampoo all over. The suds burned the fresh scrapes on my lower back, a vivid reminder of my near death in the alley, and when I got back to the bedroom, shivering in my towel, my sister was still sound asleep in the full-size bed we shared.

"Melanie. Get up." I nudged the mattress with my foot, and she rolled onto her stomach.

"Go away, Nina." She buried her face in the pillow without even opening her eyes.

"Up!" I tossed the blanket off her, holding my towel in place with one hand, and my sister finally sat up to glare at me.

"I'm not going. I'm sick." She swiped at yesterday's mascara and eyeliner, already smeared across both her pale cheek and her pillow.

I felt her forehead with the back of one hand while new goose bumps popped up on my arms, still damp from the shower. "You're not hot. Get up. Or would you really rather be here with Mom all day?"

Melanie mumbled something profane under her breath, but then she stumbled into the hall. Even half-asleep, she remembered to tiptoe over the creaky floorboard in front of Mom's room on her way to the bathroom.

When we let our mother sleep, we were rewarded with benign neglect. The alternative was much less pleasant.

I was buttoning my school uniform shirt when Melanie came back from the bathroom, pulling a brush through her long, pale hair still dripping from the shower. She looked her age, with her face scrubbed and shiny. Fifteen and fresh. Innocent. Without the eyeliner she'd taken from the Grab-n-Go and the lipstick our mother had forgotten she even owned, Mellie looked just like all the other schoolgirls in our white blouses and navy pants—shining beacons of purity in world that had nearly been devoured by darkness a century ago.

We were living proof that the Church knew best. That the faithful only prosper under the proper spiritual guidance. And about a dozen other similar lines of bullshit the sisters made us memorize in kindergarten.

"Today's the day," I said when she handed me the brush. I pulled it through my own thicker, darker hair. "I'm really going to do it." I'd almost forgotten what today was, thanks to the demon in the alley, but cold showers have a way of bringing reality into crisp focus.

"Do what? Admit that you're a hopeless stick-in-the-mud who never lets herself have any fun?" She tugged the last pair of school pants from a hanger in the closet and shoved her foot through the right leg. Thank goodness we wore the same size, because we never could have afforded two sets of uniforms on our own, and if the Church found out our mother wasn't working, they'd take us away.

Melanie wouldn't make it in the children's home. The sisters were too watchful, and she had become mischievous and careless under what the Church would characterize as neglect on our mother's part.

I'd characterize it like that too. But I'd say it with a smile.

"I think you're having enough fun for both of us, Mel." Sometimes it didn't feel possible that we were only a year and a half apart. It's not that Melanie didn't pull her own weight; it's that she had to be reminded to help out. Constantly. If I didn't beg her to take the towels to the laundry on Saturdays, we'd have to air dry all week long.

"So, what's so great about today?"

I didn't get eaten in the alley behind the Grab-n-Go. But there were only so many secrets my sister could keep at one time, and our mother took up most of those spots all on her own.

I took a deep breath. Then I spat the words out. "I'm going to pledge."

Melanie froze, her pants still half buttoned. "To the *Church*?"

"Of course to the Church." I tucked in my blouse, then pulled hers off its hanger. "We talked about this, Mellie."

"I thought you were joking." She grabbed a bra from the top drawer and took the shirt I held out by the neatly starched collar.

"I don't have time for jokes. Why else would I spend all my free time working in the nursery?"

"For the money." As she buttoned her blouse I brushed sections from the front of her hair to be braided in the back. She hated the half braid, but it made her look modest and conventional, and sometimes that demure disguise

25

was the only thing standing between my mischievous sister and the back of the teacher's hand. "The same reason I watch Mrs. Mercer's brats after school and tutor Adam Yung on Saturdays."

I glanced at her in the mirror with eyebrows raised. "You get credit for the babysitting." The Mercer kids really were brats, and she wouldn't have gone near them without a cash reward. "But we both know why you tutor Adam, and it's not for the money." He didn't even pay her in cash—Adam usually came bearing a couple of pounds of ground beef or, in warmer weather, a paper bag of fruits and vegetables from his mom's garden. Which we'd learned to ration throughout the week.

He'd never said anything, but I always got the impression that his mother sent payment in the form of perishables to make sure *our* mother couldn't spend Mellie's wages on her "medicine." And to make sure we ate.

"Stop changing the subject." She scratched her scalp with one finger, loosening a strand I'd pulled too tight. "You want to pledge to the Church just so you can teach?"

I didn't *want* to pledge to the Church for any reason. But . . . "That's the way it's done, Mellie." All schools were run by the Church, and all teachers were either ordained Church pledges or fully consecrated senior members. Same for doctors, police, soldiers, reporters, and any other profession committed to serving the community.

Adam's dad said they used to be called civil servants—back when there was civil government.

Melanie took the end of her braid from me. "Don't you think the world has enough teachers?"

"No, as a matter of fact—"

"You know what the world *really* needs?" She turned to watch me through eyes wide with excitement as she wound the rubber band around the end of her hair. "More exorcists. I mean, if you're determined to damn yourself to a life of servitude, communal living, and *celibacy*, wouldn't you rather be slaying demons than wiping noses on kids that aren't even yours? You're gonna need some way to work off all that sexual frustration."

"Don't swear, Mel," I scolded, but the warning sounded hollow and hypocritical, even to my own ears. We both knew better than to curse in public, but there was no one at home to hear or report us. "Profanity is a sin."

Melanie rolled her eyes. "Everything worth doing is a sin."

"I know." And honestly, it was kind of hard for me to worry about the state of my immortal soul when my mortal body's need for food and shelter was so much more urgent.

I plucked the two slim silver rings from the top of our dresser and tossed her one. Melanie groaned again, then slid her purity ring onto the third finger of her right hand while I did the same. "Nina Kane" was scratched into mine because I'd "misplaced" it four times during the first semester of my freshman year and Sister Hope had engraved my name on the inside to ensure that it would be easily returned to me.

Ours weren't real silver, and they certainly weren't inlaid, like Sarah Turner's purity ring. Ours were stainless steel, plucked from the impulse-buy display at the Grab-n-Go one afternoon when I was fourteen, while Melanie distracted the clerk by dropping a half-gallon of milk in aisle one.

Fortunately, the sisters didn't care where the rings came from or what they'd cost, so long as we wore them faithfully beginning in the ninth grade as a symbol of our vow to preserve our innocence and virtue until the day we either gave ourselves to a worthy husband or committed to celibate service within the Church.

I knew girls who took that promise very seriously.

I also knew girls who lied through their teeth.

I didn't know a single boy who'd ever worn a purity ring. Evidently, their virginity was worth even less than the stolen band of steel around my finger.

I grabbed my satchel on my way out of the room, and our conversation automatically paused as we passed our mother's door. In the kitchen, I pulled the last half of the last loaf of bread from an otherwise empty cabinet, and Melanie frowned with one hand on the pantry door, staring at the calendar I'd tacked up to keep track of my erratic work schedule—I worked whenever the nursery needed me. "What's today?"

"Thursday."

"Thursday the fourth?" Her frown deepened, and I had

to push her aside to grab a half-empty jar of peanut butter from the nearly bare pantry. "It can't be the fourth already."

"It is, unless four no longer follows three. Why?" I glanced at the calendar and saw the problem. "History test?"

"What?" Melanie sank into a rickety chair at the scratched table. "Oh. Yeah."

"You didn't study?" I set a napkin and the jar of peanut butter in front of her, then added a butter knife and one of the two slices of toast as they popped up from the toaster.

She shrugged. "It's just a fill-in-the-blank on the four stages of the Holy Reformation." But the way she spread peanut butter on her bread, her gaze only half focused, said she was worried.

"And those stages would be . . . ?"

Melanie sighed. "The widespread decline of common morals, the subsequent onslaught of demonic forces, the glorious triumph of the Church over the worldwide spiritual threat, and the eventual unification of the people under a single divine ministry." She was quoting the textbook almost verbatim.

"Good. Come on." I took the knife from her and made my own breakfast, then tossed Melanie a modest navy sweater and herded her out the back door, where the town perimeter wall was easily visible between the small houses that backed up to ours. The wall was solid steel plating fifteen feet tall, topped with large loops of razor wire. In the middle of the night, I heard the metal groan with every strong gust of wind. I saw the glint of sun on razor wire in my dreams.

But clouds had rolled in since my predawn activities, and the sky was now gray with them.

"December eighth, 2034," I said around a mouthful of peanut butter and bread as we rounded the house and stepped over the broken cinder block hiding the emergency cash I kept wrapped in a plastic bag. If Mom knew we had money, she'd spend it on something less important than heat and power, two resources I greatly valued.

"Um . . . the first televised possession, caught on film at a holiday parade, before the Church abolished public television to support and protect the moral growth of the people." Melanie shoved one arm into her sweater sleeve, then transferred her toast to the other hand and pulled the other half of her cardigan on over her satchel strap. "So, how dangerous could secular programming have been, anyway? It's just a bunch of videos, like the discs in Mr. Yung's basement, right? Stories being acted out, like we used to do when we were kids?"

"I guess." But according to the Church, those videos tempted people to sin.

Mr. Yung had an old TV and a disc player that still worked. I'd seen one of his videos once, but the disc was badly damaged, so I only caught glimpses of couples swaying in sync with one another, dressed in snug clothes. At the time, I'd been scandalized by the sight of boys and girls in open physical contact with one another—those would be secret shames in our postwar world. But the adults in the video didn't seem to care, and no one was driven to wanton displays of flesh or desire, that I could see.

There was no sound on the video, though, so I couldn't hear what kind of music they'd had or what they were saying.

Maybe the sin and temptation were more obvious in the parts I couldn't hear.

We turned left on the cracked sidewalk in front of our house, and I eyed the dark clouds in the sky, struggling to bring my thoughts back on task. "September twenty-ninth, 2036."

Melanie held her toast by one corner. She still hadn't taken a bite. "The first verified exorcism. Established worldwide credibility for the Unified Church, whose exorcist—the great Katherine Abbot—performed the procedure in front of a televised audience of millions."

"Good. June—"

"Did you know that wasn't even her real name?" Melanie said suddenly.

"What wasn't whose name?" We turned left again and followed the railroad tracks between the backyards of the houses a block over from ours. The train hadn't run since long before I was born, but little grass grew between the rails, which made it an easy shortcut on the days we were running late. Which was most days, thanks to my sister.

"Katherine Abbot. Her name wasn't really Katherine. The Church renamed her because they thought her real name didn't sound serious enough, or holy enough, or something like that."

"So what was her real name?"

Melanie shrugged, and her uneaten toast flopped in her hand. "I don't know."

"Then how do you know it wasn't Katherine?"

"Adam told me."

"Adam, who needs your help to add double digit numbers?" I said as we cut through the easement between two yards and back onto the street.

"He's bad at math, not history. His dad says the Church does it all the time—changes facts. Mr. Yung says history is written by the victor, and if the elderly don't pass down their memories, eventually there won't be anyone else left alive who knows how the war was really fought."

I stopped cold on the sidewalk and grabbed her arm, holding so tight she flinched, but I couldn't let go. Not until she understood. "Melanie, that's *heresy*," I hissed, glancing around at the houses on both sides of the road. Fortunately, the street was deserted. "If Adam Yung and his father want to risk their immortal souls"—or more accurately, their mortal lives—"by questioning the Church, that's their business. But *you* stay out of it."

Skepticism and profanity were largely harmless in private, and goodness knows I couldn't claim innocence on either part. But the more often they were indulged, the more likely they were to be overheard. And reported. And punished.

"You're going to have to tutor him in public. At the laundry, or the park, or something." Anywhere public exposure would keep him from filling my impressionable sister's head with dangerous thoughts she couldn't resist sharing with the rest of the world.

I wanted to tell her to stop tutoring him, but frankly, we needed the food.

"Why aren't you eating?" I glanced pointedly at her untouched breakfast.

"I told you. I don't feel good." She scowled and pulled her arm from my grip. "Next date."

"Um . . . June 2041." I pushed her toast closer to her mouth, and she finally took a bite.

"The Holy Proclamation, establishing the Unified Church as the sole political and spiritual authority," she said, with her mouth still full.

"Okay, let's backtrack." I made a gesture linking her breakfast and her face, and Melanie reluctantly took another bite. "May twelfth, 2031."

"The Day of Great Sorrow." Her face paled, and she chewed in solemn silence for several seconds before elaborating. "The day the number of stillbirths officially surpassed the number of live births. A day of mourning the world over. The Day of Great Sorrow led to the realization that the well of souls had run dry, which led to the discovery of demons among us. Which then led to the Great Purification, undertaken by the Unified Church, and the dissolution of all secular government in the Western Hemisphere. Right?"

"That's a bit simplistic as a summary. . . ." The discovery of demons was a particularly grisly time in human history, and the various factions of our former government didn't disband voluntarily or peacefully. "But probably good enough for a tenth-grade history test. Eat your toast."

We could see the school compound by then, behind its tall iron gate. She couldn't take food inside, and we had only minutes until the bell.

"Here. Take half." Mellie ripped her bread in two and gave me the bigger piece. "I can't eat it all."

I shoved the bread into my mouth and chewed as fast as I could—we couldn't afford to waste perfectly good food—and I'd just swallowed the last of it when the bell started ringing.

"Come on!" I pulled her with me as I raced down the sidewalk, and we slid through the gate a second before it rolled shut behind us.

"Cutting it close again, Nina," Sister Anabelle said as she locked the gate, her skirt swishing around her ankles beneath the hem of her cassock.

"My fault!" Melanie called over one shoulder, racing toward her first class in the secondary building, her hair flying behind her. "Gotta go!"

"What do you have this morning?" Anabelle fell into step with me as she tucked her key ring into a pocket hidden by a fold in her long, fitted Church cassock—light blue for teachers. Anabelle's robes were very simple and plain because she was still a pledge, but once she was consecrated, they would be embroidered in elaborate navy swoops and flames, signaling her status and authority to the entire world.

"Um . . . I have kindergartners today." All seniors began the day with an hour of service. I'd been selected as an elementary school aide because I already had experience with kids, from working in the children's home on weekends.

"Have you given any more thought to making an early commitment to the Church? I think you'd make a wonderful teacher."

I glanced at the brand on the back of her right hand— four wavy lines twisting around one another to form a stylized column of fire, burned into her flesh the day she'd pledged. A permanent mark to seal a permanent choice.

Anabelle's brand was a simplified version of the seal of the Unified Church, displayed on flags, official documents, currency, and the sides of all public vehicles. Each individual flame represented one of the sacred obligations, and together they formed the symbolic blaze with which the Church claimed to have rid the world of evil.

Except for the degenerates roaming unchecked in the badlands and the demons still resisting purification in several volatile regions in Asia.

But no one was worried about any of that. Not openly, anyway. The Church had it all under control—they told us so every day—and the only time willful ignorance didn't qualify as a sin was when the Church didn't want us to know something.

Which was why Melanie couldn't understand my determination to pledge. But Mellie and I were living different lives, with different obligations and responsibilities. She had three more years to read illicit books and pretend to care about math while she tutored Adam Yung while wearing stolen mascara.

I had a deadbeat mother to hide from the Church, utility bills to pay, and a decorum-challenged little sister to shield from the watchful eyes of the school teachers. The Church represented my best shot at holding all that together until Melanie was old enough and mature enough to fend for herself.

The catch? Church service was forever. Mellie would grow up and have a life of her own, but I would not. I would belong to the Church until the day I died, and even when that day came, *they* would decide what would become of my immortal soul.

I'd been mentally fighting the choice for months,

scrambling to find some other way to make things work, but my miracle had failed to materialize, and wasting the rest of my senior year wasn't going to change that.

I couldn't officially join until I turned eighteen, which was still a year and four days away, but early commitments were encouraged, and the earlier I pledged, the more likely I was to get my first-choice assignment.

Teaching. In New Temperance. Near Melanie. That was the whole point of pledging, for me.

"I was thinking of doing it during the afternoon service." I took a deep breath and swallowed a familiar wave of nausea. "Today."

"Oh, Nina, I'm so happy for you!" Anabelle threw her arms around me as if nothing had changed since I was a needy twelve-year-old, desperate for friendship and advice, and she was a senior, already pledged to the Church and assigned to mentor the girls in my seventh-grade class. Anabelle knew about my mother's problem—she'd known even way back then—but she hadn't told anyone. She trusted me to take care of Melanie and to ask for help when I needed it.

Sometimes talking to her still felt like talking to an older classmate, but the powder-blue cassock and the brand on the back of her hand were stern reminders of her new reality.

She was *Sister* Anabelle now. The Church owned her, body and soul.

Soon it would own me too.

"I have to admit, I'm happy for me too," Anabelle said, and her smile was reassuring. If she loved her job so much, pledging to the Church couldn't be *that* bad, right? "I was hoping you'd decide to pledge before the consecration. I didn't want to miss your big day!"

"Oh, I completely forgot!" Anabelle had been selected for consecration into the leadership levels of the Church just five years after she'd joined, much sooner than the average. Unfortunately, after the annual ceremony—just a few days away—she would be transferred to another town, to learn under new guidance and to experience more of the world than New Temperance had to offer.

I could hardly imagine school without Anabelle. Even with our age difference and her Church brand standing between us, she was the closest thing I had to a friend.

We were three doors from the kindergarten wing when the rain started, an instant, violent deluge bursting from the clouds as if they'd been ripped open at some invisible seam. Even under the walkway awning, we were assaulted by icy rain daggers with every gust of wind. Anabelle and I sprinted for the door, but the knob was torn from my hand before I could turn it.

The door flew open and Sister Camilla marched past us into the rain, dragging five-year-old Matthew Mercer by one arm. If he was crying, I couldn't tell—he was drenched in less than a second.

"Blasphemy is an offense against the Church, an insult

to your classmates, and a sin against your own filthy tongue!" Sister Camilla shouted above a roll of thunder.

Yes, Matthew Mercer was a brat, and yes, he had trouble controlling his mouth, but he was just a kid, and everything he said he'd probably heard from his parents.

I stepped out from under the awning and gasped as the freezing rain soaked through my blouse in an instant. Anabelle pulled me back before I could say something that would probably have landed me in trouble alongside the kindergartner.

"Blasphemy is a sin," Sister Anabelle reminded me in a whisper.

Of course blasphemy was a sin. A lesser infraction than fornication or heresy, but a grievous offense a strict matron like Sister Camilla would never let slide. Even in a five-year-old.

Especially in a five-year-old who'd already demonstrated a precocious gift for profanity.

Anabelle and I could only watch, shivering, as Sister Camilla dragged Matthew onto the stone dais in the center of the courtyard, then forced him to kneel. She was still scolding him while she flipped a curved piece of metal over each of his legs, just above his calves, then snapped the locks into place, confining the five-year-old to his knees in the freezing rain.

The posture of penitence. Voluntarily assumed, it demonstrated humility and submission to authority. And contrition. Used as a punishment, it was a perversion of the very things it stood for, just like anything accomplished by force.

In third grade, I'd once knelt in the posture of penitence in the middle of the school hall for four hours for turning in an incomplete spelling paper.

I'd never failed to finish an assignment again.

Sister Camilla marched toward us in the downpour, wordlessly ordering us inside with one hand waved at the building. At the door, I looked back to see Matthew Mercer bent over his knees, his forehead touching the stone floor of the dais, his school uniform soaked. He'd folded his arms over the back of his head in a futile attempt to protect himself from the rain.

"Pray for forgiveness," Sister Camilla called to him over her shoulder. "And hope the Almighty has more mercy in his heart than I have in mine."

Well, I thought as the door closed behind us, *he certainly couldn't have any less.*

THREE

"Okay." I crossed my legs and angled them to one side, trying to get comfortable in a chair built for five-year-olds. On the other side of the room, one of my fellow seniors had her own group of six kids assembled at the reading center while Sister Camilla taught math to six more at a table covered with little plastic counting cubes. I was in charge of the faith unit. "Who can name one of the four obligations of the people to their Church?"

Five chubby little hands shot into the air; five eager faces stared at me, hoping to be called upon. At some point between the ages of five and fifteen, that eagerness would be replaced with indifference, but in kindergarten, they still cared. They still wanted to please and to be rewarded for their effort.

"Elena."

All five hands sank and four frowns emerged, while Elena beamed at me from her chair in the semicircle. "Devotion!" Her brown eyes sparkled with triumph. "That means we love the Church and we'll love it forever!"

"Good!" But on the inside, some vulnerable part of me shriveled a little more at her enthusiasm for a child's happy lie, which would surely mature into an adult's bitter burden. "Who else?" The other four hands shot up again. "Dillon?"

He picked at the cuff of his white school shirt. "Obedience."

"And what does that mean?"

"It means you have to do what the Church says, even if you don't want to. Just like at home, when your mom says you have to eat your peas, even though they're yuck."

I smiled at him, and my knee banged the underside of the short table when I tried to uncross my legs. "That's exactly right." But the Church's "peas" were usually much more difficult to swallow. "And the third obligation?" The last three hands went up. "Jessica?"

"Penti . . . Penna . . . Pen . . ."

"Penitence," I finished for her. "Good. And what does that mean?"

"It means that when you do something wrong, you have to feel bad about it. *Real* bad. And you gotta try to fix it."

"That's right. And—"

"Like with Matthew." Elena's smile faded and her little forehead furrowed. "He didn't feel bad about what he said, so Sister Camilla *made* him feel bad."

I glanced at Matthew Mercer's empty chair, at the end of our semicircle. The rain was coming down so hard that I couldn't see him through the window. I could only see gray misery and the steady pelting of rain against the glass.

"Okay, there's one more." I dragged my attention back to the kids in front of me, in their white shirts and navy pants, smaller versions of my own uniform. "The people owe the Church devotion, obedience, penitence, and what? Robby? Can you tell us?"

"He got the *easy* one . . . ," Jessica whispered, and I frowned at her.

"Worship," Robby said. "That means you gotta love the Church."

"Good." At their age, faith was more about memorization than anything. Fortunately, five-year-olds have great memories. "Now let's move on to something more fun. Who can tell me what we learned yesterday about soul donors?"

Hands shot into the air, and for the next few minutes, the kids explained to me that since the Great Purification a century ago, donors were necessary because babies without souls die within an hour of their birth.

"Who can tell me why there aren't enough souls to go around anymore?"

Robby spoke quietly. The tone of our unit had changed, and he looked scared. "Demons ate them."

I nodded solemnly.

Actually, demons *consumed* the souls of those they possessed. But that distinction was hard to explain to small children.

Degenerates were easy to identify. Fresh demonic possessions were much, much more difficult to recognize, because when a demon possesses a human, it has access to its victim's memories. Most demons are very good at impersonating their victims. They do it for *years,* until the soul of the victim has been completely devoured.

Once that happens, if the demon can't find a new host, it becomes stuck in the soulless body, which begins to mutate and degrade, both physically and mentally. Eventually, those soulless, end-stage possessions become degenerates— mindless mutated monsters with inhuman strength and speed, and demonic appetites. They stalk the shadows in search of new souls, but because they've lost most mental function, instead of simply possessing a new host, they tear the poor victim to pieces, literally devouring human flesh in search of that vital soul.

But those details aren't taught to five-year-olds. In kindergarten we keep it simple.

"Today we're going to talk about the shortage of souls and the generational obligation of the people." That was a mouthful for a five-year-old, but even kindergartners had been hearing those phrases for most of their lives. "Do you all know who your donors were?"

Robby's hand shot up, but he answered before I could call on him. "My grandpa was my donor. I'm his namesake, so I get to put flowers on his grave every year on my birthday. But my mom cries, even though I got to live."

"I'm sure they're happy tears."

I was lying. People don't cry in graveyards because they're happy. But sometimes you have to lie to little kids. Sometimes you have to lie to not-so-little kids too.

I turned to Jessica, who was twirling a thin strand of dark hair around her finger. "What about you, Jessie? Do you know who your donor was?"

She shook her head. "My donor was from the *public registry*." She said the words slowly. Carefully. Reverently.

I blinked at her in surprise. "Well then, you're *extra* lucky, aren't you?" I tried not to think about how nervous her mother must have been toward the end of her pregnancy.

Family donations are the norm, and most donors are memorialized in the new child's name, or by the celebration of the donation along with the child's birthday every year.

It's considered an honor for the elderly to give up their

45

lives and their souls at the moment of a child's birth so the next generation can live. It's also considered an obligation. In fact, in most cases, the Church won't grant a parenting license until the prospective parents have a family donor lined up. The public registry is for emergencies. For cases when the donor dies before it's safe to induce the baby's birth, and for rare accidental pregnancies, when there is no family member willing to donate a soul for a child he or she will never see.

People who haven't already promised their souls to a family member's child are added to the public registry at the age of fifty and instructed to get their affairs in order. It's a short list. Most people want their souls to stay in the family, and those who want to grow old sometimes promise a donation to the child of a niece or nephew who's still several years away from marriage, and even farther from parenthood.

Selfish? Yes. But until the Church comes up with a law to stop it, donor procrastination is also perfectly legal.

When a baby nears birth without a promised soul, it's assigned a donor from the top of the public registry. Rarely—tragically—a town's public registry will sit empty for a few days, and inevitably during that time, babies are stillborn for lack of a soul.

"Do you do anything special for your donor on your birthday?" I asked Jessica.

"We give thanks and set a place for her at my birthday

party. No one sits in that chair, even though she's not really there. Mommy says it's symbiotic."

I hid a smile. "I think you mean 'symbolic.'"

"Yeah." Jessica turned to her classmates with an air of authority. "'Symbolic' means no one can sit in that chair, even though it's empty."

Across the room from our learning center, the classroom door opened and I glanced up from my group of kindergartners to find Sister Anabelle standing in the doorway.

"Sister Camilla, could I please borrow Nina for the rest of the hour?"

Sister Camilla nodded, and Anabelle gestured for me to hurry, so I passed out parable-themed coloring sheets and crayons for my group, then scurried into the hall.

Anabelle closed the door behind me. "They're about to start the sophomore class physicals. I thought you might want to spend your service hour there today, since Melanie's . . ." She frowned at my blank look. "Mellie didn't tell you?"

"No." But with that new bit of information, the pieces fell into place in my head. No wonder my sister was nervous that morning. The problem wasn't her history test, it was her physical exam.

My sophomore physical was the single worst day of my life. Even compared to a degenerate attack in a dark alley.

"Come on." Anabelle grabbed my arm and tugged me down the hall. "They're about to start the assembly."

We got there just as the last of the tenth-grade girls filed into their seats in the auditorium, wide-eyed and obviously scared. The boys would be addressed separately, and I wondered if they would be half as nervous as the girls were. There was no whispering or nudging in line. No one played with anyone else's hair. No one scribbled on incomplete homework papers or rushed to finish the assigned reading. They just stared at the stage, where a nurse in her pristine white slacks and matching cassock—the bloodred embroidery meant she was consecrated—stood next to the acting headmaster, Sister Cathy.

The girls looked terrified.

I knew exactly how they felt.

Anabelle and I stood against the back wall with several other teachers and volunteers, all staring out over the mostly empty auditorium. The sophomore girls took up less than three full rows.

When Sister Cathy stepped up to the podium, my stomach began to churn.

"Good morning, girls," she said, and we all flinched when the microphone squealed. Sister Cathy repositioned it, then started over. "Good morning, girls. As you all know, today is your annual physical. As you may also know by now, the tenth-grade physical is a little different from the exams you've gotten in previous years. Today, in addition to assessing your general health and development, we will also be conducting your first reproductive assessment."

My hands felt cold. And damp.

Sister Cathy made it sound perfectly reasonable. Civilized. Routine. As if there were no emotion involved. But the truth was actually brutal for the girls sitting in those chairs, hands clenched in terror. By the end of the day, every girl in Melanie's class would be declared either fit or unfit to procreate.

Those declared fit would be given a second assessment before marriage, and a third when they applied for a parenting license.

Those declared unfit would be scheduled for sterilization. Immediately.

My stomach twisted again, as if my breakfast wanted to come back up. I closed my eyes and took several deep breaths, and when I looked at the stage again, I realized I'd missed the introduction. I had no idea what the nurse's name was, or when she'd stepped up to the podium.

"The important thing to remember today, girls, is that the reproductive assessment isn't personal." She said it with an air of authority. As if that made it true. "It's not an assessment of you as a person, or of your ability to love and raise a child. Or even your ability to *carry* a child. It's a simple issue of numbers."

Numbers.

The Church was all about the numbers. I guess they had to be, since our population had been decimated by the horde a century ago. We couldn't recover most of the souls

49

devoured by the Unclean, and since no one knows how or even *if* new souls can be created . . .

"There aren't enough souls to go around anymore." The nurse finished my thought out loud, and I realized it didn't matter what her name was, or what the name of the nurse who'd spoken to my class was, because ultimately, they were both Sister Nurse. This was the same speech countless Sister Nurses all over the country were saying to thousands of fifteen-year-old girls in every town that had survived the onslaught. The same thing Sister Nurses had been saying for more than eighty years, ever since the Church imposed restrictions on reproduction.

"The Unified Church has a responsibility to make sure that the available souls go to the babies with the best chance of survival. That way, virtually all our children live."

That was a nice way to put it. The truth was that, rather than choose which infants lived or died—because *that* would be cruel—the Church chose which infants could be *conceived*.

"The decision is completely fair," Sister Nurse continued. "It's based on math and science."

I wanted to laugh. But I kinda wanted to scream too.

At fifteen years old, I was disqualified for procreation based on a history of allergies, my flat feet, and mild myopia—conditions it wouldn't be fair to pass along to the next generation. Especially when there were other

50

girls my age with fewer health issues, who could theoretically produce healthier children.

I wasn't alone. Nearly a third of the girls in my class were declared unfit. We were sterilized that afternoon, in matching white hospital gowns.

Sister Nurse spoke for another five minutes, explaining what the reproductive assessment would entail and reiterating that the girls should not be scared. Then she asked them to stand and form a single-file line.

Nothing good ever happens in a single-file line.

"Nina?" Anabelle put one hand on my shoulder as we followed my sister's class into the bright hallway. "Are you okay?" I nodded, and she got a good look at my face while the line filed slowly toward the gym, which had been set up with several exam stations separated from one another by thin curtains. Anabelle tugged me into an alcove near the restrooms and lowered her voice to a whisper. "Oh, sweetie, I'm sorry. I completely forgot." Her frown deepened. "Is that why you want to pledge? Because of your disqualification?"

"No. I'm fine. Really." Melanie filed past us, near the middle of the line, and my gaze followed her. She looked pale.

She looked *terrified*.

"You know this isn't your only choice, right?" Anabelle said. "The Church wants pledges who *want* to be in service. And you have other options. I know you don't want retail or factory work, but what about technical school? Cooking? Gardening?"

"I nearly burned the toast this morning, and I killed the bean sprout we planted in second grade." I dragged my focus from the back of Mellie's head and made myself look at Sister Anabelle. "And anyway, those aren't careers. They're jobs. Dead-end jobs, if you hate what you're doing." Like the dead-end existence that was killing my mother slowly, from the inside out.

"Okay, what about college? How are your scores?" Anabelle was irrepressible. "You could wait for the recruitment fair . . . ?"

My scores were fine. But not good enough to get me recruited by a company willing to pay for my education in exchange for my employment. My spare time was spent working, not studying, and without a recruitment scholarship, I didn't have the money for college. I didn't even have the money for dinner. The Church would provide for any higher education required for Church service, of course. But only once I'd pledged. Which brought us back to the starting point of this logic merry-go-round.

"You could still marry . . . ," Anabelle suggested softly, as the last of the sophomores filed past, their shoes whispering on bright white linoleum tile. "It won't matter what you do for a living if you're in love, right?"

I gaped at her, momentarily unable to hide my contempt.

Yeah, in a few years I could marry. If I could find a

husband who either didn't want children or had also been sterilized. But what kind of life would that be? Disqualified for parenthood because of my flat feet and occasional runny nose. Disqualified for everything but retail and factory work because I couldn't afford an education.

Could love make that kind of misery bearable? The only thing I knew about love was that Mellie read about it in her taboo books—along with a host of other improbable fantasies.

Joining the Church to become a teacher was the only way I could think of to stay near my sister yet have a life and a career of my own. Well, a career, anyway.

"I *want* to pledge, Anabelle," I insisted, speaking over the voice inside me that argued otherwise.

She studied me for a second, and she must have bought my sincerity, because then she smiled and squeezed my arm. "Great! It's good work, Nina. And I know you love the kids."

"Yeah, I—"

"Miss Kane, please step back into line," Sister Cathy said, and the rest of my sentence died on my tongue at the mention of my last name. I thought she was talking to me, until I looked up to see my sister standing alone in the middle of the hall instead of against the wall in line with the other girls.

Melanie stared at the floor, her arms stiff at her sides, and though I couldn't see her face, I recognized her posture. She was trapped between an idea and its execution, like when she was little and she realized she could sneak an extra cookie from the package but knew she *shouldn't*. Any second, she would either step back into line or . . . she wouldn't. She hadn't yet decided.

"Melanie Kane, get back in line. Now." Sister Cathy's voice was sharper this time, and suddenly everyone was watching. Mellie looked at her. Then she looked at the line of her classmates. Then she looked at the door leading into the courtyard, where rain still poured in thick gray sheets.

My heart hammered in my chest, and I felt like I was on that precipice of disobedience with her.

Get back in line, Mellie.

Running wouldn't get her out of the physical, and it *would* get her into serious trouble. The kind of trouble that would require a conference with our mother. Which would quickly land us in Church custody.

Melanie's right hand twitched, and I knew what she'd decided a fraction of a second before she lurched for the double glass doors and threw her full weight at them. The doors flew open, and she disappeared into the rain.

There was a collective gasp from the sophomore class and a startled yelp from Sister Cathy as a gust of wind and rain pelted her navy-embroidered pale blue cassock in the two seconds it took the doors to fall shut in my sister's wake. Then there was silence, except for a clap of thunder and the steady, loud patter of rain on the roof.

"Find her!" Sister Cathy shouted, soaked and obviously furious, and two of the sophomore class teachers sprinted for the exit, their cornflower cassocks flapping behind them.

I started to follow, blood racing through my veins, spurring me into action, but Sister Anabelle grabbed my arm and hauled me into the restroom alcove again.

"She's just scared," I said.

"I know," Anabelle whispered. "It would be better if you find her and get her to come back voluntarily. Ready to atone. Disobeying a Church official is a sin, Nina."

"I know." Melanie was drawn to trouble like a cat to raw meat—she thrived on it—and I'd always known that eventually she'd make a mistake I couldn't fix. I'd just hoped "eventually" would come a little later in life. And that it wouldn't involve my sister disobeying a Church official in front of dozens of witnesses, then fleeing the scene.

What the hell was she thinking?

"Is there somewhere she goes when she's upset?" Anabelle asked.

"Not lately." *But when we were little* . . . I glanced over my shoulder at the sophomores still filing into the gym four at a time. "I'll find her. Can you cover for me?"

"Of course. Go on."

I made myself walk away from the gym, then into the courtyard through a different door, when I really wanted to run. The rain had slowed a little, but the day looked gray, viewed through the steady drizzle, and my hair was drenched again by the time I got to the dais. The only sounds were the constant loud patter of raindrops, the occasional roll of thunder, and the quick tap of my school shoes on the sidewalk.

Matthew Mercer looked up from the dais when he heard me coming, and one glance at his rain-soaked misery urged me to move faster.

If they'd force a five-year-old to kneel all day in the rain for blasphemy, what would they do to a disobedient fifteen-year-old fugitive? I couldn't remember anyone else defying the Church so openly, except for . . . Clare Parker.

My stomach clenched around my breakfast at the memory.

One day, the year I was nine, Clare had refused to kneel for worship. They gave her three chances. When she still refused, Brother Phillip said refusing to recognize the Church's authority was the first sign of possession. He called in an exorcist, and two hours later, Clare was sentenced. The exorcist said that since her possession was recent, her soul could be returned to the well of souls—if it were purified by fire.

They forced her to her knees on the dais, closed the steel cuffs above her calves, then burned her alive in front of the entire school.

She was seventeen years old.

What if they thought Melanie was possessed?

Terror pumped fire through my veins and pushed my feet faster. At the rear entrance to the administration building, I turned to make sure no one was watching, then slipped inside. My shoes squeaked on the tile and left wet footprints, but there was nothing I could do about that.

Careful not to slip, I snuck through the back hall, then ducked into the laundry room. When Mellie was little, she loved to hide in the bundles of freshly laundered sheets before they were folded and distributed in the children's home attached to our school. The laundry was the only place I could think of to look for Mellie on campus, and at first I didn't see her.

I'd almost decided to climb over the fence and go look for her at home, when the pile of clean white sheets in a huge wheeled cart moved.

"Melanie? It's me. Come on out."

But she didn't move or make a sound, so I had to pull the sheets off her one by one and pile them on a table until I found my sister curled up in a ball at the bottom of the cart. Her hair was soaked, her braid destroyed. Her face was red and swollen from crying, and the terror in her eyes made her look about ten years old.

"Mellie, you have to go back. It'll be okay if you apologize and take your punishment."

Fasting? A week of silence? Public lashing? Any of those would be better than suspicion of possession.

"It's not going to be okay." Melanie sat up, sniffling, and wiped her nose with the back of one hand.

"Not if you don't get up, it won't. Hurry, before they decide you're possessed." Any reasonable person could see that she was just scared and upset. But the Church saw what it wanted to see, and it wouldn't want to see a fifteen-year-old it simply couldn't control.

Melanie shook her head slowly, and two fat tears rolled down her cheeks as she stared up at me. "I'm not possessed, Nina," she said, her voice raw and hoarse. "I'm pregnant."

FOUR

"Pregnant . . . ?" My voice sounded hollow, and when Melanie nodded, I sank to the floor on legs that would no longer hold me up.

No.

My sister climbed out of the cart, then knelt next to me on the floor, wrinkling her navy slacks and her drenched white blouse. "Nina, say something. I don't know what to do."

"Are you sure?" I grabbed her hand and squeezed it, looking for any sign of doubt in her eyes.

"Pretty sure. I missed last month entirely, and I've been feeling sick all week." She sniffled and swiped one hand across her dripping nose again. "Not just in the morning, though. Kinda off and on all day."

But for one long moment, I could only blink at her, and even once I was capable of speech, the words seemed to get stuck on my tongue. "How . . . ? Who . . . ?" She looked at the floor, and my eyes narrowed. "Adam Yung?" I demanded in a harsh whisper, and she nodded miserably. "Melanie, how did you think you'd get away with this? You knew your physical was coming up, and even if you hadn't gotten pregnant, they can tell when you've lost your virginity!"

I could get away with having sex. Because I'd been declared unfit to procreate, then rendered *unable* to procreate, the Church no longer cared whether I preserved my virtue, so long as I still presented a facade of innocence and purity to the world.

I *had* gotten away with it, several times in the months following my sterilization, when my anger at the Church couldn't be controlled without an outlet. I'd met in the dark, in the middle of the night, with boys who would hardly meet my gaze in school. A private screw-you to the system that had defined my future without so much as a "Hey, Nina, what would *you* like out of life?"

I wasn't sure I wanted kids, and I certainly hadn't been sure at fifteen. But I was *damn* sure I didn't want anyone else making that decision for me.

Had I done this? Had Melanie seen my months of rebellion—back when I'd had time for such things—and assumed that what had worked for me would work for her too?

"We weren't really thinking about that," my sister said in response to a question I'd almost forgotten I'd asked. "We weren't really thinking about anything. We were just . . . I *love* him, and he loves me, and it just *happened*, Nina!"

"Once?" I sat on my heels to keep my slacks off the laundry room floor. "You got pregnant the first time?" Not that that mattered. Once was enough.

Studying in the basement, my ass.

Melanie shook her head, and more tears filled her eyes. "We tried to stop. We knew it was wrong, but it didn't *feel* wrong."

"How does it feel *now*?" I demanded. Fornication was a sin. Melanie wouldn't have been the first fifteen-year-old to present a torn hymen at her annual physical, and if the whispers in the bathroom were accurate, several of my own classmates had already lived to tell that tale. They were sterilized, of course, and they'd been punished privately because our school didn't want smudges on its record any more than the offenders wanted to be outed as sinners.

But Melanie was giving them no choice. A pregnancy couldn't be hidden by a school uniform. Not for long, anyway.

My head spun with the details, and the consequences, and the potential outcomes, but in that deluge of possibilities, I couldn't see a single good way out of this. Not one.

"Does Adam know?" I rubbed my forehead, trying to fend off the pressure growing behind it. We were screwed.

She shook her head. "I couldn't tell him. I just kept ignoring it, hoping I was wrong, until I saw the calendar and remembered about the physicals."

"Unlicensed pregnancy is *forbidden,* Melanie. For—"

"Please don't say 'Fornication is a sin.'" More tears rolled down her swollen cheeks. "I *know* fornication is a sin. Please don't be mad at me right now, Nina. I need your help."

"I'm not mad." I was *furious*. I was so angry I could hardly think, but I couldn't deny my own hypocrisy, and being mad at Melanie wouldn't help either of us, so I pushed my anger back. *Way* back. All the way to the back of my mind, where anger at my mother festered, rotting our thin familial bond. "I just . . ." I didn't know what to do. For the first time in my life, I had no clue how to get Melanie out of trouble. "You can't have this baby, Mellie." I squeezed her hand when her tears started falling faster. "You know you can't have this baby."

There were places women could go to fix that particular problem. I didn't know where any of those places were, but I could find out. Maybe we could put Mellie's physical off if I told them she was sick, and then when she showed up for the makeup physical, we'd only have to deal with the fornication issue.

We could survive fornication, even if the Church took

custody of us and split us up. But fornication, unlicensed pregnancy, disobeying a Church official, and any other sins they uncovered when they looked into our living situation . . . ?

The more sins they charged her with, the greater the chance of a conviction.

But one look at my sister's tear-streaked face told me she wouldn't even consider what I saw as our only option.

"No! Nina, there's a *person* in here." She pressed one small fist against her flat belly, and something deep inside me cracked open and fell apart. "It's a baby—or it will be. It's *my* baby, and it's real, and it's defenseless, and I'm going to be a *great* mother."

But it wasn't that simple. She was too scared and confused to see the real problem. "We don't have a soul for him, Melanie."

"Or her. It could be a girl." Her words came out in broken, halting syllables half choked by wrenching sobs.

"The gender doesn't matter if the baby doesn't live."

"Maybe Mom will . . ." She couldn't finish the sentence, and I couldn't finish it for her. The thought was too horrible to voice.

"You know she won't." Our mother was only thirty-nine years old, and I couldn't say for sure why she'd ever had kids in the first place. The chances of her giving up her life—miserable as it was lately—for an illegally conceived grandchild she would never see were slim to none.

"One of Adam's parents, then. They love him. They won't want his baby to die."

She was right. But Adam's parents weren't much older than our mom, and . . . "Do you really want to take one of his parents away from him? Away from *Penny*?" Adam's little sister was only twelve—way too young to lose one of her parents and half of the family's income. "Would you really make them decide who should die to pay for a mistake you and Adam made?"

She looked crushed by the realization that that was exactly what she'd be doing. "What about the public registry?"

"Melanie, that's no guarantee!" And I wasn't even sure they'd put her baby on the list if the Church declared her unfit to procreate. They would never make her end the pregnancy—in fact, they wouldn't *let* her—but they wouldn't hesitate to let the child die a natural, soulless death.

"Then I'll pledge to the Church!" she cried, swiping tears from her cheeks with both hands, and I glanced nervously at the closed laundry room door. We couldn't hide forever, but we couldn't afford to be discovered before we had a plan. And my sister pledging to join the Church was *not* a good plan.

Sure, if she pledged, they'd put her baby on the very short, very elite Church registry—a list of elderly Church officials who were ready to give up their souls to support the next generation of life. But then they'd take the baby, not as a ward, like the orphans, but as an ecclesiastic dedication. A human tithe. In another town. She would never see him again, and at eighteen, he would be ordained without choice, his soul to be paid for with lifelong service to the Church by both mother and child.

"You don't want to pledge, Mellie," I said, though I couldn't make myself voice the reasons.

She wiped her eyes again and looked at me with more determination than I'd ever seen from her. "What I don't want is to let this baby die."

I stared at her. I wasn't sure I recognized my own sister in that moment. Melanie had changed in the hour since we'd walked to school. She was still young and impulsive, and still wasn't quite thinking things through, but at some point she'd come to value her unborn child's life more than her own, and that made her a better mother than ours had ever been.

"I can do this, Nina," she said, and that determination I'd seen in her eyes echoed in her voice. "I know you think I never take anything seriously, and I mess everything up, but I can do this, and if you'll help me, I may not have to join the Church. I'll do whatever you say." She took my hand in both of hers. "I'll do all the laundry, and the dishes, and anything else you need me to do, if you'll just help me keep my baby. Please, Nina!"

She was too young. We couldn't guarantee her baby a

soul. Even if it lived and the Church let her keep it, we couldn't afford to feed and clothe a baby. And I wouldn't be able to pledge and become a teacher, because Melanie couldn't do this on her own. To give her baby even a *chance* at life, I would have to spend the rest of mine in a factory.

I knew I should say no. But I couldn't.

"Okay. I'll help you. But you have to understand that there are no guarantees. If the Church decides to prosecute"—and they would if Deacon Bennett saw her as an embarrassment to the town—"you could serve serious time." Unpaid prison workers were the nation's largest source of factory labor, producing everything from paper cups and clothing to car parts and traffic signals, in every plant that had survived the war. "And even if you don't go to jail, you'll have at least two convictions on your record." One for fornication, one for conceiving a child without a license. "Those'll keep you out of college." Which was a real shame, because Melanie was smart. She had a head for numbers and a memory for facts and dates. "And they may still take the baby. But I'll do the best I can."

My sister threw her arms around me, sobbing her thanks onto my shoulder, where her tears and snot mixed with the rainwater already soaked into my shirt.

I held her for a moment, trying to squelch the sudden certainty that I'd just nominated us both for execution.

Then I let her go, hyperaware of the clock ticking over the door. We'd been sequestered in the laundry room for ten minutes. It didn't seem possible for so much to have changed in less than a quarter of an hour, but clocks don't lie.

Melanie sniffled. "So . . . now what?"

"You go home." That was the only part of the plan I had worked out so far. I waved one hand at the utility sink in the corner. "Wash your face, and don't cry anymore or you'll attract attention. Go out through the admin building so you won't have to climb the fence, but do *not* get caught in here. Follow the tracks home so no one will see you on the street either. I'll tell Anabelle you're sick—that you ran out so you wouldn't throw up on the floor—and see if she can buy us some time by scheduling a makeup physical. But they're going to find out, Melanie."

We'd just have to make sure they found out on our terms.

My sister and I parted ways in the hall, where I watched her sneak around a corner, and then I headed in the other direction, letting my wet shoes squeak on the tile floor in an attempt to cover the sound of hers. If I got caught, I could say I was looking for her. If she got caught . . .

She couldn't get caught.

When I got to the quad again, the rain had almost stopped, but poor Matthew Mercer was still soaked, and this time he didn't look up when I passed him or when a neat line of second graders filed past us both on the way to the worship center.

Back in the gym, I pulled Anabelle aside and told her that Melanie was sick, and that I'd told her to go home and rest. When I asked if she could schedule a makeup physical, she looked suspicious but promised to try.

I wanted to sneak out and follow my sister home, where I could consider our options without the distraction of teachers and classes and other students whispering—some outright asking—about Melanie's breakdown. But if I snuck out, my absence would be just as obvious as my sister's.

During third period, the front office sent a note for me to deliver to her after school. It was a formal notice for her to present herself for discipline first thing in the morning.

After school, I stuffed the discipline notice into my satchel along with my books and walked home the long way, which led me past the Grab-n-Go. I stood across the street for several minutes, watching through the window for Dale, the assistant manager, to take his afternoon break. That would leave Ruth at the register, and Ruth never looked up from her crossword puzzle long enough to notice that I'd paid for the gum on the counter but not the food in my satchel.

I hadn't come for food this time, and that fact made me even more determined to avoid Dale.

When he disappeared into the back room, I jogged

across the street and into the store, wishing for the millionth time that there was no bell to announce my presence. Ruth looked up, focused on me for half a second while I perused the selection of candy, then went back to her puzzle.

As usual, I hesitated in front of the locked display case of cola, where a single bottle had been gathering dust for most of the last year because no one in the neighborhood could afford it. Then I drifted silently toward the half aisle of toiletries and over-the-counter medications while the screen mounted at the front of the store played the news.

"The badly mutilated corpse of April Walden, the teen who went missing from Solace two days ago, was discovered in the badlands south of New Temperance yesterday, less than a month after her seventeenth birthday. Church officials believe she was killed by a degenerate."

"No shit . . . ," I mumbled, wandering slowly down the aisle, listening for any mention of the degenerate killed fifty feet from where I stood.

"Still no word on why Walden left the safety of Solace's walls, but one high-ranking Church official ventured to conjecture that she was, in fact, possessed before she ever left the town."

After that, the reporter transitioned to the latest death toll from the front lines in Asia, where brave soldiers and elite teams of exorcists were steadfastly beating back the last of the Unclean in the name of the Unified Church.

As they'd been doing all my life. The location sometimes changed as one area was pronounced cleared and troops moved to cleanse another region, but the battles themselves were always the same.

We always won, but it was never easy. Losses were inevitable. Sacrifices would be honored and remembered.

I'd taken three more steps toward a narrow white box on the top shelf when a familiar six-note melody signaled the switch to the local news, which played on the hour, every hour, to keep citizens informed about the happenings close to home. The happenings the Church wanted us to know about, anyway.

I'd sold our television almost two years before, when I realized I'd rather have a functioning microwave than hear the same pointless recitation of "news" over and over, night after night.

But this time I listened closely. A degenerate inside the town walls would *definitely* make the local news, and with any luck, the report would tell me how close the police were to identifying the mystery boy and girl who had fled the scene that morning.

"Church officials are on the lookout for a group of adolescent offenders last spotted near New Temperance, wanted for truancy, heresy, and theft. Reports indicate that the group has between three and five members, only two of whom have been identified at this time. Reese Cardwell is seventeen years old. He has light skin, brown hair, and brown eyes, but his most prominent feature is his size. Cardwell is six feet six inches tall, and his weight is estimated at over two hundred and thirty pounds."

The school picture they flashed on the screen could have been any boy at my school. He looked young and friendly, and you can't tell much about a person's size from a head shot.

"Devi Dasari has dark hair and eyes and is estimated to be five feet seven inches tall. Demonic possession is suspected for all members of the group, but unconfirmed at this time. Citizens are asked to report any suspicious activity and unfamiliar faces to your local Church leaders."

Fugitives in New Temperance . . . And if the fugitives were suspected of possession, there would be exorcists in New Temperance too.

I'd seen both suspicious activity and unfamiliar faces that very morning, and New Temperance was too small and dull a town for that to be coincidence. But one of the faces I'd seen had belonged to a degenerate—definitely not a teenager—and the other belonged to an exorcist too young and unbranded to be ordained by the Church.

Why wasn't the news reporting the dead degenerate? Were the possibly possessed teen fugitives unconnected to the demon that attacked me? Was their story big enough to eclipse reports of a degenerate *inside the town walls*?

That was almost too far-fetched a thought to process. Obviously, the news was omitting some relevant—and no doubt important—piece of the story. Probably the piece that would connect the dots.

But on the bright side, there was no report of a fifteen-year-old pregnant dissident arrested for disobeying the direct order of a Church official.

Near the middle of the aisle, I took the box I needed from the top shelf, wiped dust from it with my hand, then slid it into my satchel. At the end of the aisle, I turned left, heading toward the gum for my legitimate purchase. But I froze two steps later when Dale stepped into my path.

"Whatcha got there, Nina?" he asked softly so Ruth wouldn't hear.

"Nothing yet." I pointed past him at the display of chewing gum.

"Open your bag."

Shit! "Not today, Dale. Please." The word tasted sour, but I was willing to beg. I couldn't leave the store without what I'd come for, and I couldn't let him see what that was.

"Nothin's free," he whispered, stepping so close I could smell the coffee on his breath. "You gotta pay, one way or another." His pointed glance at Ruth was a threat to rat me out. He knew as well as I did that there were no more than three coins in my pocket—nowhere near enough for what I'd taken, even if he didn't know what that was. "Your choice."

But it wasn't, really. It was never my choice.

He gestured for me to precede him down the aisle, and I did—I knew the way—my stomach churning harder with every step. At the back of the store, he led me past the grimy restrooms and into a small supply closet, where he held the door open for me in a farce of chivalry.

I took a deep, bitter breath, then stepped inside and shoved a mop bucket with my foot to make room. Dale came in after me, and I pressed my back against the wall to put as much space between us as possible. He pulled the door closed and fumbled for the switch in the dark. A single bulb overhead drenched the closet in weak yellow light, casting ominous shadows beneath his features, making him look scarier than he really was.

Dale was a dick, and a stupid dick at best. But he wasn't scary. Demons were scary. The Church was scary. Dale was just an opportunistic asshole in a position of minor power.

"Give me the bag."

I set my satchel on the floor and pinned it against the wall with my feet. He couldn't know. No one could know.

"Fine. Take it off."

My teeth ground together as I unbuttoned my blouse. I closed my eyes so I wouldn't have to see him, but I couldn't avoid hearing the way his breathing changed. The way his inhalations hitched, his exhalations growing heavier and wetter with each button that slid through its hole.

"Take it off," he repeated when I reached the last button.

Eyes still closed, I let the material slide off my shoulders, down to my elbows. His feet shuffled on the concrete floor, and I squeezed my eyes shut tighter. A second later, his fingers were there, greedy and eager. They pushed at the remaining material, shoving my bra up, squeezing, pinching.

I let it happen. I had no other way to pay.

But when his fingers fumbled with the button of my pants, my eyes flew open. "No."

His hands stilled but didn't retreat. "It's not just a can of soup this time, is it? Or a loaf of bread? Whatever's in that bag today, I think you really want it. I think you *need* it. Well, guess what I need. . . ."

He tried for the button again, and I shoved him back, then clutched the open halves of my blouse to my chest. "I said *no*."

"You want me to call the police?"

I made a decision then. One I couldn't have made a day earlier. "Call them. I'll tell them how you've been charging a poor, hungry schoolgirl for a year and a half, corroding my morals and defiling my innocence. We'll see who they arrest."

His hands fell away and his gaze hardened, staring into mine. Trying to decide whether or not to call my bluff— and any other day, it *would* have been a bluff, because I couldn't afford for the police and my mother to meet. But thanks to Melanie's collection of offenses, they were going to meet anyway, sooner or later, and if picking "sooner" would keep Dale's hands off me, so be it.

I suffered a minor moment of panic when I realized that if I had him arrested, there would be no more free food. But then, it was never really free in the first place, was it?

"This arrangement is over." I tugged my bra back into place, trying to forget the feel of his fingers on my skin. I buttoned my shirt while he glared at me, and then I threw my satchel over my shoulder and pushed past him to the door.

I marched to the front of the store and paid for my gum. Ruth didn't even notice my untucked shirt.

"If I ever see you in here again, I *will* call the police," Dale growled through clenched teeth as I reached for the front door.

I stopped with the door halfway open and turned back to look at him. "If you ever see me in here again, you'll *need* them."

FIVE

The walk home felt longer and colder without Melanie next to me. When I passed the Mercer house, two doors down from ours, I wondered who was watching Matthew and his sister. Then I wondered if Sister Camilla had ever let the poor kid off his knees. The Church had discretion—she could keep him until his parents came and signed for him if she wanted, and there was little his parents could do or say about it without seeming to support their son's sins.

A child's behavior was widely considered a reflection of his parents' private lives, and few ever protested a child's harsh punishment for fear of being declared an unfit care-giver and losing custody of the "sinful" child in question.

The drizzle had stopped, but daylight was already fading,

accelerated by the dreary cloud cover. Soon Matthew could add his fear of the dark to his current cold, wet misery.

Our house was quiet when I went in through the back door, careful not to let it slam behind me. Mom usually slept through dinner, and most days, if we were careful, by the time she got up we'd already be in our room for the night, whispering while we finished our homework. But now things had changed. I'd planned for us to eat one of the cans of soup I'd taken from the Turners, with a slice of bread each, but was that enough for an expectant mother? Should I make both cans? Or give her the last of the peanut butter as well?

I'd just burned my bridge at the only store within walking distance, which meant that when the soup and peanut butter were gone, I'd have to break into the emergency cash for bus fare to an actual grocery store and either pay for some food or risk getting caught shoplifting by employees whose habits I didn't know.

One more year.

If Mellie and Adam had waited one more year to give in to their hormones, I would have been old enough to work full-time.

But then, I had no high ground to stand on. I couldn't even claim to have loved the boys I'd used in my carnal rebellion against the Church. At least my sister had that—someone who loved her. And surely once she told him about the baby, he'd want to help feed it.

And its mother.

Melanie's satchel hung over her chair at the kitchen table, but that was the only obvious sign that she'd made it home. When I opened the bedroom door, my sister sat up on the bed, her eyes wide with fear until she recognized me in the dying light from the half-covered window. "Did she wake up?" I whispered, pulling the door closed behind me.

Melanie shook her head, and I knew with one look at her rumpled school clothes that she'd been in bed all day, not because she was tired or sick, but because moving around the house would have increased the chances of our mother waking up to find her at home.

"Anabelle scheduled the makeup physical for next week, but she couldn't get you out of this." I reached into my satchel for the disciplinary notice and handed it to Mellie. She set it on her scuffed nightstand without reading it. She knew what it was with a single glance at the heading on the paper.

"And I picked this up for you on the way home. I figure we should be sure before we start borrowing serious trouble." I pulled the stolen cardboard box from my satchel and tossed it onto the bed. Even if I'd had the money to pay for it, I couldn't have—you have to show identification and a parenting license to buy a pregnancy test.

Melanie picked up the box with shaking hands. "I didn't even think of that."

"I know." My sister was smart but impractical. She

thought about things all day long, but rarely about anything that would put food on the table or clothes on our backs.

"Should I take it now?"

I set my satchel on the end of my bed. "The sooner, the better."

Melanie opened the cardboard box—her hands still shaking—and read the directions while I changed into the same jeans and long-sleeved tee I'd worn the previous afternoon. "I'm pretty sure you just have to pee on the stick," I said, when she still seemed confused by the time I was fully dressed.

"I know. But when I do that, we'll *know*. For better or worse, we'll know for sure, and I'll have to stop pretending everything could still be okay."

"Everything *will* be okay, Mel. One way or another. I promise." She gave me a small, terrified smile. "Now, go pee on the stupid stick."

I followed her to the bathroom and stood in the doorway while she took the test and then covered the end of the stick with its plastic cap and set it on the bathroom counter. We both stared at the indicator while she flushed the toilet and rinsed her hands.

The directions said we had to wait two minutes before reading the results, but the second line appeared in the result window in less than half that time. Before Mellie could even dry her hands.

Phantom obligation settled onto my shoulders, and I felt

my connection to the outside world severed, as surely as I'd felt the snip that severed my genetic line—not physically, but *absolutely*. There would be no college, no teaching, and no career. For me, there would only ever be New Temperance and whichever factory job would put the most food on the table and diapers in the pantry.

"That's it, then." Melanie sank onto the toilet seat, the test stick held between her thumb and forefinger as if it might break. "This is really happening." Two fresh tears rolled slowly down her cheeks. "I'm actually pregnant."

"You little *bitch*!"

Melanie's gaze snapped up and her eyes went wide. I turned to find our mother standing in her bedroom doorway, one bony, blue-veined hand clutching the doorjamb. Her faded tee hung from her shoulders straight to her bare thighs, too big on her thin frame, and her skin was paler than I remembered. Paler than it had been the day before, somehow. I could see most of her veins through her flesh.

My mom grabbed my arm and hauled me out of the way with more strength than should have been possible from such a frail form and wasted muscles. Her grip bruised. She stepped into the bathroom doorway, her thin feet straddling the threshold, and somehow she seemed to take up more room than she should have.

Melanie tried to back away from her, but she was trapped between the toilet and the tub.

"How far?" My mom's voice was rough. Scratchy, as if she'd been gargling gravel.

"I don't . . . ? Wh-what . . . ?" Melanie stuttered, and the pregnancy test fell from her hand to clatter across the floor.

Mom picked it up, and her knees cracked when she moved. I frowned, staring at her ankles. Had the bones always been so prominent? She glanced at the test, then threw it at Melanie.

Mellie flinched. The plastic stick hit the tile beside her right ear and broke into several pieces. I did an automatic inventory of the bathroom, trying to anticipate what would be thrown next and how badly it could hurt my sister if Mom's aim improved.

Ancient, heavy hair dryer. Empty hand soap bottle. Stick of deodorant.

"How. Far. Along?" our mother demanded carefully, deliberately, and I wasn't sure whether she was going slowly for her own benefit or for Melanie's. "How old is the belly rat?" She shot an angry look at my sister's flat stomach.

"I . . . I don't know." Tears trailed down Melanie's cheeks, and the rims of her eyes were red. "I've only missed one cycle."

Mom nodded sharply, her thin hair brushing her bony shoulders, and her gaze lost focus. "We'll fix it. I know someone who can do it safely, but it's a drive. . . ."

"No . . ." Melanie slid to the floor with her arms crossed over her abdomen, her knees pulled up to her chest. "No, I won't. Nina's going to help me keep it."

"Nina's going to . . . ?" My mother turned to me. Her eyes flashed white for a moment, as if they were reflecting more light than was actually available. Like cat eyes in the dark. I took a step back. Something was wrong. More wrong than usual.

"I'll be almost eighteen when the baby's born." I met her angry gaze and held it. "I can work full-time. I can take care of us. *All* of us." I hoped that including her under my umbrella of support might help, even though we hadn't been under hers in nearly two years.

Not that I expected her to last much more than another year. The drugs were killing her—but not fast enough. She'd live past the birth out of spite, just to keep the baby from getting her soul. Because my mother was a selfish bitch.

That was the first of many survival lessons I'd learned.

"Nina's not going to do a thing," my mom spat, glaring at me. Then she turned back to Melanie. "And *you* are going to do exactly what I tell you. Change your clothes. Now. Put on something dark."

When my sister didn't move, my mom lunged forward and hauled her up by one arm, though Mellie had to outweigh her by fifteen pounds. She pulled Melanie down the short hall and threw her into our bedroom, where my sister stumbled, then half collapsed on the bed.

"Don't worry. I'll talk her down," I whispered to my terrified sister as Mom stomped past me into the living room, headed for the kitchen. "Just . . . change out of your school clothes. Put on anything."

Our mother had never been warm and fuzzy. I had no childhood memory of hugs and kisses, or birthday presents, or being pushed in a park swing. In fact, I didn't understand that those things were the norm until the night of my third-grade Church creed recital, when all the other parents had rushed the stage afterward to pull their children into praise-laden embraces.

My mom hadn't even shown up.

But she used to be functional, at least. She did what needed to be done when we were too young to do it ourselves. I was around nine when I realized she thought of us as a second job, but I never did figure out why she'd bothered with parenting licenses and her two allotted pregnancies in the first place if she really knew someone who could have taken care of the infestations in her womb.

I followed my mom into the kitchen, where I stood in the doorway watching her, trying to understand what she was mumbling. She seemed to be having two different conversations with herself—or maybe half of one—and I didn't understand any of it.

"Twenty years . . ." She pulled the teakettle from a lower cabinet, then let the door slam shut. "Planning. Searching. Negotiating. Waiting. All for *nothing*."

The next part was lost to the clang of the teakettle in the sink and the *shhhh* of running water as she filled it.

". . . and they ruin it all! One gets herself sterilized, and the other can't keep her pants buttoned!" She slammed the kettle down on one of the front burners, then lit the gas beneath it and turned the flames up so high they licked the side of the kettle, baking the peeling paint.

"Worthless!" My mother threw open the cabinet over the toaster, then cursed and slammed it shut. "Where's the tea?" she demanded, whirling on me. I didn't think she'd even noticed me there.

"We're out." We'd been out of tea for eight months, since she'd stopped drinking it, at least at home. Since she'd stopped eating, talking, and coming out of her room even to yell at us. Over the past year, her angry, resentful tirades had faded into listless neglect as my mother retreated into her own head, into her room, and into nights spent out and days spent sleeping. Or unconscious. Or both.

"Do you have any idea what youth is worth?" she demanded, as if she'd already forgotten the tea.

I shook my head and backed into the living room when she stomped closer, her eyes wild, wisps of pale hair floating around her face as if they were so thin gravity couldn't touch them.

"*Gold*, Nina. Youth is the gold setting, and innocence is the glittering diamond in the center. Throwing your own away wasn't enough, was it? You had to let her do it too. This is *your* fault." She wagged one bony finger at me. "All she had to do was keep her skirt down for a few . . . more . . . years." My mother turned back to the kitchen and threw open another cabinet. "She would have been enough to keep me going. To keep *us* going. But now she's worth half the listing price. Worth *nothing,* if we can't get that *thing* out of her."

"What? Mom, I don't know what you're talking about." I understood the individual words, but they made no sense together. No sense I wanted to see, anyway. Yet with each word she spoke—each mention of worth, and listing price—the goose bumps on my arms grew taller. Fatter.

"Of course you don't. Because she's the smart one. You're the fighter and she's the thinker, but none of that matters now. It *never* mattered, but you never figured that out. Because you're not the thinker. But that's okay, because I don't need you to think."

She spun again, so fast she should have lost her balance, but she didn't fall. Somehow, though her thin frame lacked both grace and stability, her balance was flawless and her strength was . . . terrifying.

What the *hell* was she on?

"Keys . . ." She opened drawer after drawer, only to slam them shut again when she couldn't find what she wanted. "Where the hell are my keys?"

"Mom, you can't drive. You're . . . not well."

"Not well!" Feverish laughter bubbled out of her mouth and spilled into the room. It seemed to bounce off the walls and strike my skull at exactly the wrong angle. "I'm not well. I haven't been well in a long time. But that's about to change." She closed her eyes, and when she opened them again, her gaze pinned me to the spot where I stood. "Fine. You drive."

"I can't." Because I'd sold the car. *"Why?"* I demanded through clenched teeth, when the anger and confusion and fear became too much to think through. Too much to breathe through. And I only realized in retrospect that I wasn't asking about her tantrum, or about what she was trying to make Melanie do. "Why did you have us in the first place? You don't want us. You don't even like us. *So why the hell are we here?"*

My mother turned to me slowly. Her eyes flashed again like they had in the hall, as if they were reflecting some light source I couldn't see.

"He made you, didn't he?" I guessed in a horrified half whisper. "My dad. He made you have us, didn't he?"

In my mind—in the stories I'd made up for Melanie when we were little—that was always how it went. Our father fell in love with our mother a long time ago, when she was still young and beautiful. Long before the drugs ruined her body and fried her brain. She was his weakness—the only flaw in a kind, caring man who'd loved us until the day he'd died, when Mellie was still a baby.

I had no memory of him—nothing to contradict the story the way I told it.

"Your *dad*?" She laughed again, as if the very concept were ridiculous. "Nina, you never had a dad. I married Oliver to keep the Church out of my uterus, but he wasn't your father. Your father was a very special man with a very special gift, and it took me almost two years to find him. I danced and touched and flirted, and he made a small genetic donation, and Oliver—Melanie's father—never suspected a thing." Her gaze was colder and harder than I'd ever seen it, and then suddenly it was blurred by the tears filling my eyes. "Oliver wanted you to be his. I needed you to be someone else's. But ultimately, you were mine." Her eyes narrowed. "You *are* mine."

My blood boiled in response to the lies she was spewing. They *were* lies. They *had* to be. "You're crazy. The drugs have finally baked your brain."

"I'm not an addict, Nina." The kettle whistled, and she took it off the burner without a pot holder. The handle left an angry red mark on her palm, but she didn't seem to feel it. "Drugs didn't do this to me." Her sweeping gesture took in her entire body. Then she turned and stood on her toes to pull a box from the top cabinet, and her shirt rose to reveal emaciated thighs.

I turned off the burner while she set the box on the countertop, flipped open the torn cardboard lid, then pulled out a white pill bottle. "Vitamin E, for my skin and my immune system." She set the bottle on the counter, then dug out another one. "Vitamin C, to regenerate antioxidants and firm up collagen. Can't you see how *well* it's working?

"Vitamin K." She set another bottle on the counter, then dug out a fourth and a fifth and a sixth. "Calcium. Niacin. Vitamin A. The rest of these you've probably never heard of." She tilted the box so I could see another half-dozen bottles inside. "The drugs I take are to slow what's happening to my body, and I'm paying on credit. Which means that someday I'll have to make good on my debts. You would have figured it all out by now if you were smarter. Your sister would have figured it out if she were older. But I managed to create the perfect combination of youth and ignorance with the two of you. I probably couldn't do it again if I tried."

She looked at me then. *Really* looked at me, studying my features like she hadn't in years. Maybe ever. And somehow, her scrutiny was even scarier than her neglect had been. "You were perfect, and you never even knew it. You were my perfect, lovely little shell, just waiting to mature. Beautiful on the outside. Flawless on the inside. Until you weren't."

For just a moment, as I tried to puzzle through the indecipherable tangle of sentences that dangled from her tongue, I thought she might cry. Her eyes were damp. Sad.

But then her gaze went hard and her jaw clenched in

anger. "I drank half a bottle of vodka the day I got the call. My daughter had been declared unfit for reproduction. They'd already snipped your tubes and tied neat little knots in our future by the time they bothered to tell me. Over a runny nose and flat feet! There was nothing I could do."

My head spun. I backed away from her until my calves hit the couch, and then I sat, because the alternative was to collapse on the floor.

I'd wanted my mother that day like I'd never wanted her before or since. When I woke up in my infirmary bed, near the end of the line of girls all waking to the same devastating realization, I'd wanted my mother to hold me. To hug me and tell me that everything would be okay. That they could come at me with scalpels and sutures and sever my bloodline along with my fallopian tubes, but they could never cut out my thoughts, and they could only kill my dreams if I let them.

I still had worth. I still had hope. My future was whatever I wanted to make of it.

That was what the other mothers said to their newly sterile fifteen-year-old daughters. I could hear them. But the chair by my bed held only my little sister, her eyes as wide as saucers and as wet as the ocean. She was as scared as I was angry, and together we could only cry.

"You ruined everything for us that day," my mother spat. "I *planned* for you, and I *saved* for you, and I carried you *so* carefully. You and your descendants would have been my future—a long line of made-to-order hosts. A genetic gift to myself. My legacy. Instead, you got yourself sterilized, ruining *decades* of planning, and your sister, whose value depended entirely on youth and purity, got herself knocked up. You're a perfect pair, the two of you—beautiful and largely worthless. An exquisite catastrophe."

I couldn't make any sense of that last bit, because the first part kept playing in my head.

You ruined everything for us that day.

Had I? Had my sterilization been the trigger for our mother's descent into depression and neglect? And madness, evidently? Was I the reason she'd stopped even trying to be a parent?

My hands were damp with nervous sweat, so I wiped them on my jeans, but I couldn't do anything about the ache deep in my chest.

"Nina?" Melanie said, and I looked up to find her standing in the middle of the living room in jeans and a dark blue shirt, staring past me at our mother, who now clutched her car keys in her burned right hand. "What is she saying?"

I opened my mouth to tell her that everything would be okay, but the words melted like sugar on my tongue—sweet yet insubstantial.

"I'm explaining the state of things to your sister." Our

mother turned back to the teakettle. "Nina's a little slow today, but I think she's finally starting to understand just how badly the two of you have screwed things up for our happy family. But mostly for me."

Listing price. Made-to-order hosts. Genetic donation.

A picture was forming in my head, but it wouldn't come into focus.

"Fifteen is young." Mom was talking to herself now, as if she'd just thought of something new, but I couldn't even process what she'd already thrown at me, much less whatever screwed-up epiphany she was having. "Maybe youth will balance out a loss of innocence. Some of it, anyway." She whirled around then and eyed Melanie as she'd eyed me minutes earlier. "Thin but well shaped. Pretty," she muttered, and her gaze lost focus again. "Of course she's pretty. Her genes were carefully selected. This one will age well if she's not overworked." She blinked, and her gaze focused on Melanie again. "You might still be worth something after all."

"Nina . . . ?" Mellie was close to panic, and I wanted to help her, but I was confused. Lost and drifting in a sea of words that made no sense. Dots I couldn't connect.

"I could crunch the numbers," Mom continued, wandering around the kitchen now as if we weren't even there. "The profit margin is narrow, and I'll need a new genetic donor"—she glanced at me, and chills shot through every bone in my body—"but it's not a total loss. I'll just have to get a credit extension . . ." Her gaze fell on Mellie again, and my sister started to tremble. "Assuming I get fair market value."

And she must have been right about Melanie being the smart one, because my little sister figured it out first. Part of it, anyway. I could tell from the raw horror shining in her eyes and the way she backed away from us slowly, as if she were afraid to move too far, too fast, and trigger some sort of predatory instinct in our mother.

"No . . . ," Melanie moaned. "Nina, she's going to sell me."

"What?" How could you sell a *person*? Who would buy a fifteen-year-old girl?

Then I remembered Dale-the-dick and his favorite form of currency, and my blood curdled in my veins. *No . . .*

"You would sell your own *daughter*?" Melanie whispered, but her angry gaze was much bolder than her voice. Her eyes demanded answers.

Our mother laughed, and the cruel sound resonated in every cell in my body. "I don't have daughters. I have very carefully conceived investments. You were *born* to be sold." Then she turned to me. "And you to be bred. Strange how sometimes life just laughs in your face, isn't it?"

"She's crazy," I whispered, edging toward Melanie with my arms out, as if I could shield her. Our mother had lost what was left of her mind. And her heart. What kind of parent would sell her own child?

And we *were* her children. Melanie had her fair hair and skin. I had her eyes, pale blue, and virtually colorless when we got angry.

Mellie only shook her head. "Not crazy, Nina. She's possessed."

An ice-cold lump of terror fell into my stomach and lodged there.

It wasn't possible. Not in New Temperance. Not half a mile from the school and less than two miles from a worship center. Not in my own *home*.

The news reported the occasional isolated domestic possession, along with footage of black cassock–clad exorcists sent in to deal with the problem, but there hadn't been a documented possession in New Temperance since Clare Parker, and few people believed she really was possessed. Clare's execution was a display of power. A threat to all future sinners. And it had worked.

But my mother was . . . something else.

She smiled at me slowly, and her eyes flashed. I knew in that instant that Melanie was right.

My mom was a demon.

SIX

My mother watched me from across the kitchen doorway, and my heart felt like it was going to *explode*. It was beating too fast, and everything in my living room looked really crisp and clear, as if my eyes were working better than my other senses. As if they could make up for not seeing what had been there all along.

My sister's feet whispered on the worn carpet behind me as we both retreated slowly. Suddenly my hands felt empty. I felt like I should be holding a weapon now that I knew my mother was a demon, but that didn't make much sense. She'd been a demon for who knew how long, and I'd never needed a weapon before.

But then, she'd had nothing to fear before we knew her secret.

"Mellie, go next door and use the phone." I was whispering, but my voice felt like a hammer bludgeoning fragile silence in the wake of our demonic discovery. "Call the Church."

"Yes, call them." My mother's smile was slow and cold, and it was all for Melanie. "They'll probably set me on fire around the same time they scrape the embryo from your womb. Or maybe they'll just cut the whole thing out of you. Won't have to worry about unauthorized breeding if you haven't got the parts for it, huh?"

"Melanie, *go*," I said, but I could feel her behind me, so close I could smell her shampoo, and I could practically taste her fear. "They won't do that." They wouldn't kill the baby. But they *would* use it against her, trading its life for her service and obedience.

They would make an example of her. Of both of us. They'd say we should have known. They wouldn't believe that my mother had been possessed right under my nose and I'd had no idea. I could hardly believe that myself.

I'd seen the withdrawal from life, the neglect and disinterest, and the obvious illness, yet demonic possession had never occurred to me. Why? Why did I see drug use instead? Because the changes happened slowly?

Or because there wasn't really much of a change at all?

And that was when I truly started to understand the scope of the lie we'd been living. My mother hadn't changed because she was possessed. She'd changed because she was deteriorating. Because her soul was almost completely devoured and her health was starting to decline. Her body was starting to mutate.

To degenerate.

But . . . it should take *years* for a possessed host to become a degenerate. Nearly two decades, under optimal circumstances. There was no telling how long our mother had been in the possession of the Unclean.

For a moment, that thought almost made me happy, because it offered relief. The problem wasn't that we were unlovable; it was that our mother wasn't *capable* of love. Because she wasn't our mother. She wasn't even human.

Then that thought began to resonate, and I couldn't let it go, even though interrogating a demon was a *really* bad idea.

"How long?" I asked as Melanie tugged me backward. Away from the demon.

How long had Leona Kane's body been possessed by the monster calling itself our mother? Since her descent into drug-fueled withdrawal from life? Since before my sterilization? Since my third-grade recital?

Longer? It *had* to be longer. Degenerates aren't built in a day.

"Ask your sister," the demon in my mother's skin said. "I think she's finally figured it out."

"Mel?" I squeezed her hand. I wanted to look at her—to see for myself if she knew something I didn't—but I couldn't afford to take my focus from the demon. "How long, Mellie?"

"Always," Melanie whispered, and fresh horror washed over me. "Or very close to it."

Our mother's head nodded, as if the demon behind her eyes was proud of at least one of its . . . investments. "I always knew she was the smart one." Her gaze found me again. "Fortunately, I don't need you for your brain."

"We were never supposed to be her children," Mellie continued in a horrified, haunted voice. "We're her business. Souls to steal. Bodies to wear. Right?"

"In your case, a body to *sell*," the demon corrected, and Melanie shuddered all over. "Nina is my next host, born and bred for that very purpose. But you, dear Melanie, are an investment. My payment plan. You can't imagine what a young, healthy body is worth to the right people." And by *people*, of course, she meant demons. She shrugged, and the gesture looked painful, as if her joints resisted the motion. "You would have been worth more as an eighteen-year-old virgin—of legal age—but at least you're not a total loss. I'll just consider this a lesson learned. Next time, staple the investment's knees together."

"Next time?" I was cold with shock. My teeth wanted to chatter. "You're going to do this again?" *Stop talking and run.* Every survival instinct I had was demanding my retreat. But I *had* to know. "Have you done this before? Did you breed our mother for this?" Demons could not be born, nor could they age. They could only move from host to host as each body wore out, consuming one irreplaceable soul after another. Had this demon *conceived and raised* our real mom, only to steal her body and soul when she came of age?

"I bred both Leona and her brother when I was in possession of their mother. The money from his sale kept me fed and clothed while I searched for your father." She glanced at Melanie. "And *your* father. How else is an independent demon supposed to make a living?" She shrugged, and both of her shoulders creaked with the motion. "Leona was never really your mother, though. She never met either of your fathers. She never carried you, in her womb or in her arms. She never changed a diaper or warmed a bottle. That was all me." The demon clutched a possessive handful of her shirt. "Leona was just a host and an incubator, who turned eighteen on the day I harvested her. The day I left her mother's dying body in favor of her young, healthy one. She thought she hated her mother, like you thought you hated yours, but she never got the answers you have now."

"How could you sell your own children?" Melanie demanded from my left, one hand laid protectively over her abdomen.

"We sell what we have." The demon took in my look of horror and seemed to enjoy it. "We *all* sell what we have. And you don't have much, do you, Nina? What did *you* sell?"

"Shut up." Was the demon seriously questioning my morals?

"What did you sell, Nina?" she repeated, and Melanie looked at me with round, sad eyes.

"I fed us," I spat, backing away from her again. "I did what I had to do so we could eat, when *you* would have let us starve. What kind of business sense does that make, anyway? How were you going to sell half-starved host bodies?"

"I wouldn't have let you starve," she insisted, but she was lying. I could see it. For whatever reason, maybe because she was sick—and she was *obviously* sick—she'd lost sight of the goal. She'd abandoned us as investments, like she'd abandoned us as children. "I know what I'm doing. She"—she glanced briefly at Melanie—"is worth enough that I won't have to breed any more brats for another generation or two. Which is good, because you took that option right off the table, didn't you?"

I didn't answer. I *had* no answer.

"Sit." She plucked the kitchen phone from its dock. "I have to make a call."

We didn't sit. Melanie's hand tightened around mine again, and we backed slowly toward the front door because we already knew what our not-mother was about to discover.

"It's dead!" She threw the phone across the room, and Mellie flinched when it smashed through the window over the kitchen sink.

"The service was cut off six weeks ago." I fought the urge to look back and see how close to the front door—and potential escape—we were. "That's what happens when you stop paying." We'd had to prioritize. Phone or heat.

I didn't have anyone to call, anyway.

"Sit!" she roared. The demon actually *roared*, and my fingertips started to tingle with a strange warmth, like pinpricks of fire. When we didn't move, she lunged through the kitchen and halfway into the living room in a single step, and though I'd seen it before—that very morning—I was startled all over again by a demon's ability to make human bodies do things our physiology shouldn't have been capable of.

Our "mother" had abandoned her human guise entirely now. She moved as if her body had too many joints. As if her bones were too long. And maybe they were. She wasn't yet as deformed and animalistic as a degenerate, but her body was no longer fully human either. When had that happened? Was that why she slept all day—so we wouldn't notice?

Melanie screeched and let go of my hand. She tried to run, and the demon lunged for her. I stepped between them, and the demon bowled me over. My head smacked against the floor—concrete covered by thin carpet—and the room spun around me.

The demon launched herself off my abdomen, driving the air from my body as she pounced after Mellie like a cat. I forced myself up, gasping, when she dragged my sister away from the door and tossed her toward the couch. Melanie stumbled foot over foot and caught herself with one knee on the center cushion.

"Run," I gasped, still trying to catch my breath. But Melanie collapsed on the couch, crying, her knees tucked up to her chest.

"Where would she go?" the demon demanded, hunched in an agile squat between me and my sister. "We are everywhere. Seen but unseen. Known but unknown."

"She's lying." I backed away from Melanie, trying to draw the mother-monster my way so my sister could run. But Mellie only cowered. "The war is over. We won." The only surviving remnants of the demon hordes roamed the badlands as degenerates, and they were reportedly few and far between. And gradually dying off as they slowly starved for souls.

"Yes." The demon advanced on me, swaying sluggishly like a bridge in the wind. As if she might pounce again at any second. "*We* did."

"What does that mean?" I said as Melanie finally climbed off the couch and crawled toward the kitchen, and suddenly I wished we'd found a way to pay the phone bill. The Church could already be on its way.

"We are endless, Nina. We are *legion*." The demon stood straighter and frowned, as if my lack of a reaction disappointed her. "That statement would have scared the shit out of your grandparents. But my point is that there are more of us than you could *ever* imagine. We outnumber the grains of sand on the beach, the drops of water in the ocean. The seas in hell rage with us, rising and falling in waves, cresting and crushing one another. We bleed and moan and starve, yet we cannot die. We think of nothing but escape, yet there is nowhere to go. Nowhere but here. And for every one of us that breaks through, anchored in your world by the souls we devour, there are *thousands* still waiting, begging, fighting for the chance. But souls are finite and your bodies are fragile hosts. There will never be enough of either to go around. The only way to stay here is to find a new host before the old one dies, and every time one of us fails in that endeavor, another will rise to take its place. You. Cannot. Win."

Despair pinned me to the spot where I stood. Was she telling the truth? Were there really thousands of demons in hell for every one that had broken into our world? If so, why bother to fight? Humanity would fold in the end anyway. How could it not?

Then Melanie's gaze met mine over our mother's shoulder, and I remembered why we should fight. Why we'd been fighting for more than a century, though no one else seemed to realize the war was still raging.

Demons might win in the long run. In the future. That seemed inevitable. But *this* demon wasn't going to win *this* fight. She wasn't going to sell my sister and claim my soul.

This demon was going down.

"Run!" I shouted at Melanie. My sister stared at me in surprise for the half second it took our mother to whirl toward her. Then she took off for the back door, sneakers squealing on the scratched, faded linoleum.

The demon snarled and lurched after her, but I grabbed her thin arm.

She turned to me, her eyes flashing with a cold, bright white light. Her mouth opened wider than should have been possible with a human jaw, and terror shot through me like a thousand bolts of lightning. Suddenly I realized I had no idea what to do next. I hadn't thought beyond distracting her so Melanie could get out.

The demon snarled again—at me this time—and the back door slammed shut as she jerked her arm free from my grasp and lunged for the door. And that was when I understood that she couldn't hurt me. At least, she couldn't *kill* me. Not if she still wanted my body.

I sprinted several steps and grabbed a handful of my mother's shirt, then jerked the material as hard as I could. She made a strange strangling sound as the collar pulled tight against her throat. I yanked again, and she stumbled backward toward me.

"Keep running!" I shouted, with no idea whether or not Melanie could hear me. "Don't stop and don't come back! I'll find you after—"

After what? After I killed the demon?

Demons couldn't be killed; they could only be exorcised. But I wasn't an exorcist. The best I could do was kill the host body—my own *mother's* body—and even if I managed that, what was to stop the demon from then taking over my body? Which had been its plan all along.

Exorcist. I needed an exorcist. For the first time in my life, I was desperate to get in touch with the Church. But the phone was dead.

"Help!" I shouted, and the demon whirled on me, ripping her shirt from my grasp. "Someone call—" My mother's bony hand clamped over my mouth.

"They won't get here in time," she whispered, but her voice seemed to originate from inside my head, where the words echoed over one another in an endless, cacophonous loop. "By the time they arrive, this body will be dead and your body will be mine, and you—the part that makes you Nina Kane, anyway—will have been extinguished like the fragile, flickering candle flame you are."

My left hand burned, pinpricks of fire beneath my skin, a horrible itch I couldn't reach to scratch. My jaw ached—her hand was crushing my face.

"They'll think I'm you. Melanie will think so too. She'll think she's safe until the day I sell her to the highest bidder. Which will have to be before she starts to show, since 'Nina' wouldn't make her end the pregnancy."

Melanie would never fall for that, even if the demon did

have access to my memories. But my sister's knowledge wouldn't save her.

Terror skittered through every inch of me. I grabbed the demon's arm but couldn't make her let go. I tried to scream, but only a muffled moan escaped through her fingers. I tried to shove her, but she couldn't be moved.

"Shhh," she breathed into my ear, walking me backward. My pulse raced in terror and I stumbled, fighting to remain upright. "This shouldn't hurt a bit."

But it already hurt. My heart beat so hard it was surely about to burst. My silent screams bounced around in my head, bruising me in places that shouldn't have been able to feel pain.

She pushed harder, faster, and my feet couldn't keep up. I tripped, and she lifted me with her free hand, without uncovering my mouth. My feet no longer touched the floor.

An instant later, my back slammed into the wall. Pain shot along my spine and air burst from my lungs, through my nose. White dust drifted around us; she'd dented the drywall with my body.

Her hand left my mouth, but before I could scream— before I could even suck in a desperate breath—her lips closed over mine. Her mouth was cold, and her chill threatened to invade my warmth. My skin already tingled with the cold everywhere she touched me. But then she exhaled, and her chill crawled inside me, her life

105

force invading mine. Soon whatever it was that made her a demon would overwhelm whatever it was that made me human. Then I would be gone. Extinguished like the candle flame she'd called me.

And I couldn't fight her. I couldn't make it stop.

I pushed, but she stood firm. I pulled, but she resisted. I kicked, but my feet found no target.

I could feel that warmth—my soul—being absorbed. She was swallowing me whole.

I screamed, and she swallowed that too.

Then, in the distance, I heard the sirens. Melanie had gotten to a phone, even though I'd told her not to stop. She'd called someone. Help was coming. But it would be too late.

Tears poured down my face, leaking beneath my closed eyelids, and still the mother-monster sucked at my soul. I opened my eyes, but she was all I could see. The sirens still wailed in the distance, but time seemed to have slowed. The world sounded . . . stretched. Warped.

And finally I understood. I was losing consciousness.

No. I was dying.

The only thing I could feel, other than my mother's freezing lips and the dwindling warmth of my own soul being devoured, was the hot tingling in my left hand and the frantic ticking of my internal clock, counting down toward the end of my life. I had seconds left. I could feel it.

One more try. I owed it to Melanie. If the demon

possessed me before the authorities arrived, she'd be alone with a monster. Or in Church custody.

I tried to push the monster off again, this time with my tingling left hand. The moment my fingers touched her chest, something exploded between us. Something brighter than light and hotter than fire. Something I'd only seen in person once—that morning, when the rogue exorcist had saved my life.

The demon screeched and dropped me, and my feet finally hit the floor. Normal human warmth returned, like a flood washing over me. The monster tried to back away but couldn't disconnect from the fierce light still shining between us, so bright I wanted to close my eyes. But I couldn't look away from her or from the light glowing beneath my hand, still pressed to her chest.

She tried to scream and choked on the sound. She tried to run but was frozen in place.

Sight and sound zoomed back into focus around me. The wailing sirens abruptly stopped altogether, and distantly, I realized the police had never even gotten close.

Were they out on a different call? Had Mellie not stopped to call them? I was both relieved and terrified by that thought.

My hand still burned. That tingling beneath my skin had become the roar of a blaze that should have devoured my fingers but consumed the demon instead. She hung from the fierce light between us now, like a coat on a hook, limp and slowly swaying, though she seemed to weigh nothing.

I wanted to make it stop but didn't know how, and my ignorance scared me almost as badly as the fire I couldn't explain. As badly as the demon hanging from my open hand.

My front door flew open and crashed into the living room wall. I screamed, and the light in my hand blinked out through no conscious effort of mine.

My mother's body crumpled to the floor like a heap of clothes.

Smoke rose from a jagged, scorched hole in her sternum, where my hand had been an instant before.

I'd burned a *hole* into my mother's *chest*.

No, that wasn't my mother. My real mother died before I was ever born.

The room spun. My lungs refused to expand. My vision swam and blurred.

"Don't move!" The man in the doorway aimed his gun at me, and the world snapped back into focus. His black linen cassock was fastened with distinctive silver buckles matching the elaborate silver embroidery on the dramatic flare of his wide cuffs. The tails of his cassock were split up both sides to his hips, for ease of movement, and that split revealed his snug black pants.

His right cheek was branded with a stylized column of fire, scarred into his very flesh.

Even standing there in total shock, I recognized him instantly. Him, and the three others behind him, fanned out on my front lawn—a terrifying sight in their black Church robes and silver-buckled boots.

Exorcists.

No wonder the police hadn't come. They'd called in a team of specialists. *Real* exorcists, trained, dressed, branded, and given authority by the Church.

But the cavalry had arrived too late. I'd already . . .

What *had* I done?

It had looked for all the world like I'd done to the mother-monster what Katherine Abbot had famously done to that demon on television nearly a century ago. But that wasn't possible. She was an exorcist. She was *the* exorcist. A naturalist, the Church had called her, because she'd needed no training. She was *born* an exorcist. There hadn't been one like her since.

Except maybe the Church was wrong about that, because what else could you call the boy in the alley, if not a natural-born exorcist?

That thought led to an even bigger question as I stared at the black-clad men aiming guns at my head.

What the hell were they going to call *me*?

SEVEN

"Put your hands up!" the man at the door shouted. "Did you see what she just did?" he said in a softer voice, that part obviously aimed at the men behind him. "She lit that bitch up!"

Yes, that was what I'd done. I'd lit the bitch up, as if my hand were a match and my mother were a kerosene-soaked rag. I'd lit her up, and now she was dead, and the demon inside her was *fried*. I'd lit her up, and that was when the world stopped making sense, because my mother was a demon, and I had a five-fingered torch for a left hand, and the exorcists were obviously scared of *me*.

A second man in a black cassock crowded the first, trying to see over his shoulder and into my house, where I still stood like an idiot, not sure what to do other than keep breathing.

In and out. In and out. Not so fast, Nina. You're going to pass out.

"She's a——"

"Yeah, she is." The first man cut the second one off before he could say something I was pretty sure I wanted to hear. I was a what?

"We have to take her to——"

"Yeah, we do," the first man snapped.

Whatever happened in the next few moments would change everything for me, and for Mellie. Everything. I knew that. Yet I felt powerless to influence the outcome.

"Turn and face the wall, and put your hands over your head!" the first man shouted, and I realized his aim had never wavered. There was a dead demon on the floor, but he was pointing his gun at me. As if I were the bad guy.

"But I didn't——"

"Silence!" he shouted, and I jumped, startled. "Turn around and put your palms flat on the wall."

Before I could decide whether to obey, something moved on the lawn at his back. The neighbors had come to watch our private drama, but they were being herded back to their own houses by the remaining two exorcists, in cassocks so dark they seemed to be part of the night itself.

The onlookers went willingly, because exorcists were rare and scary and carried nearly infinite authority. But they also went slowly because exorcists were rare and scary, and they might never have another chance to gawk at one. Or at the skinny girl across the street whose mother never left the house during the day. The girl who traded what little she had—*what did* you *sell, Nina?*—for food and wiped snotty noses on weekends to keep the lights and the heat on. The girl who was about to be taken away in handcuffs by real, live exorcists, which few in New Temperance had ever seen in person.

The small crowd was moving on, slowly, reluctantly, except for one young boy and girl, standing side by side on my lawn. Wearing identical expressions of terror.

Melanie. And Adam Yung.

"Wait!" Mellie cried as a man in a black cassock took her by the arm.

"Don't touch her!" Adam's dark hair gleamed in the light from the front porch. He dodged the man reaching for him, then grabbed Melanie's hand, but as the exorcists pulled her away from both me and Adam, Mellie began to struggle.

Then her mouth opened.

Don't say it! I shouted in my head, but of course she didn't hear me.

"That's my house. That's my sister!"

"No!" I yelled, drawing their attention back to me. If they thought there was something wrong with me, they might think there was something wrong with my sister too. "Leave her out of this. She has nothing to do with it."

"Melanie!" Adam was being restrained at the edge of the yard.

"Nina!" Mellie tried to push her way past two of the exorcists, and at the exact moment a third turned to help them, wood splintered in the kitchen and someone kicked in my back door.

"Nina!" a new voice shouted. I whirled toward the sound of my name and saw the boy from the alley standing in my kitchen. The boy with the green eyes.

"Don't move!" the exorcist team leader shouted again, and I turned to him on instinct, just in time to see one of the men on the lawn aim his gun at my sister, who'd become quite belligerent.

"No!" I screeched, and though I couldn't hear the footsteps at my back over the shrill sound of my own voice, I could feel them reverberate in the floor beneath my feet. "Don't touch her! She's pregnant!"

I regretted it before the words even left my mouth, but I'd had no choice. They would have hurt her if she didn't stop fighting, and she wouldn't stop fighting until they hurt her.

At my last word, silence descended. Melanie stopped struggling. Adam blinked at her, stunned, from across our small yard. The exorcist lowered his gun, and the other two let my sister go. What remained of our lawn audience stared in shock because the skinny girl who traded favors for food, and who was now being arrested by a team of exorcists, also had a pregnant fifteen-year-old sister.

Clare Parker and her public execution were no doubt eclipsed in those moments as we made New Temperance scandal history.

Warm fingers folded around my hand, and the boy's green-eyed gaze met mine as the world fell apart around me. Then he began to pull me backward into my kitchen. "We have to go," he whispered, and though no one else could have heard him, his words seemed to trigger the return of the planet to its regular rotation. Only, it felt like things were spinning even faster this time.

"Stop!" The team leader raised his aim to my head again.

The boy lifted his right arm. Sound thundered from the gun in his hand and echoed mercilessly in my head. The man in the doorway stumbled backward onto the front stoop. Moonlight glinted off his silver buckles and shone on something leaking onto his cassock as he fell.

"Let's go! Now!" the boy shouted, and before I could fully process the fact that he'd just shot the exorcists' team leader, he was pulling me through my kitchen toward the back door.

"Wait!" I insisted as the rest of the team raced across the lawn toward my house, guns drawn. "Melanie!"

"They won't hurt her if you leave her," he said. "But they *will* shoot through her to get to you if we try to take her with us."

The exorcists gathered around their injured leader, and

one of them spoke into a wireless radio, calling for help. The other two still aimed guns at us.

"If you don't come with me now, they're going to take you, and I can't help you once you're in Church custody," the boy said while they yelled at him to drop his weapon. "We have to run."

I didn't understand everything he'd said, and I wasn't even sure I'd heard all of it. But his point sank in.

Run.

I was more than familiar with the concept—I'd been caught shoplifting at two different grocery stores the year my mom stopped paying the bills, and both times I'd gotten away by following that very imperative.

Run.

He must have read my decision on my face, because he pushed the screen door open, and when I stepped out onto the stoop, already shivering from the cold, he snatched my coat and satchel from the kitchen chair where I'd dropped them after school, then followed me out.

The screen door slammed shut and gunfire exploded from the front yard. Bullets thunked into wood behind us. The kitchen window shattered, and glass sprayed the dead lawn. I ducked. Melanie screamed. People started shouting. Then the boy was pulling me down the steps and across my tiny backyard. He shoved my coat at me, and by the time he'd wedged his first foot into the chain-link fence and started to climb, I could hear more sirens.

"How did you find me?" I demanded, shoving both arms into my coat. Then I followed him up the fence.

"Been looking all day," he said, and if he was winded, I couldn't tell. "In the end, I just followed the sirens."

I wanted to ask how he'd known the sirens would lead to me, but there was no time to talk after that. The minute my feet hit the grass in the yard that bordered mine, footsteps pounded behind us as the exorcists—at least two of them—gave chase. When I glanced back from the cover of darkness, flashing lights were painting the whole neighborhood in frantic bursts of red and blue.

The first cop car screeched to a stop in front of my house, and a second later an ambulance swung into the driveway, but the boy in the dark clothes pulled me forward again before I could see anything else between the houses.

We ran and climbed fences and dodged streetlights, huffing with exertion, our breath exploding in little white puffs that shone in the moonlight and trailed behind us with each step. Soon we outran the flashing lights, and right after that, the sirens stopped. Speedy medical care could no longer help the exorcist—he'd been shot in the chest.

My mother had been beyond help long before the police had arrived.

I tried to think of nothing as we ran—nothing but putting one foot in front of the other without tripping—but racing through a neighborhood I already knew by heart didn't take much focus, and my brain was working much faster than my legs. The questions I hadn't been able to put into words with my mother's body cooling at my feet were suddenly there all at once, shooting through my head too fast to truly contemplate, much less voice. With the sharp wind stealing my breath, each inhalation felt like swallowing cold steel needles.

And still we ran, his warm hand around mine, pulling me through my own neighborhood from one backyard to the next, then across the first major street with hardly a glance in either direction. A horn blared as a car screeched to a stop two feet away, but the boy just kept pulling me, faster, farther.

The night was a blur of cold air and dark buildings, broken only by bright patches of light at every intersection. Our footsteps pounded, pounded, pounded, but that sound changed when we ran from concrete onto grass, then onto gravel, then back to concrete. At last, when my fingers were numb from the cold, my legs were sore from the run, and my lungs ached and burned with every breath, the boy pushed open a dented metal door in the center of a long, narrow alley, then tugged me into the building. And finally, we stopped moving.

I leaned over with my hands on my knees, gasping for breath, my heart thudding so hard my chest felt like it was going to explode. I'd never run so fast or so far, and even though we'd outrun the police and the exorcists, I still felt like I was being chased. No, *hunted*. I felt like I was being tracked or stalked by something I couldn't see— something I could *almost* see—and even though it hadn't found me yet, whatever it was, it was still searching. Looking. Scenting me out. And it *would* find me. I knew that like I knew to breathe or I'd die.

But I didn't know *how* I knew.

I pulled my hand from the boy's for the first time since we'd left my house.

"It's okay," he said when he noticed me scanning the room, peering into the shadows for this threat I couldn't see but couldn't shake off. "I don't think they saw which way we went."

"It's not that." I wasn't sure how much he'd seen, why he'd been near my house at just the right time, or why he was helping me, but my naïveté had died around the time I lost my first baby tooth. He knew all he was going to know about me until I knew a little more about *him*.

His eyes narrowed as he studied me. "You feel something?" he said, and I blinked as if I didn't know what he was talking about, because I *shouldn't* have known what he meant, and he shouldn't have known what I felt—the pursuit of . . . whatever was chasing me.

None of this made sense.

"I feel like my mother's dead and I don't know how that happened." I breathed deeply while the burning in my lungs slowly faded. "I feel like my pregnant sister is in Church custody and probably terrified. I feel like I shouldn't be standing in an abandoned warehouse with some guy I don't know."

I feel like my life is a book, and someone turned the page before I was ready, and now I can't follow the story.

"That wasn't your mother." His green eyes practically glowed, reflecting moonlight shining in from a broken window overhead. He brushed his palms on his dark jeans, and when he turned to gesture through a doorway at the body of the warehouse, I realized that his black hoodie was threadbare and almost worn through at the elbows. "Come sit, and I'll explain what I can."

A new possibility crept in to overwhelm the fears that had driven my flight from the police. I shook my head slowly, hands curling into fists at my sides. I didn't know the alley we'd run through. I didn't know the building. I didn't know the boy. And I had no idea how he knew about my mother.

Or how he'd found me.

I lurched for the door we'd just come through, suddenly sure I'd made a horrible mistake. What if I'd run from the police and the exorcists straight into the arms of some pervert stalker/murderer? Or even another demon? Sure, he'd killed the degenerate hunting me and helped me flee the men aiming guns at my head, but that didn't mean he didn't have his own dangerous agenda.

"Nina, wait!" he said the moment my hand touched the cold doorknob. "I have blankets. And food. And . . . answers. Some of them, anyway. You must want some answers."

I hesitated because he hadn't tried to physically stop me from leaving. And because the lure of answers was more than I could resist.

"If you go out there, they *will* find you." He set my school satchel on the floor between us, obviously a demonstration of goodwill. "And asking your friends and neighbors for shelter would be like painting targets on their backs. Your face is probably all over the news already, along with whatever lie they've cooked up to explain what happened at your house tonight. They'll probably say you're possessed. They'll definitely say you're a murderer."

I turned slowly, my hand still on the doorknob at my back, and the boy was watching me. "Murderer?" The word wouldn't sink in.

He nodded. "Matricide. And they'll probably tack on a charge for theoretical infanticide, because in killing your mother, you've denied some poor baby the chance to inherit her soul."

"But . . . she wasn't my mother. She was a demon. No one could have inherited her soul." The soul she'd stolen from my *real* mother years before I was born. The soul that was almost completely devoured by now, if her physical degeneration was any sign.

"Yeah." He shrugged and shoved his hands into his pants pockets. "They'll probably leave that part out."

"How do you know what they'll do?"

"That's what they did to us." He leaned against the grimy wall of the warehouse's entryway. Through the open door on his left lay the rest of the building—one huge, open room, as far as I could tell. "They broadcast lies in public, then hunt us in private, hoping for tips from the people they've turned against us."

And that was when I made the connection—part of it, anyway. "You're one of them. One of the fugitives they're hunting." *Possession is suspected.* "You're the reason the exorcists are in New Temperance." If he and his gang hadn't brought them here, the police would have been first on the scene at my house, and things might have gone differently. Maybe. Things certainly couldn't have gone much worse.

Another shrug from the boy, who had yet to introduce himself. "Sorry about that."

"Where are the rest of them? The news says there are . . . more of you." They'd shown two pictures, but I couldn't remember the names. . . .

"There are, but my friends don't know about you yet."

I frowned as another layer of confusion settled over me. "What don't they know about me?"

"That I found you. That a degenerate found you first. That the Church knows you exist."

"The Church has always known I exist. My mother

had a parenting license." And, evidently, a demonic parasite. Admittedly, an odd combination. "Why were you looking for me? Why was the *degenerate* looking for me?"

"It's kind of a long story. Do you wanna . . . ?" He gestured toward the larger room again, where, presumably, there was somewhere to sit.

"I'm not going anywhere with you." Well, anywhere other than the dark, creepy, abandoned warehouse I'd already followed him into. "I don't even know who you are." I kept my back pressed against the door in case I needed to make an escape.

"Fair enough." He smiled, and his green eyes sparkled in that beam of moonlight. "I'm Finn."

"Finn who?"

He shrugged. "That's all I know."

"You don't know your last name?" *Yeah. Right.* "I thought you had answers."

"I do. But not that one." He cleared his throat, apparently nervous now that I'd stumped him with what should have been an easy question. "Listen, the rest of this is kind of a long story, and I'm freezing, so why don't we talk over there?" He tossed his head toward the far corner of the warehouse, where I could barely make out some camping equipment and blankets. "There's another exit on that side of the building, if the urge to flee strikes again."

But I wasn't ready to let go of the doorknob, and he could tell.

"Okay, how 'bout this? Here." Finn knelt and slid a long scrap of wood toward me on the floor. "If any of this starts to feel creepy or dangerous, you can beat me with that and make your escape. Only, I'd consider it a personal favor if you'd avoid the face," he said with a crooked grin that was probably supposed to look disarming. And almost did.

"*All* of this feels dangerous and creepy."

"I know. But if it gets any worse, you can . . . take a swing." He mimed swinging a baseball bat, and when my expression didn't change, his grin faded. "Okay, look. It's dinnertime and I'm starving, so I'm going to make some soup. If you're hungry, or if you want to hear what I know about all this—and about your family—I'll be over there."

My chest ached at the thought of my sister, and the possibility of getting answers was more than I could resist. Still, I didn't know him, and I had no evidence that anything he'd said so far was true. Though it all made a certain kind of strange sense.

When I didn't respond, Finn turned and picked his way through scraps of paper, assorted packing materials, and machine parts toward what was obviously his base of operations. Whatever those operations were.

After a minute of watching him, trying to plan my next

move, I scouted out the other exit he'd mentioned, then threw my satchel over one shoulder and squatted to pick up the wooden board. Then I followed him. I was armed— kind of—and had the nearest exit in full view, and I was wanted for matricide. What did I have to lose?

EIGHT

The closer I got to his makeshift campsite, the more of it came into focus in the near dark. He had a two-burner camp stove with a dented pot on each burner, and a small stockpile of canned goods lined against the wall behind it. Three regular bed pillows were arranged in an arc around the front of the stove, like cushions, and in the middle sat a battery-powered camping lantern. As I picked my way through the junk cluttering the warehouse floor, Finn turned on the lantern, which threw a soft circle of light over the immediate area and cast the rest of the warehouse in deep shadows.

Several blankets were folded next to the double row of cans, and when I sank onto the pillow across from his, he reached over and tossed me one.

"Thanks." I sniffed, and when I smelled neither filth nor mold, I unfolded the blanket and wrapped it around my shoulders. "So, what? Home is anywhere you can safely warm up a can of soup?"

"In the traditional sense, yes. In the more esoteric sense?" He hesitated, then frowned. "Yes to that one too."

I had no idea what he meant by the "esoteric" sense of home, and I decided not to ask. He didn't seem violent now that his gun was safely stowed, and if he was crazy, I didn't want to know that until I'd had both dinner and answers. Starting with the most important.

"What will they do with Melanie?"

"Your sister?" he asked, and I nodded. "They'll charge her with fornication and unlicensed pregnancy. They'll interrogate her for information about her baby's father, and about you."

"Interrogate." The ache in my chest sharpened into a painful, piercing fear. "What does that mean, exactly?"

He shrugged. "I'm not sure, since she's pregnant. Normally, they'd starve her, or keep her awake for days on end, or drug her, or even beat her, but the baby makes her a wild card, so their move depends on their endgame."

"What do you mean?"

"You told your whole neighborhood about the baby, so everyone knows that if they hurt your sister, they'll be hurting the baby too, and the last thing they want is public sympathy for a pregnant underage outlaw."

"So she's safe for now?" Hope felt like a tiny flame warming me from the inside, beating back my chills just a little. Until he doused it with the cold, hard truth.

"None of us are safe, Nina. Least of all your sister. A bird in the hand is worth two in the bush, and she's the only bird they've got their hands on at the moment. But they'll be looking to change that. They'll be looking for you, obviously, and for me because——"

"You shot an exorcist."

Finn looked up from the row of cans he'd been studying, and light from the lantern fell on half of his face. "Yeah. He wasn't my first. But if it makes you feel any better, I only shoot in self-defense. Or friend-defense. And those weren't real exorcists. They were just soldiers in black robes. Walking propaganda." He picked up two cans, then twisted to show them to me. "Beef stew or spaghetti and meatballs?"

"Beef," I said, and he set the other can back in line, its label facing forward like all the others'. "How do you know those weren't real exorcists?"

"I know because *you* are an exorcist, and *those* 'exorcists'"—his voice practically dripped with derision as he settled onto his cushion again—"were terrified of you."

You are an exorcist. That was the first time anyone had said it out loud. I hadn't even dared to *think* it, but hearing him say it felt like . . . validation. Corroboration.

Confirmation that I wasn't crazy. That I hadn't imagined the whole thing.

He shrugged. "Also, I know they were fakes because *all* the Church's exorcists are fakes."

"Wait, what do you mean? How can they all be fakes?"

"They can't actually exorcise a demon." When I started to mention news footage of exorcists on the front lines, charging into battle against the Unclean, he stopped me. "They're soldiers. They know how to shoot, and if they'd wanted you dead, they would have shot you on the spot. That's what they're good at. But killing a possessed host doesn't exorcise the demon. That just releases it, which means the demon is then free to search for another host. That's harder for the demon to do once it's been disembodied. Going from one body to another, they just . . ." He shrugged. "They do this cold-kiss thing. I hear it's pretty horrible."

"I can verify that." I shuddered at the memory.

"Disembodied demons have to find someone who's sick or hurt or under some sort of chemical influence. Or even just someone sleeping. If the demon finds a body before he's sucked back into hell . . . ta da! You have a newly possessed citizen, which means the 'exorcists' have failed."

"But what about all the Latin and the holy water and the symbols of faith?" Elements we'd come to associate with exorcists after a lifetime of seeing them on the news and on posters, decked out and armed for battle in their iconic, silver-trimmed black cassocks. "What about their training?"

"Bullshit." Finn dug out a can opener from a shallow box full of utensils. "Demons can't even *understand* Latin unless they've possessed someone who speaks it. Which is why they always speak the local language, no matter what that is. So if you're trying to fight evil with stupid incantations, you'd have just as much luck with pig Latin as with the real thing."

Wow. "What about holy water?"

He clamped the halves of the can opener over the top rim of the stew can, then twisted the handle. "That might piss them off if you hit them in the face, but I suspect the spray-bottle approach works better against naughty cats than against demons."

I almost laughed. Almost.

"Symbols of faith? Like the column of fire?" Exorcists wore them on chains hanging from their necks, echoing the brands burned into their cheeks.

"Seriously?" Finn tossed the can opener back into the box, where it rattled against the other utensils. "That degenerate this morning tried to eat your face off—which would have been a real shame, by the way." He grinned, and I actually felt myself blush. As if we had nothing more important to discuss than how much he liked my face in its not-devoured state. "Do you really think she would have run off screeching if you'd been wearing a bonfire charm?"

I pulled the blanket tighter around my shoulders.

"I guess that would have been a *little* out of character for a monster so intent on consuming my nose." And my soul.

"Exactly. Faith-based symbols don't work, because not only do demons have no faith, they're not in spiritual opposition to any faith either. In the land of opposites, demons and the Church would not stand on opposing sides. Demons and *humanity* would stand on opposing sides. All of humanity. Sinners and saints. Men and women. Children and adults. Consecrated and civilians. It's not just the Church versus demons. It's *us* versus demons. All of us."

"Wait. So then . . ." I couldn't finish that thought. My mind was blown. The world no longer made sense.

The Unified Church was the final authority. It had been since the demon horde had killed off two-thirds of the world's population—devouring many of its souls—and devastated three-quarters of the American landscape. The Church was strict and cruel and domineering, but it had saved us when no one else could. It had exorcised the demons, and walled in the surviving cities to protect us from the remaining degenerates roaming the badlands. That was why people had put the Church in charge in the first place.

If it hadn't exorcised the demons, then . . . "How . . . ? Why . . . ?"

Finn pulled the detached lid from the can of stew, then

gestured at me with it. "I like you. You ask all the right questions."

"So, what are the answers? If the exorcists are fakes, and the Church can't fight demons any better than anyone else, why are they in charge?"

"*Great* question." He tilted the open can over the empty pot on the right burner, and thick beef vegetable stew poured out in chunky globs. "And if I had the answer, I'd give it to you."

"Okay. But . . . the Church *used* to have real exorcists, right? Otherwise, how would we ever have won the war?"

"Exorcists aren't born every day, but I think it's reasonable to assume the Church had a few at one point."

"Like Katherine Abbot, right? The naturalist?"

"Naturalist." Finn shook his head and tossed the empty can into a plastic trash bin against the wall, where it landed with the clatter of can against can.

"You're saying she wasn't a naturalist?"

"I'm saying there *are* no naturalists." He twisted a knob on the front of the tiny, shin-high stove, then lit a match and stuck it through the burner. Fire flared in a ring beneath the pot, and he adjusted the height of the flames by turning the knob again. "Or, more accurately, there are *only* naturalists. You can't be trained to drive a demon from a stolen body by scorching its life force with the power of your own."

Was that really what I'd done? How was that even possible?

"You have to be born with that ability." His gaze met mine across the indoor campsite, and flames from the stove made shadows dance on his face. "And you *were* born with that ability, Nina."

I shifted nervously on my pillow. "Why would the Church have a bunch of fake exorcists? What happened to the real ones?"

Finn shrugged, digging in the utensil box again. "You're as qualified to answer that one as I am. You're an exorcist. Why aren't you down at the worship center right now, in line to get your cheek branded?"

"Because the only Church officials who know I'm an exorcist just aimed guns at my head!"

He finally pulled a plastic spoon from the box and used it to stir the stew. "Yeah, they tend to do that."

"Doesn't the Church need us if they don't have any real exorcists?"

"Who knows what the Church thinks it needs?" He met my gaze over the camping lantern. "*Humanity* needs us. I know that much. Demons hunt us. The Church will *take* us. I know that for a fact. They took Carey James. I don't know what they did with him, but I know they took him *alive*."

"Who's Carey? An exorcist? Your friend?"

"He *is* an exorcist, yes. Just like you."

Like me? Why not like *us*?

"But I never met him," Finn continued, stirring the stew again, and my stomach started to growl. I hadn't eaten since lunch at school. That felt like ages ago. "I know his sister, though. Her name's Grayson. You'll like her. Everyone likes her."

He pulled two paper bowls from a package and set them on the floor in front of the stove.

"What do you know about my mother?" I asked as Finn twisted a knob and the flame beneath the pot died.

When he turned away from the stove, he looked sad. "I know she was possessed and probably had been for quite a while."

"Since the day she turned eighteen." How could I not have known?

Finn poured beef stew from the pot into the first bowl. "This isn't your fault, and you couldn't have stopped it. There's no way you could have known. You had no frame of reference, right?"

"What do you mean?" I took the bowl he pushed toward me and held it for warmth, even when the blanket slid off my shoulders.

Finn set the pot back on the burner and picked up his own bowl, then settled onto the pillow across from mine. "She's been possessed your whole life, right? So you don't have any experience with a normal mother to contrast yours with. There's no way you could have known."

Maybe not. But I *should* have known.

If Mellie hadn't gotten pregnant and derailed my mom's plans, would I have *ever* known? We'd been avoiding her for months. Her symptoms had gotten dramatically worse, and we hadn't noticed, because we didn't want to see her or deal with her. We just wanted her to wait until I turned eighteen before overdosing and passing quietly out of our lives.

But that wouldn't have happened. She would have possessed me and sold Melanie, and . . . well, I wasn't sure what her plan was after that, since my body couldn't produce a new host for her.

Finn chewed his stew quietly, watching me. He'd set a bottle of water at my feet, and I hadn't even noticed.

"What else?" I put my bowl down and picked up the water. "What else do you know about her? About us?" How had he found me?

"Tell you what." He glanced at my untouched bowl. "I'll tell you whatever you want to know, as long as you keep eating. You're going to need plenty of energy if we're going to make it out of here without getting caught."

I had no home. I had no clothes except what I was wearing. I had no food except what belonged to Finn. I had no information except what had come from him. And I had nowhere to go and no one to trust. There was nothing left. Except Finn.

He must have seen doubt in my eyes, because he smiled,

and when he smiled, I could see nothing of the boy who'd killed a degenerate and shot an "exorcist." When he smiled, he looked normal. Friendly. Trustworthy. And that very thought put me back on edge.

I didn't know him well enough yet to think of him as trustworthy.

"Relax." His smile had slipped a little as he was confronted with my skepticism. "If I wanted to kill you, I wouldn't have saved your life. Twice. If I wanted to turn you in for the bounty, I wouldn't have welcomed you into my home amid wealth and luxury I don't share with just anyone." He spread his arms in a grand gesture, taking in the grease, dirt, and trash all around us. "Is there any other fear I can put to rest for you?"

When I only pulled the blanket around myself again, he laughed. "Fine. If I were planning to . . . you know . . ." He waved one hand at my entire body. "I wouldn't have given you a slab of wood with nails sticking out of it." He pointed to the two-by-four still lying next to me within easy reach. "I'm as protective of my parts as the next guy. More protective than some. So . . . are we good?"

I thought about that for a minute. Then decided to ignore the question. "Do you really think there's a bounty for me?"

He chuckled again. "The Church usually calls it a reward, but yeah, they've probably put a little cash on the line to encourage your neighbors to join the manhunt."

Would that happen? Would the Mercers call the police if they saw me? What about Adam and his family? Would they turn me in if they thought that would help Melanie?

I wasn't sure how much Finn actually knew about what I was facing, but I was sure he knew more than I did. "So . . . I eat and you talk?" I said, and he nodded, spooning the last of the broth from his paper bowl. "Deal." I picked up my bowl, hoping Melanie was eating as well as I was, wherever the Church had put her. Thinking about my sister brought up more questions about our mom, which had never been far from the surface. "What else do you know about my mother?"

"I know she was a breeder." Finn opened another can of stew while we spoke, and I realized I was already starting to feel better physically, thanks to the warm blanket and food. "Your mother—well, the demon masquerading as your mom—conceived you and your sister specifically either to provide herself with a new host body or to sell you to some other demon in need of one."

"One of each," I said, and he nodded.

"Two kids means a breeder can keep one and sell one—maximum profit with minimal risk." He set the can opener in the box, then carefully removed the detached lid from the can and tossed it into the plastic bin. "Some of them really shop around before they commit to a . . . um . . . to a look." His gaze took me in, jeans, tee, blue blanket, and all. "Your mother must have been *beautiful* at some point."

My face felt suddenly warm. Under the vigilant eyes of the sisters at school, there was no flirting. No overtly lustful looks, even from those of us who'd already dabbled in sin, fumbling around in the dark with few sounds that could rightfully be considered communication.

But Finn didn't seem the least bit self-conscious about kind of complimenting me.

My gaze caught on his intense focus, and I had to grasp for the dropped thread of a conversation I'd almost forgotten.

Oh yeah. My mom.

"She was pretty." Actually, before she'd gotten sick, my mother'd had the kind of beauty that drew attention from strangers. The kind that attracted trouble. Just like Melanie.

"Well, that was no accident," Finn said. "At some point in the past, she spotted one of your ancestors and decided those were genes she could work with. Breeders tend to stick with a particular bloodline until it hits a dead end."

I was that dead end. And for the first time in nearly two years, I was able to view my sterilization with something other than total despair and blistering fury. My inability to breed now felt like a huge middle finger flipped at my mother and her demonic machinations.

"They don't seem to care about gender either," Finn continued, stirring the second can of stew as I slowly finished my first helping. "In fact, I don't think demons themselves actually have genders, so if you'd been born a boy, your mom would have been looking for the perfect face/uterus combo to implant with the next generation of her—his—demon seed."

Suddenly my stew lost all flavor.

"They usually space the kids pretty close together so that the older rarely figures out what's going on before the younger is ready to harvest." Finn shrugged and dumped the second can of stew into the pot. "It's always safest to harvest one at the same time you sell the other."

"Harvest?" I set my bowl down and wrapped the blanket tighter around my shoulders, but the chill seemed to be coming from inside me, at the thought that there were more kids out there like me and Mellie—born and bred to host the Unclean. "How common *is* it?"

Finn shrugged. "More common today than it was yesterday, and it'll be more common tomorrow than it is today."

We are everywhere. Seen but unseen. Known but unknown. My mother's words rang in my head, and suddenly they made sense.

The Unclean were hiding in plain sight, among us. Breeding their own hosts. Existing right under the Church's nose.

"How many breeders are there?" My voice sounded hollow. Empty. "Are we talking dozens?" Or hundreds? Thousands?

"Who knows?" he said.

We outnumber the grains of sand on the beach, the drops of water in the ocean, my mother had said. But had she meant demons in general, or breeders specifically?

"How do you and your friends fit in?"

"Carey and Grayson were bred for hosting. That's how I know about breeders."

I pushed my empty bowl toward him with the toe of my sneaker. "So, what, you and your friends go around rescuing ill-fated children from their demon breeder parents?"

"Um, no." He stirred the stew one more time, then turned off the gas and lifted the pot from the burner. "As noble an enterprise as that would be, it's impractical."

"Because otherwise, running from the police and hiding out in abandoned warehouses is the height of practicality?"

"Of course not. Which is why we can't keep adding to our ranks. Beyond the obvious numbers issue, most of us are exorcists and *all* of us are wanted by the police. We wouldn't be doing your average orphaned breeder kid any favors by letting him tag along."

"So you just leave them for the Church?" Like he'd left Melanie. And suddenly I realized he would have left her even if we could have somehow taken her.

"We have no other choice." He poured more stew into both bowls, and I got the feeling he was using that task to avoid having to look at me. "It's hard enough to get from town to town with just the five of us."

"How *did* you get into New Temperance?" Passage through most town gates required identification and paperwork, and kids couldn't leave town limits—*any* town limits—without an accompanying parent or Church official.

And, of course, citizens were *highly* discouraged from venturing into the badlands.

Finn's grin was back. "We *might* have stowed away in a cargo car with a shipment of Church cassocks. Which is why we can't collect every orphan we meet. But you're an exorcist. We need you." He pushed my bowl toward me, and the spoon sank until only an inch of white plastic stuck out of the stew. "And if the Church had gotten to you first, no one ever would have heard from you again. Including your sister."

My hands tightened around the edges of the blanket as I realized how differently the whole thing might have played out if he'd come in just a little earlier. "Did you know about . . . ? Did you know I could . . . ?" I took a deep breath and started over. "Did you know I was an exorcist?"

"This morning? Not for sure. I just knew that degenerate was stalking you, so you could be the one we came for."

My heart thumped too hard. What the hell did that mean?

Finn stirred his stew aimlessly. "But then you disappeared, and I spent half the day watching your school, waiting for you to come out so I could find out if you were the one." He leaned as far forward as he could without sliding off his cushion. The lantern lit his face from below, lending a threatening cast to his eager expression. "The degenerate from this morning was only the first. More will find you, and you can't take them all on by yourself. You need us, Nina. You need us every bit as much as we need you."

NINE

My fist clenched around the edge of the blanket. "Why are degenerates hunting me, Finn?"

"They have your scent. How old are you?"

"Seventeen, next week." Fear dropped adrenaline into my bloodstream.

"Degenerates can sense an exorcist nearing maturity, and when we saw them converging on this area from all over the badlands, we knew you'd be here. We didn't know who you'd be, or whether you'd be in New Temperance or Solace, so we split up to widen our search. We're here to keep the degenerates from killing you and the Church from taking you."

"And now we're camping out in an abandoned

warehouse, hiding from the police? And the fake exorcists?"

He nodded and took a bite from his bowl. "And from the Church in general. And the degenerates."

And the degenerates . . .

I wasn't leaving town without my sister. "So, are your friends in New Temperance?" I reached for my stew, and suddenly my arms felt heavier than the full bowl.

"They are now. We have another . . . place. It's nicer than this one," he added, and I could hear the apology in his voice. "But it's not safe for you to be on the move yet."

My hand shook as I tucked the blanket tighter around my legs. The heater was only two feet away. Why was I trembling? "Because the police are still looking for us?"

"Yeah, but our real problem is that you just exorcised your first demon, and—"

"Whoa . . ." The warehouse tilted around me, and I almost dropped my bowl. "Something's wrong."

Finn set his bowl down and glanced at the watch on his left wrist. "Yeah, that's about right. How's your head? Any pain?"

"What's happening?" Vertigo washed over me, and I threw one leg out to keep from falling sideways.

"Okay, hang on. Let me help." He stood and grabbed the extra pillow next to his.

I blinked, trying to draw the room back into focus,

then set my paper bowl on the ground and pushed it back with a shaking hand. My pulse raced, and that only made me dizzier. "What's in the stew, Finn?"

"This has nothing to do with the food, I swear." He squatted next to me and set the extra pillow beside mine. "Here. Lie down."

But I scooted away from him clumsily. The warehouse spun, and suddenly my clothes felt like chain mail instead of cotton.

Panic danced in my chest and I tried to stand, but the signal *Flee!* got lost somewhere between my brain and my muscles. My other leg shot out and my foot flipped my bowl. My arm collapsed behind me and my shoulder slammed into the bare concrete. "What's wrong with me?" I demanded, and my words were slurred.

"You're gonna be fine. Try to hold still, Nina. Don't fight it or you'll hurt yourself."

Terror made my pulse trip when he reached for me. "Fight what? What's wrong with me?" My words were a mishmash of soft syllables, like verbal baby food. The warehouse was going dark from the edges of my vision inward, as if the night was spiraling in on me.

"Just close your eyes and try to relax. . . ."

The rest of his instructions got lost as the world went dark, and the last thing I saw was Finn's green eyes staring down into mine while he lifted my head and slid a pillow beneath it.

* * *

My ears regained function first, and I heard Finn talking but couldn't tell what he was saying. I heard sound, but that sound had no focus.

The first words that made sense were spoken by a girl I didn't know. "Where the *hell* are you?" Her voice was peppered with static.

I blinked, and the ceiling of the warehouse appeared above me, a distant, dark blur. *Why can't I move?* Fresh panic fluttered in my chest.

Finn sighed, and I heard footsteps as he paced to my right. "I found an empty warehouse on Morgan Street. On the north side of town, near the old train depot."

"Morgan . . ." Paper crinkled over the connection, and I realized she was looking at a map. Whoever she was.

"We're fine, Devi." Finn sounded exhausted. Frustrated.

I tried to move my right arm, and my fingers twitched.

"*We're* fine? How do you know he's fine? Have you asked him?"

Him? Had Finn told her I was a guy? Was she his girlfriend? Kids our age rarely defined illicit relationships with titles or commitment, but there were exceptions, like Mellie and Adam. Did Finn think his girlfriend wouldn't notice my complete—if not entirely functional—set of girl parts?

"Thirty-eight hours!" Devi shouted. "I've been looking for you for nearly *two days*. Don't you *ever* disappear on me like that again!"

Yup. Definitely a girlfriend.

Finn paced closer to me that time, which brought him into my field of vision, behind the camp stove. He was almost in focus. "I found her."

Her? *Me,* her? Then who was "him"?

"That's no excuse!" Her shrill shout made my ears ring. "Grayson says there's a small horde somewhere in your area, and you're all alone with a rookie. What happens if they find you?"

"Shit!" Finn rubbed his forehead in frustration, and I flexed my right hand, forcing all four fingers to move at once. They brushed soft material, and I realized he'd covered me with a blanket. "She's been triggered. If they're that close, they've already scented her. We have to move."

"Did your brain leak out your ears this morning? Stay there. We'll come get you. Hopefully, we can take out a few of them along the way to even the odds."

I lifted my left arm from the blanket, and when Finn turned toward the motion, he found me looking at him.

"Gotta go. She's waking up."

Both of my arms were working, as were my fingers. My toes twitched in my sneakers when I tried to move them. My body was slowly surrendering to my control, but that did little to alleviate my anger and fear, when I didn't know how I'd lost control of it in the first place.

"Do *not* get him hurt, Finn," the girl on the radio said,

static breaking her order into several bursts of sound I had to concentrate to make sense of.

Finn clipped the radio to the waistband of his jeans, then stepped over the portable heater and knelt next to me. "Hey."

"'Hey'? Seriously?" I spared a moment to be grateful that my voice worked when the rest of me seemed to be malfunctioning. "I pass out under your care, then wake up half paralyzed to hear that some kind of 'horde' is in our area, and that's your opener? 'Hey'?"

Finn shrugged while I glared up at him. "I almost went with 'Get up and help me pack before we're overrun by a horde of degenerates,' but I was afraid that might lead to more panic than the situation actually warrants."

"There's a limit to how much panic that situation warrants?" Because I was pretty sure the only thing worse than fighting one mutated demon was fighting a whole horde of them.

"Degenerates aren't exactly a rarity in our line of work, so if you panic every time you get the opportunity to do what you were born to do . . . well, let's just say that the number of exorcists who panic is inversely proportionate to the number of exorcists who survive."

"Good to know."

"Still, you *should* get up before we're overrun by that horde of degenerates."

I pushed myself into a sitting position, and the blanket

fell into my lap. My head spun. When I started to tip over, Finn put one hand on my shoulder and one on my lower back to steady me. His hands were warm through my shirt when the rest of the warehouse was cold, and they felt good. I wanted to enjoy the feeling, but I didn't know him. I didn't know why I'd passed out or what he'd had to do with that.

The number of girls who let strange boys touch them in abandoned warehouses after waking up from unexplained blackouts was probably inversely proportionate to the number of girls who survived.

I cleared my throat and sat up straighter, and he let me go. "What the hell happened? What did you do to me?"

"Nothing, I swear."

I started to argue, but he spoke over me as I struggled to make my legs obey commands from my brain. "Nina, there are some things you don't know yet. Things I was going to explain when you woke up, but you were out for longer than I expected, and now we're kind of . . . out of time."

"Because of the horde of degenerates?"

"Yeah. Although the Church's 'exorcists' and the police are also looking for us. So we need to pack everything we can carry before my friends get here."

Running for our lives. Again. Was this how he lived? "Fine. I'm a little busy relearning how to walk, but I assume you can talk and pack at the same time?"

He smiled, and I tried not to notice how green his eyes were in the light from the lantern. "I'm a proficient multi-tasker, yes."

"Good. How long was I out?"

"Almost seven hours."

"Seven hours!" I glanced up at the windows near the ceiling, searching for any sign of daylight while I did the math. "So it's, what, three in the morning?"

"Just after."

"Why am I so weak?"

"You'll be fine in a few minutes." Finn backed away from me, and when I didn't fall over, he grabbed a duffel I hadn't noticed before, then sank to his knees in front of the box of utensils. "Your body did most of the hard work while you were passed out." He dropped a small box of plastic utensils into his bag, then followed those with the can opener and a large box of matches. "Most exorcists start coming into their abilities around the time they turn seventeen. I'm not sure why that is, but Reese thinks, evolutionarily speaking, the exorcists whose abilities matured before their bodies did were hunted and killed by degenerates."

Reese! That was the other name mentioned on the news. Reese and Devi. Reese was the big guy, and Devi was . . . I wasn't sure *what* Devi was.

"He thinks those who matured later were better able to defend themselves, so they lived to pass on their genes.

Either way, seventeen seems to be the magic number, give or take a few months."

"And because I'll be seventeen next week my abilities have matured, so the degenerates can, what? Smell me?"

Weird.

"Or sense you. Or something like that." Finn disconnected a small propane tank from the camping stove, then folded in the sides and closed the lid, so that the stove looked like a small metal suitcase. The dented outside said it was well used, but the shiny inside and lack of burnt-on crud said it was also well cared for. "But they can only sense you during that transitional period, between the time your abilities start to manifest and the time you gain full control over them all. Which can't happen until you're 'triggered.'"

"Wait, abilit*ies*? Plural? I can do something other than fry demons with my bare hands?" Because, honestly, that one was both awesome and scary enough on its own.

He slid the camp stove into the bottom of his duffel, then tightened the seal on the propane tank and slid that in after it. "That's the big one, but yes, you'll develop a few other advantages that help you hunt both degenerates and demons in their prime."

"Like what?"

"Like . . . speed. And strength. They can run fast, so you have to be able to run fast. They're strong, so you have to be strong. But like I said, those additional abilities have to be triggered." He glanced up at me with a shrug. "That's what we call it, anyway."

And he'd told Devi that had already happened. "How?" When I realized my head was no longer spinning, I shook out the blue blanket—the best I could, still seated—and folded it in my lap.

"By exorcising your first demon." He grabbed a flashlight standing on end near the rows of cans and dropped it into the duffel bag. "In your case, that was your mother."

"Superpowers as a reward for matricide. This just keeps getting weirder."

Finn glanced at me in surprise, and I remembered that he hadn't read Mr. Yung's old picture novels, and he probably had no idea what I meant by "superpowers." But then he smiled.

"They're not superpowers, and you'll only be able to use them to their full extent when there's a demon near, but yeah. I guess it's kind of weird if you're not used to it."

"So why did I pass out?"

"Because it takes a lot of energy for your body to implement those changes. That happens to everyone, and obviously you're most vulnerable when you're unconscious. Which is why we're here." He made a sweeping gesture to take in the entire warehouse. "I wasn't sure how soon you would shut down, and I didn't want to be running when that happened. But now we have to go. Can you stand yet?"

I planted both palms on the ground, then carefully got to my knees on the pillow beneath me. "Did it ever occur to you to *tell* me I was about to lose control of my own body?"

"I was getting to it when you passed out." He grabbed the blanket I'd folded, and refolded it into a longer, narrower shape, then stuffed it into the duffel on one side, as padding for the other supplies. "How do you feel?"

I stood slowly, my arms out for balance, and when the warehouse didn't pitch around me, I let out a sigh. "Fine. I feel pretty good."

"Great." He tossed me my school satchel, and I caught it easily. "Take all the cans you can carry."

I stepped over the lantern and two pillows, then knelt in front of the double row of canned goods. "Who's Devi?"

Finn made an annoyed sound deep in his throat, and some small bit of dread inside me eased. She was definitely *not* his girlfriend.

"Devi's a friend. Well, more like the irritating girlfriend of a friend. She only speaks in commands and seems to think she's the boss of the whole world, but she comes with the territory, and she carries her weight, so what can you do?"

I unzipped my bag and picked up two cans, but Finn

rolled his eyes and snatched the satchel from me. "You're not going back to school, so this is all worthless." He turned my backpack upside down and dumped all my textbooks and notebooks onto the grimy floor.

A surprising bolt of disappointment shot through me at the realization that he was right.

I dropped the first two cans into my empty bag, trying to find points of commonality between my life before I'd killed my mother and this new existence on the run with dangerous abilities I didn't yet understand and a beautiful green-eyed boy I didn't really know. But I couldn't find any. The before and after halves of my life seemed to have nothing in common except *me*.

And Melanie. She was still my sister, even if my mother wasn't really my mother and my school was no longer my school and my future was now a huge question mark scribbled over the path I'd always assumed my life would take.

I couldn't leave her.

"Where are we going?" I dropped two more cans into my bag, then picked up another two without glancing at the labels.

"Today? To our current home base. It's much more comfortable, and it has running water and a functioning bathroom."

Good. I'd been trying to ignore the pressure in my bladder ever since I woke up. "And after that?"

Finn shrugged. "We don't have an agenda, but we'll stay in the area long enough to hunt down most of the degenerates scenting you, unless the Church gets too close to finding us."

I wouldn't leave Melanie, even if that happened.

I zipped my full bag and stood, mentally preparing myself for how heavy it'd be, and was surprised when I lifted it with very little effort. Did the increase in my strength mean the degenerates were getting closer?

When I turned to Finn, I found his little campsite virtually gone. He'd managed to fit most of his equipment into that one huge duffel.

"Where did you get all that, anyway?" I waved one hand at the pillows and cans remaining.

"I . . . um . . . I'm pretty good with acquisitions. I'll show you later." He threw the bulging bag over his shoulder with as little effort as I'd needed to lift my satchel. "Ready? Devi and Reese should be here any minute, and hopefully they've thinned out the horde a little on the way."

"How big a horde are we talking about?" I clutched the strap of my satchel. A strange itch had developed in my legs, way too deep to scratch. My muscles *ached* with it, as if I'd been in one position for too long and now my body wanted to stretch. To move.

"Grayson said it was small, so ten or twelve, I'd guess, unless Devi and the others have made a decent dent."

That itch in my legs swelled, extending through my arms and down into my feet—a physical sense of urgency, as if my muscles knew we should have been running but my brain didn't yet know why. I dropped into a squat and bounced on the balls of my feet, then set my satchel down and bent to touch my toes, hoping stretches would alleviate some of that itch to move. To run.

"What's wrong?" Finn set his duffel on the floor and ducked to catch my gaze. "You feel something?"

"Yeah. I'm not sure what, though. I just . . . I feel like we should be moving. Fast. *Now*." I could sense something strong and dark racing toward us and felt *compelled* to run in the opposite direction.

"It's the horde. While you're transitioning, they can feel you and you can feel them."

"Yeah, well, I feel like they're getting closer. Really close." I picked my bag up and tugged on his arm. "Let's go."

He pulled his hand from mine, and I would have been disappointed if I weren't too scared to focus on anything but the burning in my muscles, urging me to run. "Devi and Reese are on their way, and we'll be stronger in a larger group. Especially considering you've never really fought a degenerate."

But my instincts weren't telling me to fight. They were telling me to flee. Right then. As fast as I could. "I have to go." I settled my satchel higher on my shoulder, and he let go of me with obvious reluctance. "Come with me, Finn. We'll go to your safe house and meet the others there." My legs felt like tightened coils about to explode from the tension. My feet ached to run. My head was alive with thoughts that had no form or meaning, like the fuzz on the TV during a rare news outage.

"Nina, look at me." He put one hand around each of my arms, and his green-eyed gaze searched mine. Only it felt more like an assessment of my mental state. "Calm down. Ride it out. You want to run because your body knows you can't fight them all on your own. But you're *not* on your own, and if we're not here when Devi gets here, she'll kill me." Shadows hid most of his face, but the determination in his voice was very clear.

Screw Devi! Finn was an exorcist. He'd been through what I was going through, right? So why couldn't he understand that my body was giving me a command I had no choice but to follow? I couldn't stand still for one more minute, with my muscles burning and my—

His mouth met mine, and I almost choked on surprise. Then his hand slid behind my neck and his head tilted, and I had a second to decide whether to bite his tongue off or kiss him back.

I'm not sure why I kissed him back.

Maybe because he was the only person I'd spoken to in the past twelve hours, other than my sister, who hadn't tried to kill me, possess me, grope me, or arrest me. Maybe because I'd never been kissed by someone who wasn't clumsy and hurried, or ashamed of what he wanted, or using me for an entirely different reason than I was using him. Maybe because kissing Finn felt good when I needed to feel something that wasn't scary and dangerous and terrifyingly uncertain.

What I *do* know is that I committed to that kiss like I'd committed to little else in life. My fingers brushed over short stubble at the back of his jaw on their way into his hair. He sucked my lower lip into his mouth and I let him have it, then I gave him more. I *lived* in that moment, fighting panic and urgency with the boldest, most breathtaking and brazenly immodest human contact I'd ever felt.

Then something caught the back of my shirt and I screamed as I was ripped away from Finn, reaching for him, my fingers grasping. I twisted, my heart pounding, ready to scratch and claw at the degenerate who'd snuck into our sanctuary, surely the first of dozens ready to chew me to death and slurp up my insides.

My feet met the floor and someone swung me around by one arm.

A girl's face came into focus in the dark, and she was definitely not a degenerate, though she did look mad enough to rip my arms off. Before I could truly process the fact that I'd just been caught in carnal contact—yet another sin on top of the charges already leveled against me—she said my name.

"You're Nina?" Her dark eyes narrowed as she studied me, though she couldn't have seen much in the shadows. Her grip on my arm bruised, and my heart kept racing, even though she was human, thus unlikely to eat my face off or devour my soul.

I nodded, too surprised to ask the questions rapidly coalescing from the chaos in my head.

"Well, Nina, we'll get along just fine if you remember to keep your *mouth* off my *boyfriend*."

TEN

"I'm not her boyfriend." Finn stepped into sight on my left, carrying my satchel with his duffel over one shoulder. "Let her go, Devi."

I jerked my arm from her grip and took my bag when Finn held it out. "Who's her boyfriend?"

"Maddock. We look a lot alike, in a certain light." He turned to Devi. "She hasn't met him yet."

"But he's okay?" Fear resonated in her voice, beneath an obvious strength and hostility.

"Like I'd let him get hurt."

Devi looked far from mollified. "I want to talk to him."

"So do I. We'll both have to wait until we get to the safe house. Where's Reese?"

"Keeping watch in the alley," she said, and when Finn strode past her, headed for the back door, she grabbed his arm, and I realized she talked as much with her hands as with her mouth. "Finn. I want. To talk. To Maddock."

That was when I decided I didn't like Devi.

"We don't have time for this. Come on."

"Where's Maddock?" I jogged to catch up with Finn, stepping over trash and dodging broken, oily machine parts while my satchel bounced on my back.

"You didn't tell her?" Devi called, stomping after us.

"Tell me what?"

"I haven't had a chance to explain everything yet." Finn shot me an apologetic glance. "We're kind of a complicated team, in case that isn't obvious." He pulled the door open and gestured for me to step into the alley. "You'll meet Maddy and Grayson when we get there. For now we all need to concentrate on surviving the trip. Stick close to me, and if I say run, you run. Got it?"

"Finn!" Devi snapped softly.

Finn followed me into the alley. He never even glanced at her.

Though she was still clearly furious, Devi got quiet as soon as the door opened, obviously hyperaware that we weren't the only ones who could hear her now.

"How do you feel? Are they any closer?" Finn whispered, and it took me a second to realize he was talking to me. And that he was using my transitional state like a radar gun for degenerates.

I closed my eyes and discovered that that panicky sense of urgency was still there. I'd just been too distracted by Devi—and kissing Finn—to think about it for the past two minutes.

"Don't do that," Devi whispered, so close to my ear that I jumped. I opened my eyes to find her frowning at me from the doorway, her long, thick, dark ponytail trailing over her shoulder.

"Don't do what?"

"Don't close your eyes. You can't fight what you can't see."

"How close are they?" Finn asked, and I tensed when footsteps reverberated from the darkness at the other end of the alley.

"Close." Those footsteps set me even more on edge, but Finn and Devi didn't look scared, so I was assuming I shouldn't be either.

But then, maybe they never looked scared. Maybe fighting degenerates was so routine for them that they didn't even remember what fear felt like. I wasn't sure whether to envy them that or feel sorry for them.

The shadows shifted and a man stepped into the moonlight several feet from us. He was *huge*. At least half a foot taller than Finn, and nearly as broad as the back door of the warehouse. But when he came closer, I realized he wasn't any older than the rest of us. He was just . . . big.

"Nina? Hey. I'm Reese." He reached out to shake my hand, and his nearly swallowed mine.

"Hey." In spite of the sizable new addition to our forces, it took every bit of my self-control to keep from bolting down the alley and into the street, then racing in whatever direction my legs chose.

Reese turned to Finn. "She looks antsy. She's been triggered?"

He nodded. "About eight hours ago."

"Then maybe we shouldn't take her to our local base," Devi said. "As long as they can sense her, they'll hunt for her, which will lead them straight to us."

"You want to *leave* me?" Panic rang in my voice. I'd never successfully fought off a degenerate, and I could feel the horde getting closer, like I could feel the rush of my own pulse. But I couldn't outrun them all.

"We're not leaving her," Finn said.

Devi's dark eyes glistened in the moonlight when she rolled them. "Of course not. We need her, whether I like her or not. But maybe we should stash her somewhere until she finishes transitioning. Somewhere they can't get to her, obviously."

"And where might that be?" Reese crossed thick arms over an even thicker chest.

"I don't know, but it seems stupid to point a big flashing arrow at our home. Right? You *want* to lead them to Grayson?"

Reese looked startled by the thought, and then he frowned, considering. "Wherever you put her, degenerates will circle her like sharks around blood, and a bunch of monsters clawing up the outside of a building would definitely draw the Church's attention. It'd have to be outside of town. So maybe one of the ghost towns?"

My heart dropped into my stomach.

There were thousands of ghost towns in the United States alone—entire communities wiped out nearly a century ago during the war. Most of the smaller ones had been completely swallowed by the demon horde right at the beginning, every single citizen either killed or possessed. Some towns had been razed, burned to the ground by the occupying horde or by the army fighting it.

Most of the towns that were still standing at the end of the war had been abandoned in favor of cities and larger towns, which had managed to build strong walls and post armed guards to keep out the remaining, roving degenerates. Now those "ghost towns" dotted the vast expanse of the badlands, in what used to be the heart of America.

There were four ghost towns within an hour of New Temperance by bus. We'd been to two of them—one razed, one standing abandoned—on school field trips, and they were *beyond* creepy. The only thing scarier than living in a town ruled by the Church would be living in a town *not* ruled—thus not protected—by the Church.

"Seriously?" My pulse raced and my legs ached to move. "You're just going to abandon me in a ghost town?"

"No." Reese smiled at me in the dark, and moonlight

shone on his teeth. He had a friendly smile. "I'll stay with you. You've only got eight or ten more hours of transition, and after that we'll meet everyone else at home base."

Finn took my hand. "Stash her if you want, but I'm staying with her."

"*Damn* it, Finn," Devi whispered. "You are *not* taking Maddock with you."

"Wait. What's the point of stashing me if we're going to have to kill any degenerates that surround the place anyway? Can't we just kill them now and not get followed anywhere?"

Devi's brows rose, and she seemed to be reassessing me. "You up for that? Have you ever faced a degenerate?"

"Yeah." I shrugged, and a can from my satchel poked my spine. "It didn't go so well, but if anyone has a spare gun, I'm sure I can point and shoot."

"No guns," Reese whispered. "Even if the noise wasn't a problem, you can't shoot degenerates. Well, you *can,* but that only releases them to find a new host in our world. You have to exorcise demons to send them back to their world."

Oh yeah. "Then why does Finn have a gun?"

"Because you can't exorcise regular people." Devi's grim focus narrowed on me. "Answer the question. Are you ready for this?"

The brain-rattling squeal of stressed steel ripped through the night, a block over at the most, followed by a familiar screechy roar. That burning sensation in my legs flared, and my hands began to flex as if they wanted a weapon. "No choice," I mumbled, and the three of them were instantly on alert. They headed for the east end of the alley at a jog, though no one had so much as pointed in that direction. I trailed behind, as close to Finn as I could get without stepping on his heels.

"How many?" he asked, and Reese cocked his head, moving silently on concrete even in heavy boots.

"Three within a block. Maybe three times that trailing behind, in the main wave."

"I thought only exorcists in transition could feel degenerates." I tugged my satchel strap higher on my shoulder and tried to make my feet as quiet as theirs, but my sneakers seemed to crunch on every loose bit of asphalt.

"He's not sensing them." Devi paused at the end of the alley to glance both ways. "He's hearing them. Reese's ears are like a cat's." When she saw no traffic—or demons—she waved for us to follow her across the dark street and into the next alley, where the stench of rotten food emanated from a restaurant's trash bin. "I used to think he was brain damaged because he was always staring off into space, but it turns out he was just listening to stuff we can't hear. Handy in moments like this. Not so much when you want privacy."

Fascinated, I glanced up at him as we ran, which only made it harder for me to keep up. "Cat ears?"

A monstrous screech-roar rang out from behind us, bouncing off buildings and concrete, and my legs began to itch and burn again. Any early risers in the area would have heard that. Fortunately, the nearest neighborhood was more than half a mile away.

"Shouldn't we move faster?" Our pace had slowed, and my body wanted to *run*.

"We want the ones in front to catch up with us so we can kill them. Then we'll draw the rest to a location of our choosing. Someplace away from the residential areas where people might hear the commotion and call the cops." Devi glanced at Finn without missing a step as she jogged. "There's a junkyard on the north edge of town, about a mile from here. Industrial district. Should be pretty deserted this time of the morning."

Finn gestured for us to take a right on the next street. "I saw it yesterday while I was scouting out the town." While I was in school, presumably. "We'll have to climb the fence, but that should work."

The junkyard owner, Mr. Johns, had bought my mom's car for parts a year before. A few months later, he'd bought an old stereo and our rollaway dishwasher for probably twice what they were worth because he could see that I needed the cash. But even the nicest man in the world would call the police if he saw degenerates swarming his business.

Fortunately, the junkyard didn't open until nine. Mr.

Johns was probably still asleep in his bed. On the other side of town.

"How's this?" Finn stopped jogging and the others stopped with him as I huffed to a graceless halt several feet past them, my full satchel bouncing on my back. I wondered if I was missing some kind of silent signal. Or maybe my transitional brain wasn't yet tuned to the exorcist mental frequency.

Reese and Devi glanced around the broad alley we'd stopped in, assessing its usefulness. The path was wide enough for a garbage truck to drive through, and it was scattered with industrial trash bins. The wall on my left was brick, and the one on my right was chipped concrete. There were no windows, and the only light was what shone in from streetlights on either end and what moonlight filtered through the shifting clouds overhead.

If we had to make a stand in town, this was the place.

"Looks good," Devi said, and while her whisper still hung on the air, Reese tensed and turned to face the way we'd come.

"Three, closing in."

I could feel them. They were hungry. *Ravenous.* Their muscles burned from the chase, but they didn't seem to notice. Their blood pumped, and I could feel the synchronized throb of their pulses inside me, like a second heartbeat. And as I set down my satchel and mimicked Finn's fighting stance—feet spread for balance, arms bent, hands empty and ready—I realized that the degenerates' heart-beats weren't just in sync with one another's. They were in sync with *mine*.

They could feel me, just like I could feel them.

"They're close," I whispered, and Reese nodded in confirmation. "What's the plan?" Three degenerates. Four exorcists. I might not get a chance to kill one.

I wasn't sure whether to be frustrated or relieved by that thought.

Devi laughed, and the sound bounced off the walls around us. The degenerates heard her, and their pulses tripped faster, triggering an increase in my own heart rate. "The plan is to send the bastards back to hell, then dance on their corpses."

"She's kidding about the dance." Reese's gaze was focused on the end of the alley, his eyes narrowed in concentration as he listened.

Finn stepped up to my side. "No, she's not."

Before I could decide which of them to believe, another screeching roar speared my brain. Claws scraped concrete at the end of the alley. My pulse jumped, and a degenerate leapt out of the shadows. He landed in a squat on all fours, bony knees bent, long, wiry muscles standing out under the pale skin exposed beneath his filthy, shredded pants.

His shirt hung in tatters, one sleeve completely missing, and his shoes were long gone.

His eyes gleamed and he looked right at me, his bald

head crusted with dried blood in places and shiny enough to reflect moonlight in others. His mouth gaped wider than should have been possible, saliva gathering at the corners. He threw his head back and screeched, and chills skittered up my spine.

I tried to suck in a breath, but my throat closed in terror. The degenerate leapt for me, and I shoved my left hand forward, trying to call up the fire that had burned the demon from my mother's wasted body. But my fingers trembled and remained dark as the monster soared toward me in the air, and time seemed to slow around me.

My heart lurched into my throat and as I dove to the right—my backup plan—Reese's left hand shot up and out. He snagged the scraps of the degenerate's shirt as it flew over him, then plucked the demon from the air like picking an apple from a low-hanging branch.

Reese slammed the monster into the concrete, and the degenerate and I hit the ground at the same time. My palms skidded on loose asphalt. I heard a violent explosion of air as collision with both Reese and the ground drove breath from the demon's lungs.

Finn pulled me up by one arm, and I had an instant to realize Devi was laughing at me before a bright glow lit the alley. Squinting, I turned to see that Reese had the degenerate pinned on its back, his hand glowing against the monster's chest as the demon kicked and bucked and clawed beneath him.

Reese made it look easy. Maybe it *was* easy for him, considering his size and obvious strength. I watched him in awe, but I couldn't imagine ever doing what he'd just done—snatching one of hell's natives from the air, then driving the demon back to hell before it had even caught its breath.

After a couple of seconds, the degenerate stopped snapping and struggling, and the glow from Reese's hand faded. He stood and brushed his palm on the front of his shirt, then turned a broad grin on the rest of us. "First kill. Again." He focused on Devi. "What's in the pot?"

She scowled. "Only three. Finn hasn't chipped in yet." She pulled a small wad of bills from her back pocket and handed them to Reese while Finn added a dollar of his own to the pile. "Neither has Nina," Devi pointed out, watching me expectantly while more scrapes and animal-istic hissing echoed from two different directions.

"She doesn't have to." Finn turned to me, and my skin crawled as the other degenerates closed in on us, but my new friends didn't seem worried, and after seeing Reese in action, I was starting to see why. "You don't have to," Finn repeated, to me this time.

"I'm in." I dug a dollar from my pocket—part of my remaining laundry money—and handed it to Reese, who winked at me. Normally, I wouldn't have voluntarily parted with a single dime of my hard-earned pay, but consider-ing that the exorcists had fed me, protected me, and saved my life twice in less than a day, a dollar seemed like the least I owed them.

Reese caught my gaze as he stuffed the crumpled bills into his front left pocket. "Your turn. You ready?"

I frowned. "Do I have to . . . ?" I mimed snatching a demon from the air overhead, and Devi laughed again.

"If you ever get that good, I'll eat my own underwear."

"Make it Reese's shorts, and you've got a bet." Finn slid his arm around my waist, and warmth grew in my cheeks in spite of chills both from the cold and from the sound of the degenerates bearing down on us.

"Heads up!" Reese shouted before Devi could reply, and by the time I swung my gaze skyward, Finn was already pulling me out of the way.

Another degenerate landed where I'd stood an instant earlier, catlike on stretched limbs and clawlike fingers. Her bare feet were too long, and what remained of her hair hung in her face, half hiding mad eyes too murky to be any color other than black. Her skin had once been dark, and maybe smooth, but now it was ashen and mottled, and it clung to her mutated bones.

And this one smelled. Sweat and dirt and foul fluids matted the filthy dress to her torso, and I was glad to see the cloth was mostly intact.

Then I was *horrified* to see that her dress was actually a Church cassock, maybe originally pale blue. This demon had once been a teacher.

So much for faith protecting the faithful.

She snarled at me, and Devi shoved me forward. I stumbled to within three feet of the monster, and Finn cursed Devi behind me, but this time he didn't pull me back. They were going to let me take this one. Or maybe they were going to let this one take *me*.

"Breathe," Finn whispered. "Your body knows what to do."

Yeah, well, my head didn't. My special exorcist hand didn't seem to be in the know either.

The degenerate crawled toward me on her hands and feet, each motion eerily smooth in spite of limbs that no longer seemed to fit her body and joints that cracked with every movement.

Devi heaved a dramatic huff. "Just do it alr—" Then something hit the pavement behind me, and I heard her and Finn struggling with what was hopefully the third and last degenerate in the advance wave.

"They're fine," Reese said from my degenerate's other side. "You focus on this one."

And I would have. Except that this time when the degenerate opened her mouth, instead of hissing at me again, she pounced.

The monster's clawed hands slammed into my chest and the alley tilted. My backside hit the ground an instant before my head, and the crack of my skull against concrete was enough to stun me. I tried to suck in a breath, but my lungs wouldn't expand. A heartbeat later I realized why—the degenerate was perched on my chest.

She lunged for my throat. I threw my right arm up and braced my forearm against her neck, holding her snapping jaw inches from my face. She roared in fury, and my ears rang while her finger-claws tore at my coat. I forced my left hand between us, and when no light appeared in my palm, I groaned in frustration, then shoved her with every bit of strength I had. I didn't expect much from the effort, and I didn't *get* much from it. But I got enough.

The degenerate fell backward onto the concrete and I scrambled to my knees. An instant after that, I dropped my full weight on her, as I'd just seen Reese do.

She snapped and tried to throw me off, but I clenched her waist between my knees and her throat in my right hand, then held on tight while she bucked and sputtered beneath me. And finally my left hand was tingling.

"Hold . . . still . . . you filthy . . . bitch!" But she didn't hold still, and I couldn't make her, so I slammed my palm down on her sternum as hard as I could and shoved that heat building inside me into my hand.

The glow was weak but immediate.

She bucked harder and tried to screech, so I squeezed her neck with my other hand, and something crunched beneath my fingers. Her trachea?

Transitional strength. It had to be.

"No!" Reese shouted. "Don't kill her. *Exorcise* her."

"What does it look . . . like I'm . . . doing?" I demanded, riding out another desperate thrash while the degenerate clawed at the arms of my coat, reaching for my face.

"It looks like you're riding a half-dead dog," Devi said, and my temper spiked. And with that pulse of anger, the glow beneath my palm exploded in light so bright I could hardly stand to look at it. The degenerate gave one more weak twitch beneath me, then fell still. I didn't get up until the glow was completely gone, leaving me half blind while my eyes readjusted to the shadows.

"Nice," Finn said as I stood on shaky legs and wiped my hands on my jeans. I understood why they did that now—degenerates were filthy.

"It was adequate," Devi said, while I stared in awe at the demon I'd just exorcised. "But slow. Let's go before the rest of them are on us." She glanced at Reese, brows raised in silent inquiry.

"They're closing in," he confirmed, and I could feel them coming as I picked up my satchel. Too many of them. Devi was right. I was too slow.

"Come on." Finn picked up his duffel, then grabbed my hand, and when I turned to follow him, I had to step over the degenerate he and Devi had dispatched—a big one, bald, but not quite as long and angular as the former woman I'd fought.

We took off into the dark again, and this time I was in the lead with Devi because I knew the way. We raced across roads and through dark parking lots, avoiding streetlights as much as possible, in case anyone was up early enough to see four teens being chased through New Temperance by a mini horde of degenerates.

By the time we got to the junkyard, I was panting. I'd run my required laps in school, and I'd certainly done my share of running away from things—mostly people—but those were sprints. I'd never run as far or as fast as I did that morning, drawing the demons to the north side of town, away from houses and businesses, and carrying at least twenty pounds of canned goods.

Relief washed over me when I spotted the six-foot chain-link fence, its gate chained closed and locked. But that relief was followed by a bolt of dread and fear. The junkyard wasn't our safe haven.

It was our battleground.

I was the last one over Mr. Johns's fence. The clinking rattle of chain-link and the cold metal jerking and swaying in my hands with every new foothold from my fellow exorcists would forever be associated with the memory of that night. With my mother's death and my sister's arrest. With the confusion in my head, the ache in my heart, and the fire in my palm. I threw one leg over the top of the fence, my satchel bouncing on my back, and dropped to the dirt from four feet up. By the time my feet hit the ground, I could hear the degenerates.

Seconds later, as we receded into the junkyard, mostly

shielded from both moonlight and streetlights, the monsters came into view through the fence. My heartbeat stuttered and my eyes strained to filter the forms of monsters from the darkness. I could feel them—the rush of their pulses blending with my own—but I couldn't distinguish their individual shapes until they crept into the glow of a string of streetlights across from the fence.

For a moment, I couldn't breathe.

Mutated and emaciated, they formed a rough line facing ours. I counted ten. Some stood, too tall and angular, as if they'd somehow been stretched. Others squatted, a complication of limbs and joints that seemed to be put together all wrong, from mismatched human parts.

At first, they only watched us, some growling, others scenting the air as if to confirm what they already knew from the internal connection we shared. That I was there. That I wasn't running. That my soul—the only one they could sense, thanks to my transitional state—was up for grabs.

Then one of them lurched forward and his movement triggered the rest. The demons launched into motion almost as one, and I stood steady between Finn and Reese, determined—if not truly prepared—to face the wave of violence about to crash over us.

ELEVEN

"Keep track of your stats, people," Reese called as the monsters ran, leapt, and raced on all fours, barreling through the glow of the streetlights, bearing down on us so fast they looked like a storm of shadows closing in. "He with the highest body count claims the first shower."

"Or she," Devi said from his right. "Don't get cocky."

"It's only cocky if you talk a better game than you play."

"My point exactly," she shot back, but Reese only laughed, and I realized this was their routine—a way to make light of the death and violence that defined their existence.

The first degenerate hit the fence with the *crashclink* of

chain-link, and my nerves crested in a burst of destructive energy like nothing I'd ever felt. Finn let go of my hand and moved over to give us more room. Reese charged forward with a growl of his own as the first monster landed on our side of the fence in an impossibly deep squat, and in my peripheral vision, Devi tensed, silently preparing for battle.

Reese grabbed that first degenerate by her ripped shirt, and while they struggled, the second and third demons launched themselves at the fence. The second cleared the metal entirely and landed on the ground in front of Devi. The third perched near the top of the fence, his long, bare toes curled around metal wire while his deformed and knobby hands gripped the metal rod defining the top edge.

Finn lunged forward and I followed, my pulse racing so hard I could near nothing as loud as my own heartbeat. He grabbed the degenerate's wrist and pulled with a low grunt. The monster screeched and fell end over end to land on his back in the dirt. Finn was on him in an instant, his hand already glowing, and when I looked up, I saw that the front of the junkyard was *alive* with light now.

A glow faded from Reese's palm as another built around Devi's, and while I stood there like an idiot, Reese rose from the degenerate he'd just exorcised. "One!" he half shouted, and before the word had even faded from my ears, he'd pulled another demon from the fence.

"One!" Devi stood and kicked a deformed dead woman in the side, then grunted in surprise when another landed right in front of her.

"One!" Finn called. Then, "Nina, heads up!"

I turned just as the sixth degenerate dropped from the fence and snarled at me. I took a step back, flexing my left hand, praying for that light to appear while the demon advanced, snarling and snapping in anticipation. Finn stood behind him, the glow still fading from his palm and imprinted on my vision. He reached for the demon approaching me, but then one pulled him off his feet and he was suddenly ensnarled in another fight.

I was on my own.

"Two!" Reese yelled, and another bright glow appeared on my right, highlighting the degenerate just two feet in front of me now. His chin was too sharp and thin flesh clung to the points of his elbows. His eyes flashed with light, and I couldn't tell what color they'd been before, but now they were black, as if the demon inside him had rotted the very color from his irises.

"Two!" Devi shouted.

The degenerate pounced, and I lurched to my right. I only meant to move out of the way to avoid being pinned. Instead, my feet hit the ground six feet away. Stunned, I turned and the junkyard spun around me, the glow from Reese's palm streaking across my vision twice before I finally stilled, dizzy and confused. My intended 180 had become two and a half revolutions, as if I were stuck on my own personal merry-go-round.

I threw my hands out, trying to regain my balance.

The snarl and the flying shadow hit me at the same time. Pain slammed into my chest. My back hit the dirt. Jaws snapped near my nose for the third time in less than a day. I threw my arms up, and teeth sank into the left sleeve of my coat. Rancid drool dripped on my cheek, and I turned my head, shuddering in revulsion while my pulse raced in fear.

The demon shook his head like a dog with a bone, and pain ripped through my arm from wrist to shoulder. I shouted and tried to jerk my arm free before he tore it off, but he wouldn't let go, and the ache in my bruised bones was *fierce*.

"Two!" Finn shouted.

Desperate, I swung at the degenerate's temple with my free right hand, and to my shock, his head snapped to the side and his pointy teeth were torn from my sleeve.

"Three!" Reese called, and Devi echoed him an instant later.

The demon groaned, stunned, and I saw my chance. I pressed my hands into his chest and lifted him as far from me as I could, then tucked my knees and wedged my feet between us. Then I kicked.

The demon flew up and out, snarling in the air, arms and feet trailing uselessly. He crashed into the fence and I stood just in time to see Devi grab his shirt and shove him face-first into the ground. "Four!" she shouted, slamming her palm down on the degenerate's back. The glow in her hand consumed the demon.

"Hey! That one was mine!" I yelled, and Reese laughed.

Devi shrugged. "Then next time exorcise it instead of playing with it."

"I wasn't . . . It nearly pulled my arm off!" I did fast math in my head, still trying to catch my breath. Three for Reese, four for Devi and two for Finn. "Wait, that should still leave—"

Something slammed into my back, and the earth flew up to meet me. My face hit the dirt, and air was driven from my lungs, through my throat.

"Nina!" Finn shouted. Footsteps pounded toward me, then stopped abruptly.

"She wanted a kill, Finn," Devi said. "Let her have one."

Something hot and wet dripped on the back of my neck, and I sucked in a desperate breath, forcing my lungs to expand in spite of the weight pressing me into the ground. Claws raked through my hair, and I felt as much as heard a dozen tiny pops as individual strands were ripped from my scalp.

The monster growled, and hot, unspeakably foul breath washed over me as it sniffed near my ear. It seemed to be looking for my face. My skin crawled and my pulse raced.

"Nina, do something!" Devi shouted, and footsteps pounded toward me again, but stopped when the degenerate screeched in warning. Exorcists were fast, but so were demons. They couldn't get to me before the monster ripped my head off and slurped out my brains.

The degenerate clawed at my coat, and pain ripped through my back as he shredded both cloth and flesh. And that was when anger started to rival my pain and fear.

If I was about to die, I wasn't going to go out facedown in the dirt.

I reached up and back, fumbling for a grip on anything, and my fingers closed over cool, taut skin. Ignoring another wave of revulsion, I pulled as hard as I could. The degenerate shrieked, and his claws ripped into my flesh again as I pulled him off me with a primal grunt of effort. I was stronger now, but the angle was awkward. Nearly impossible.

As soon as I was free, I scrambled to my feet. The degenerate squatted a foot away, hissing, and my hand started to burn. So I threw myself at him.

We crashed to the ground and I sat on his stomach, then pressed my glowing left hand against his chest. The demon screamed like a wounded cat, and my hand burned and burned and burned.

Two seconds later it was all over. I sat on a deformed corpse staring sightlessly at the dark sky as the light between us faded.

"You okay?" Finn pulled me up by both arms and folded me into a hug. I squeezed him back, in spite of the pain from my injuries, burying my nose in the warmth and scent of his neck. I'd never been so exhilarated in my life—adrenaline pumped through my veins from both the fight and the intimate embrace.

"One," I said, panting, and Devi laughed. Reese grinned at me over Finn's shoulder.

"That adds up to ten," Devi said. "Let's go home."

* * *

Climbing the fence with injuries sucked, and my super speed and strength seemed to have abandoned me entirely in the wake of my first real demon battle. And after the fence, there was still an almost two-mile trek to their real hideout. No one talked much during the walk, and I was relieved to realize they were tired too. Even Reese seemed subdued; the only thing I heard from him during the trip was an offer to trade his five dollars for the first shower.

The only thing I heard from Devi was an incredulous laugh, which was evidently Devi-speak for "no way in hell."

In spite of Finn's promise that their "real" hideout was more comfortable than the warehouse he'd obviously set up just for my vulnerable transitional period, I expected them to take me somewhere similar. An unused office building or storefront. There'd always been lots of those in New Temperance. In addition to two-thirds of its human population, the United States lost a good deal of its industry during the war, even in the surviving towns and cities strung together only by deteriorating highways and necessity.

So I was more than a little surprised when, less than an hour before dawn, we turned toward one of the residential neighborhoods near the northeast portion of the town wall. There were a couple of unused apartment buildings in New Temperance, just like there were abandoned businesses, but none of them were in the neighborhood we seemed headed for, unless they knew something about my hometown that I didn't.

When we finally turned in to the rear grounds of a complex I knew, I pulled Finn to a halt with me. "Here? You're staying *here*?" Anabelle had lived there with her parents, before she'd joined the Church. Many more of my classmates lived in that very complex. "This is possibly the worst place to hide in all of New Temperance. I bet there aren't even any empty units."

"There was one," Devi said, and I didn't like the way she said it. Something was missing from her voice. Sincerity, maybe.

"It's okay," Finn said. "Really."

I decided to trust him because he hadn't let me down yet. And because my shoulder was throbbing and my back was both burning from the demon scratches and cold from the air flowing in through the new ventilation in my old coat. I needed a shower and some antiseptic. And some breakfast.

They led me to a door on the first floor, near the back of the complex. Anabelle's parents still lived one floor up, and maybe two doors over.

"Shhh . . ." Finn put one finger across his lips while Reese dug a key from his pocket and opened the door. They let me go in first, and I stopped cold after four steps.

"This isn't an empty unit. This apartment is *furnished*!" There were still pictures hanging on the walls. Keys on hooks by the pantry. Coats and scarves peeking out of an open closet.

"It's empty *now*." Devi pushed past me into the living room, then into the dining area, where she took off her jacket and draped it over the back of a chair. "Close the door." She shot a look at Reese over my head, then focused on Finn as she walked backward toward the bathroom. "I'm taking a shower. When I get out, I want to talk to Maddock. Got it?"

Finn nodded and Reese locked the door.

Before I could start demanding explanations, the second of three doors in the tiny rectangle of hallway opened and a girl appeared, young, petite, and fresh-faced. She reminded me of Melanie, and that made my chest ache.

Her light brown curls bounced as she raced across the living area and threw herself at Reese, who actually had to lift her off the floor to give her the kiss she obviously wanted.

I couldn't help but stare. Kids in New Temperance didn't kiss in front of people. We kept our sins secret. We stored them in the dark with our hopes and our fears and everything else never meant to see the light of day.

"That's Grayson," Finn mock-whispered. "They're . . . close."

"So I see." I looked away from them as if I saw couples kiss on the mouth every day. As if I weren't scandalized by the fearless audacity of their affection. "Where's Maddock?"

Reese set Grayson down, and she studied me for a moment, then looked up at Finn, her brown eyes narrowed in censure. "You didn't tell her?"

"Come on." Reese took Grayson's hand. "Let's give them a minute."

"Why?" She frowned. Then her gaze traveled to where my hand was linked with Finn's, and I dropped it, mortified to realize I'd grown so used to the feel of his hand that I'd forgotten I was holding it. "*Ohhh* . . . Uh-oh."

"Uh-oh? What's uh-oh?" My chest felt bruised again. Something was wrong. "What's wrong with Maddock? Is he scary-looking or something?"

Finn laughed, but the sound wasn't natural. "Actually, he's kinda pretty."

Grayson let Reese pull her toward an open doorway, through which I could see the end of a double bed.

"Reese." Finn dropped his duffel on the floor and shoved his hands into his pockets. "Do you mind?"

Reese turned to meet Finn's gaze and frowned. Then he nodded. Grayson let go of his hand and gave Finn a small smile in acknowledgment of something I still didn't understand, then went into the bedroom and closed the door.

"What?" Goose bumps had risen on my skin. Why did Reese get to stay, but not Grayson? What weren't they telling me? "Where's Maddock?"

Finn looked right into my eyes and he tried to grin, but the result looked more like nerves. "Um . . . The thing is . . . you're looking at him."

TWELVE

My eyes narrowed at Finn. "I don't . . . I don't know what that means." I'd heard the words, but they didn't make any sense.

Finn ran one hand through his hair. "I know. This is . . . This is harder than it's ever been before. Um . . ." He glanced up at Reese, who stood pressed against the far wall as if he were trying to give us privacy without leaving the room. "You ready? I don't know how else to do this."

I twisted to see Reese nod. Once. Solemnly. When I turned back to Finn, his eyes were closed. They stayed closed for one of the longest seconds of my life.

When they finally opened, they were the wrong color.

Finn's green eyes were now blue. Not blue-green. Not aqua. Bright blue, and as clear as the Caribbean Sea had looked in a film I'd seen in geography my freshman year.

"What the hell?" I took two steps back in confusion. Then I took three steps forward in fascination, and we were inches apart.

He blinked, once. Twice. Finn's forehead furrowed, and then he backed away from me so fast he almost fell. "I . . ."

His newly blue eyes widened in bewilderment. He looked . . . lost.

"I . . . ," he said again. Then he looked over my head. *"Devi!"*

The bathroom door opened and Devi came out wrapped in a very short brown towel, her long, dark hair dripping wet. She didn't seem to care that she was practically naked in front of two different guys, with all the lights on, and they seemed no more surprised to see her in a towel than I would have been surprised to see my sister in one, in the privacy of our own home.

But Devi wasn't their sister, and this wasn't their home, and they weren't really family.

Did the boys walk around in towels too? I'd never seen a guy in as little as Devi wore.

And suddenly it occurred to me that even during the carnal rebellion following my sterilization, I'd actually seen and truly experienced very little.

That was when I noticed that Devi didn't wear a purity ring.

She took one look at Finn's weird blue eyes, and then her face erupted into a huge smile for the first time since I'd met her. She looked *stunning* in that moment. Immodest and forbidden and relieved and . . . happy about something I hadn't yet wrapped my mind around.

"Maddock!" She shoved me over and threw herself at him, and the only thing holding her towel on was the fact that it was pinched between their bodies. While she kissed Finn. Whom she'd called Maddock. Who kissed her back. And had blue eyes.

"What the *hell*?" I turned to Reese, who held up one finger, an obvious request for me to wait a second.

Wait for *what*?

He closed his eyes, and when he opened them an instant later, his brown eyes were green. Finn-green. Unmistakably.

"Nina?" It was Reese's voice. But they were Finn's eyes.

"I don't . . ." I retreated until my back hit the wall, my heart thumping so hard I could practically hear it.

"What's going on?" Finn said from behind me. Except that what I was starting to understand—in the sense of still being totally lost—was that the Finn I'd met wasn't really Finn. He was Maddock. "How long was I gone?"

"Almost two days!" Devi let him go and resecured her towel, preserving what little modesty she had left. "Finn found the new exorcist, then lost her, then she exorcised her mother's demon and the Church tried to arrest her for matricide, and he played hero. Then he *flirted* with her while she was vulnerable, and now she's thoroughly confused." She turned to me, one hand on the seam in her towel. "Nina, this is Maddock. *My* boyfriend."

"Wow." Maddock stepped forward and stuck his hand out almost formally, as if his girlfriend weren't standing there half naked. Tears blurred my vision when I shook his hand. He moved differently from Finn. He held himself differently from Finn. "Good to meet you," he said, and his voice sounded like Finn, but his words didn't. "Sorry I missed all the action."

When he let go of my hand, I brought my fingers to my lips, where I could still feel the ghost of Finn's mouth on mine. Only my memory was really of Maddock's mouth.

I glanced at Reese. Then back at Maddock.

"Oh shit." Maddock turned to his girlfriend. "He kissed her, didn't he?"

She made a disgusted face. "It was completely gratuitous."

This coming from a girl in a towel.

Maddock actually laughed, and even that sounded different from the way Finn had laughed with the same voice. "Did you play nice?"

Devi gave him a coy smile, and long, straight hair fell over one of her dark eyes. "Don't I always?"

He laughed again. "Do you ever?"

She shrugged and pouted, and wet hair brushed the curve of her backside, over her towel. "What can I say? I don't like to share." Devi pulled Maddock toward the bathroom. "Let's get you cleaned up." She plucked his damp T-shirt away from his chest, then let it go. "Finn got you all sweaty."

"Sorry about this, Nina." Maddock hung back while Devi tugged on his arm. "I'm sure Finn didn't mean to tell you like this." He glanced up at Reese. "Right?"

Reese nodded. Then he blinked Finn's green eyes.

The bathroom door closed behind Devi and Maddock, and pipes groaned within the walls when they turned on the shower. I should have been fundamentally shocked by the bold implication of that sound, but I was too busy being fundamentally confused about everything else.

I turned to Reese, and my vision cleared a little as the tears standing in my eyes fell. "You're Finn now?" He nodded and his mouth opened. But then it closed, as if words had abandoned him. "Are you still Reese?"

Another nod. "The body is Reese. Always was, always will be, if I have anything to say about it. But the rest is me. At the moment."

"Can he . . . Can Reese . . . see me?"

"No." Finn ran one hand through Reese's light brown hair. "He's still in here, but he's kind of . . . asleep. He can't see or hear any of this."

"I . . ." There were too many questions to ask. I didn't know where to start. Then suddenly I did. "Are you a demon?"

"*No.*" He shook Reese's head emphatically, but kept his distance from me, as he had in the alley behind the Grab-n-Go almost twenty-four hours earlier. As if he were afraid I'd back away if he came closer.

"But you're possessing someone else's body. How can you be sure you're not a demon?"

He sat on the arm of an overstuffed chair against the wall shared by the small kitchen. "Are *you* a demon?"

"Of course not!"

Reese's brows rose over Finn's eyes. "How do *you* know?"

I crossed my arms over my chest and clung to the righteous anger building inside me, because that was infinitely better than confusion. "I know because I'm not evil, and I can't possess people, and I don't come from hell, and I'm not thousands of years old!"

"All that is the same for me, except for the part about possessing people. And I don't have any choice about that. Besides, if I were a demon, I'd have been sucked back into hell years ago." He met my gaze again, and it felt weird to see Finn's eyes in someone else's face. "Do you want to sit?"

"I want to understand."

"I know. Me too." He gestured at the couch behind

me, and I sat because the alternative seemed to be passing out from a combination of shock and exhaustion. "Want something to drink?" He was already pulling open the refrigerator door before I could answer. The fridge wasn't new, but it was newer than the one at my house. And this one actually held food.

Finn emerged from the kitchen with a bottle of water in one hand and a clear, unlabeled bottle of amber liquid in the other. He held both up, silently asking me to choose. I pointed to the water. I hadn't had alcohol since I was fifteen, newly sterilized and determined to prove to myself that my body was still my own, no matter what the Church had done to it.

The Unified Church had no official problem with alcohol, but overindulgence in anything was considered a sin, and any consumption of alcohol by a minor was considered overindulgence. But that had nothing to do with me turning down the . . . whiskey? I didn't want a drink because I needed a clear head, and I needed to stay awake until I was sure I was safe, at least for the moment. And I couldn't do that until I knew how and why Finn was in Reese's body instead of his own.

He set the unlabeled alcohol on the counter and carried two bottles of water into the living room, where he handed me one, then sank onto the opposite end of the couch, facing me. "Okay." He cracked open his bottle. "I know this is weird, and I owe you answers. Probably more answers than I actually have. So . . . ask me anything."

The questions tumbling through my head were so tangled up that separating one from the rest didn't seem possible. Then my gaze caught on a framed photo standing on the end table. In the picture, a woman in her forties laughed with a girl not much older than I was, who could only have been her daughter.

"Whose apartment is this?"

Finn frowned with Reese's fair features. "After all this, that's your first question?"

"Yeah. Who are the women in that picture? Where are they?"

He twisted to pick up the photo, then studied it while he spoke. "As near as we can tell, the girl is in college. There's a university pennant on the wall in her room."

There used to be lots of colleges in the United States. Lots of choices and opportunity. After the war and the necessary restructuring, only a dozen or so remained. None of those were within a day's drive of New Temperance, which meant the daughter was unlikely to come home and find her apartment occupied by teenage outlaws.

"And her mom?"

"Her mother's name is Angela Reddy. Ms. Reddy is dead, as of two days ago."

"What happened to her?"

"Maddock exorcised the demon. The host's body died in the process," he said. "Fortunately, her rent's paid up until the end of the month, so . . ."

"So you killed her, then moved into her apartment."

"She was a demon, and she doesn't need this place anymore, but we do." His brows rose in a very un-Reese-like challenge. "Have you ever slept in one of the ghost houses? Or in a tent in the badlands?"

My skin crawled at the thought. Rumor had it, some of the ghost houses still held the bones of the people who'd died there a century before. Many of the houses had become nests for degenerates. And a tent in the badlands? I couldn't even wrap my mind around the danger that represented—nothing but a sheet of nylon between me and whatever monsters roamed the barren ruins of the Midwest. Tents may be waterproof, but they certainly weren't degenerate-proof.

Still, the apartment . . .

"It wasn't coincidence, was it? I mean, the first demon you ran across in New Temperance happened to have an absentee daughter and a paid-up apartment at the back of a complex near the town wall's north gate?"

"There are no coincidences." Finn set the photo on the end table and wedged his bottle of water into the crook of his bent leg. "There are more than a few demons in New Temperance, and we couldn't take them all on, even if we wanted to. We're here to get you out, which means we need to fly under the Church's radar as much as possible, which means minimizing food and supply runs. The best way to do that is to set up camp in a furnished apartment.

Of all the demons we saw during recon, the one who lived here had the most ideal setup." He shrugged Reese's broad shoulders. "So we sent her back to hell and moved into her apartment."

I nodded, still trying to process all of it. It made a certain brutal sense. "How long do you think it'll be before someone notices her missing from work?"

Another shrug. "A few more days, hopefully. Devi called in and said she had the flu. They practically begged her to stay home."

I cracked open my bottle of water, then stared at it. I was sitting on a dead woman's couch, drinking a dead woman's water. Hell, I was now a dead woman's daughter. How was it possible that without changing at all, the world we lived in now looked nothing like the world I'd thought I understood twenty-four hours before?

"How do you do it?" I sipped from the bottle, struggling to bring my thoughts back on track, then screwed the lid back on. "How do you . . . get in there?" I waved my empty hand at Reese's body.

"I don't know." He looked surprised by the sudden change in subject. "I've never really thought about it. I just kind of . . . step in. Figuratively speaking, of course, since I don't actually have any feet."

"Why not? Where's your body?" That was probably the strangest question I'd ever had to ask.

"I don't have one."

All the questions skittering around in my head stuttered to a stunned halt, and the abrupt internal silence left me reeling. Grasping for his meaning. "What do you mean? How can you not have a body?" A sudden horrible possibility made my heart ache for him. "Are you . . . dead?"

He actually laughed, and even in Reese's voice, the laughter sounded like Finn. "I'm not a ghost, Nina. I just don't have a body. I never have, at least not as far back as I can remember."

"How is that possible? Are you human?"

"Of course I'm human!" He wasn't laughing now, and I realized I'd hurt his feelings. I felt bad about that, but my initial fear had taken root again, deep inside me, and I couldn't think past it.

People have bodies. Demons don't, at least in our world—who knows what they look like in their world?

Only demons could possess someone else's body. Only demons would want to, right?

True, I'd never heard of a bodiless demon not getting sucked back into hell, but I'd never heard of a bodiless human *at all*. Was one really any less believable than the other?

"I'm sorry, Finn, I just . . . I don't understand. I mean, if you don't have a body, how do you know *what* you are?"

"Well, I guess I don't. Not for sure." He shrugged. "But I know what I'm *not*. I'm not a demon, Nina. I have a soul.

In fact, that may be all I have." He held my gaze, waiting for my response, and just like every time he'd looked at me since the moment we'd met, there was no sign of doubt in his green eyes. He meant everything he'd said. Including the fact that he didn't know for sure what he was, and I didn't know how to process that.

"Okay," he said, when I'd opened and closed my mouth twice without managing an actual response. "I know that's a lot to chew on at once, but I need you to understand something." When I nodded, he took a deep breath and continued, in Reese's voice. "I may not know for sure what I am, but I know *who* I am. I'm left-handed, no matter whose body I'm in. I love spicy food and hate licorice, no matter whose tongue I taste it with. My favorite color is blue—the exact shade of the deepest blue in your eyes," he said, his gaze glued to mine, and something deep in my stomach flip-flopped so hard and fast I almost lost my balance sitting still on the couch. "I've learned a lot about who you are too."

I shook my head, denying what couldn't possibly be true. "We met less than twenty-four hours ago."

"It's not the amount of time that matters, Nina. It's what you do with it."

"What did you do with the time?" My voice was only half a whisper. That was all I could manage with him looking at me like that. As if nothing else in the world existed. As if there was only me, and this moment.

"I paid attention."

"To me?"

"To everything. To the green peas you picked out of your beef stew. To your secondhand clothes." He ran one finger over the frayed hem of my long-sleeve T-shirt. "To the way you frown when you're thinking, as if your disapproval should be enough to change whatever's wrong." He blinked and his focus deepened somehow, as if he could see right through my eyes and into my soul. "I paid attention to the fact that you got your sister out of the house and faced down that demon yourself, with no idea you could actually handle the fight. And I paid very close attention to the way you kissed me back."

My cheeks flushed bright red at the bottom edge of my vision, and the memory of that kiss warmed me everywhere else.

He reached for my hand and I let him take it, but my fingers wouldn't relax in his grip, because it wasn't *his* grip. It was Reese's. I frowned. This new hand was broader, its fingers longer. This hand felt different. It didn't feel like Finn. This hand swallowed mine like it had when I'd shaken Reese's hand.

I'd been introduced to this hand as Reese's, and because of that, it would always feel like Reese's hand to me.

That was when I realized I had no idea what Finn's hand actually felt like, because Finn didn't have a hand, and he never would. Maybe he really never had. The hand

I'd held earlier was Maddock's, and the mouth I'd kissed had been his too. It wasn't Finn's soft, wavy hair. It wasn't his short cheek stubble. Finn couldn't grow stubble because he didn't have a face, and he never would, and that meant I'd never know what he really looked like, because he didn't look like *anything*.

Yet he could *look* like *anyone*.

"Nina . . . ?"

But those green eyes were Finn's, and they were staring right through me. Finn's eyes could see everything I was thinking but not saying. I could tell because of how sad those eyes suddenly looked, and his sad green eyes made me want to cry.

The bathroom door opened, and Maddock and Devi came out wrapped in matching towels before I'd figured out what to say to Reese-who-was-really-Finn. How to explain that yes, I'd kissed him back, and I didn't regret that, but I wasn't sure I could deal with the fact that he didn't have a body, and that whatever body he borrowed might randomly step out of the bathroom in a towel with another girl, and that I'd never really be able to see the guy who'd saved my life and helped me fight and stood watch over me while I was unconscious.

I wanted to be as straightforward and bold as he was, because he deserved that, but I had no experience with being straightforward and bold. I had experience with lying, and clothing myself in darkness if in nothing else, and stealing, and paying a high price for the things Mellie and I couldn't survive without.

And running. I was used to running, and that impulse took over when I saw a chance to escape.

"I . . . I really need a shower. I'm so sorry." I hated myself before the words had even left my lips, but that didn't stop me from bolting into the bathroom while Devi and Maddock stared at me, or from locking the door behind me.

I *did* need a shower, but what I needed even worse was time to think. It was too much—all of it. Demons in New Temperance. Glowing heat from my left hand. Pregnant Mellie. My pulse synchronizing with the horde of degenerates hunting me. A fearless boy I liked and was attracted to, who turned out to have no face or body of his own.

I couldn't process any of it without a few minutes to myself.

I turned on the shower and dropped my clothes on top of the smelly pile Maddock and Devi had left in the corner, then relieved my screaming bladder while I waited for the water to heat up. I was already standing naked beneath the hot flow of water before I remembered I didn't have anything to change into. Or anything to dry off with. The linen closet was right outside the bathroom, and I'd forgotten to grab a towel.

And for some reason, after everything that had gone horribly, tragically wrong over the past twenty-four hours, having no towel to dry off with became the straw that broke the new exorcist's back.

I cried in the shower.

I let everything out because there was no more room for holding it in. I cried for Mellie and her doomed baby. For Adam and his parents, and the decision they'd soon have to make. I cried for the mother I'd never met, and for the people who'd been possessed by the demons I'd helped exorcise.

Then I cried for the future that had been rewritten for me twice, first by a surgeon's scalpel, then by the demon who'd tried to possess me as a replacement for my mother's deteriorating body.

"You know we can all hear you, right?"

I jumped at the sound of Grayson's voice, then slipped and had to grab the towel rack at the end of the shower to keep from busting my butt on the bottom of the tub. When I'd regained my balance, I stuck my face under the faucet to rinse away the tears, then peeked around the shower curtain, my hair dripping on the linoleum.

Grayson sat on the toilet lid, a folded green towel on her lap. She blinked up at me with big brown eyes, then tucked shoulder-length curls behind one ear. "I'm just sayin', if you were looking for a private cry, you're out of luck. The walls are pretty thin here. They're thicker in some of the old ghost houses, but there's very little running water in the badlands, so it's kind of a trade-off."

So much for a few minutes to myself.

"How did you get in here?" I closed the curtain and stepped beneath the flow of water again, then grabbed a bottle of strawberry-scented shampoo.

"I opened the door. Devi broke the lock yesterday 'cause she had to pee while Reese was in the shower. Someone probably should have told you that."

Mental note: no lock on the bathroom door.

Related mental note: Devi breaks things.

"Grayson, right?" I stared at the clear, pinkish shampoo pooled in my skinned palm. "What do you want, Grayson?"

The toilet seat squeaked as she shifted, and she spoke loud enough to be heard over the patter of water all around me. "I want my brother back. I want Reese to exercise more caution and less impulse. I want Finn to be happy. Also, I kind of want some pizza, but even if we had the money, calling for delivery is out of the question, thanks to the fugitive lifestyle."

My mom used to order pizza sometimes, when we were still little and she was still healthy. And employed. I could remember the aroma of onions and pepperoni, and the grease that had soaked through the bottom of the box.

I gave Grayson a frown she couldn't see through the curtain. "I meant, why are you in here? While I'm showering."

"Oh. I brought you a towel."

"Thanks." I smeared the shampoo on top of my head and began to lather, and the artificial strawberry scent brought back memories of helping Mellie rinse suds from her hair when she was five and I was seven. Mom had decided we were old enough to bathe ourselves, but my sister's long, thick hair was virtually unmanageable for a kindergartner.

Melanie loved smelling like strawberries.

"Also, we didn't get a chance to talk much when you came in, so I thought, if you're going to be with us, you and I might want to get to know each other."

"That's nice of you." I tilted my head back to rinse my hair, and the pressure on my throat made my voice sound strained. "But I'm not sure I'll be staying with you."

"Why not?" Now *her* voice sounded strained. "We took a lot of risks to find you. We could have been killed. Finn saved your life."

"I know, and I can't tell you how grateful I am, but the Church has my sister. I can't leave her."

Grayson was quiet for a moment. "Is she an exorcist?"

"No, she's only fifteen." And based on the fact that we had different biological fathers, I was betting she never would be an exorcist, even at my age. "And she's pregnant."

Grayson's soft "Oh" echoed deep within my soul. "They have my brother too. He's not pregnant, obviously. But he's an exorcist."

I let the suds slide down my forehead, then closed my eyes. "You left him?"

"No. When they came for him, he made me hide. I can't fight the Church, and it's not like they'd give him back if I just smiled and said 'Pretty please.'"

No, they would have taken her as well, because if her brother was an exorcist, she might be one too.

"I don't know where he is. Or if he's alive." The ache in her voice made my heart hurt.

"How did it happen?" I asked as I rubbed conditioner into my hair. I didn't actually expect her to answer, but I really wanted to know just how much she and I had in common. "Finn said your parents were breeders, like my mom?"

"Yeah, but we didn't know that then. We didn't know Carey was an exorcist. We still don't know if I'll be one. I was your sister's age when Carey was triggered, almost a year ago. Now I understand that his abilities came in kind of early, so our parents didn't have a chance to harvest him before the degenerates came for him. He was still two months away from his seventeenth birthday when the first one found him. It happened on our way home from school. His hand started glowing and instinct took over. He fried his first demon in broad daylight, in front of several witnesses."

I rinsed the conditioner from my hair and pretended I couldn't hear the pain in her voice, because I didn't know how to gracefully acknowledge it.

"Someone must have called my dad at work, because he came home early. He tried to harvest Carey, but we didn't know what was going on. We thought he'd lost his mind. We thought he was trying to kill us." Her voice hitched with the obviously painful memory. "We heard sirens, and Carey told me to hide. The police shot my dad, then took my brother. They didn't know I was there. I don't know what happened to my mom.

"Maddock and Devi showed up later that night, looking for Carey, and found me instead. I was alone and terrified. I've been with them ever since. Almost a year now."

So she was sixteen. She looked younger than that. She reminded me of Melanie, even though physically they had little in common.

"What about Finn and Reese?" I lathered the bar soap and had already washed my face when I realized that our dead hostess had a special squirt bottle of soap just for face washing.

"Finn was already with them. He and Maddock are a package deal. Reese came next, after me. We'd been making our way through the badlands for a couple of months, driving when we could find gas, walking when we couldn't."

I shuddered at just the *thought* of wandering through the American wasteland, easy prey for degenerates, demons, and human predators alike.

"Then Finn and I noticed that the degenerates in the

area seemed to be . . . flocking. They were all going the same direction. We figured that had to mean there was a new exorcist about to transition, so we went looking for him."

I rinsed my face and lathered everything else while she talked, grateful for the seemingly endless hot water. Even when the water heater worked at my house, the supply never lasted very long.

"We found Reese in Diligencia. He hadn't been triggered yet, and his parents were normal. Comparatively." By which I assumed she meant that they weren't breeders.

"So, he left his parents?"

"His dad didn't make it. His mom sent him with us to protect him. He came with us to protect *her*."

Because those wanted by the Church were dangerous to the people who loved them. I'd already figured that much out.

I turned off the faucet, and before I could ask for the towel, she draped it over the curtain rod.

"So, you and Reese are . . ."

"We're together," she said as I dried myself behind the curtain, and I was surprised by the difference in her tone from one sentence to the next. I could hear how much she cared about Reese, and how happy she was with him even though she'd lost her brother and was living on the run from the Church.

"I figured that out for myself. I was gonna say you two are . . . bold." Actually, I was thinking "shameless," but I was afraid she might take that as an insult. "Aren't you afraid of . . ." But I couldn't finish that thought. They were already wanted for sins worse than carnal contact, so what did she and Reese have to lose by loving each other? What did *any* of them have to lose?

"Never mind." I wrung water from my hair with the towel. "I'm just not used to seeing . . ."

"Public display?" She laughed. "It's not really public when we're on our own, but I know it's a shock after school and the Church and everything. It felt weird for me too, at first, but we spend so much time together as a group, hiding from everyone else, that we kind of live in our own little world. With our own norms."

I peeked around the curtain again. "So, what's your norm?"

Grayson smiled softly. "There's not a lot to laugh about, running from the Church and hiding out in ghost towns. Our norm is whatever feels right. Whatever makes us happy."

I wrapped myself in the green towel, then pushed back the shower curtain, and this time when I looked at Grayson, she didn't look like a stranger. She looked . . . familiar. I saw some of the same things in her brown eyes that I'd often seen in Mellie's: Intelligence. Personal strength. Determination. And a strong, stubborn core of optimism—just enough to keep her from ever admitting defeat.

Grayson was what Melanie could have been under slightly less horrible circumstances. If our mother hadn't neglected her "investments." If Finn and his friends had found us sooner. If I had kept a better eye on her "tutoring sessions" with Adam.

I tightened the towel beneath my arms and stepped out of the tub, and that was when I saw what else Grayson held. Jeans. And a blue tee. They looked clean.

"I was going to lend you some underwear too, but Reese said you might think that was weird."

"Thanks." I accepted the jeans and pulled them on beneath my towel. They felt uncomfortable without underwear, but uncomfortable was better than naked. "Reese is back?"

"Yeah. Finn left. He was upset."

Crap. He'd saved my life—twice—and I'd questioned his humanity. He deserved better than that; it wasn't *his* fault I was having trouble dealing with his . . . state. "Where does someone with no body go when he leaves?"

Grayson shrugged. "Anywhere he wants." She handed me the T-shirt. "Sorry there's no bra. Mine won't fit you." She eyed the modest cleavage the edge of my towel was tucked into, then glanced down at her own nearly flat chest. "Devi's might, but I wouldn't ask her for anything right now."

"Because she and Maddock are making crude noises from behind closed doors?" I couldn't pretend that didn't creep me out, considering that half an hour earlier I'd thought Maddock was Finn, and an hour before that I'd been kissing him.

She smiled again—a cute little grin of private amusement—and tucked stray curls behind her ear while I pulled the tee over my head. "No, actually . . . Devi's mad."

"Mad crazy, or mad angry?" I pulled the shirt down, then tugged the towel out from under it and hung it over the curtain rod to dry. "Because I'd believe either of those."

Grayson sighed. "Here's how it works. When Finn's upset, Maddock's upset, and when Maddock gets upset, Devi gets mad on his behalf, and when Devi gets mad, she makes us all miserable. So . . . you need to fix this."

I wiped the fogged-up mirror with my skinned left hand and studied my face. "Fix what?" I looked tired, and I'd found several new scrapes and bruises in the shower, but I was intact, which was more than I could say for the degenerates we'd fought on my first night as an exorcist.

"Finn likes you," Grayson said, and my hand clenched around the comb I'd just found in the vanity drawer. "A lot. I'm not sayin' you have to like him back, but if you do, please don't let his weird personal situation scare you off."

"His weird personal situation?" I started tugging the comb through my wet hair. "That may be the biggest understatement I've ever heard."

"It took me a while to get used to it too, but I promise you it's worth the effort. He's not a demon, Nina. He has a soul. I think he *is* a soul. We're all he has, and he loves every single one of us—even Devi—and that's not something a demon is capable of."

"I know." I turned to face her, leaning against the counter while I combed my hair. "But I don't know how to process the fact that when he talks to me I'm hearing someone else's voice, and when I touch him I'm holding someone else's hand. I mean, I don't know if I'm ever going to be able to dissociate Finn from Maddock's face and voice."

"He probably should have told you earlier," Grayson said. "And you should definitely take it slow. But—"

Someone knocked on the bathroom door, and I opened it to find Devi standing in the tiny rectangle of hallway, long, dark, still-damp hair twisted over her shoulder in some thick, complicated braid I'd never be able to master. Maddock and Reese were visible behind her on the couch, staring at a television I couldn't see from the bathroom.

I expected Devi to start yelling, or doing whatever

Devi does when she's mad, other than break things, but she actually looked kind of . . . worried. "They just announced a special report from New Temperance coming up on the morning news. Nina, I think you're about to be on television."

THIRTEEN

"New Temperance made the national news?" My hometown was among the smallest of the cities and towns that survived the war, and little of interest ever happened inside our walls. In my entire life, New Temperance had made the national news only once—the day school officials burned Clare Parker.

I followed Grayson and Devi into the small living room, where the guys moved over to make room for their girlfriends. I sat alone in the only armchair, angled to face both the couch and the screen.

Angela Reddy's television was bigger than the one I'd sold, but still smaller than many I'd seen, and its resolution was very clear, like the bigger monitors mounted in most public buildings.

"Where's Finn?" I said while the international head-lines scrolled across the screen accompanied by "peaceful" music I'd heard a million times. I was already glancing around the room for him before I realized that even if he were there, I probably wouldn't see him.

Could he be seen when he wasn't in someone's body? Could he be heard? Could he see and hear us?

Grayson took Reese's hand. "Not back yet." She looked certain, and I wondered how she could possibly know that for sure.

"What do you care?" Devi's brows rose in challenge. "You've already called him evil and rejected him. He may not have a body, but he has a heart, you know."

"I know." My cheeks burned. "I didn't mean to—"

"Leave her alone, Dev," Maddock said. "Don't you re-member how weirded out you were when you first met Finn?"

Devi scowled, and even with her dark eyes narrowed, her nose all scrunched up, and her face bare of makeup after her shower, she was still fiercely beautiful. "Why are you taking her side? I'm the one who's going to have to share my boyfriend if Demon Spawn and Invisi-Boy ever make up."

"Oh, I doubt you'll be the only one shouldering that burden. . . ." Reese smiled.

"So, you guys don't mind him just . . . hijacking your bodies?"

"He's supposed to ask first," Reese said with a shrug.

"And he's pretty good about that. He spends most of his corporeal time in Maddy's body because that's where he's most comfortable, but I don't mind pitching in when he wants to interact with the world and Maddock's unavailable. Or while they're . . . occupied." He waved one thick hand at Devi and Maddock.

That sentence insinuated several things I didn't want to truly contemplate. But I couldn't run from Finn and his situation forever.

"So, when he's not . . . *in* one of you, where is he?"

"Wherever he wants to be," Maddock said. "He's not limited by physical barriers, like doors and walls, but he seems to be ruled by time and space just like we are."

"Wait, what?"

"Maddock keeps trying to apply science to a situation where it clearly doesn't belong," Devi said thinly.

"Of course it belongs," he insisted. "Finn can't just wish himself across town. He actually has to *go* there, just like the rest of us. Only, we can't see or hear him walking unless he borrows someone's body."

"Wait, how can he walk without—"

A familiar three-note fanfare from the television stole the words from my tongue and the thought from my head. My heart started pounding the minute the national news anchor, Brother Jonathan Sayers, took his position behind the news desk, shuffling the papers in front of him so we could all see the gold embroidery on his purple cassock sleeve and the sacred flames branded on his right hand. Sayers was a national icon. I'd seen him nearly every day of my life.

My foot tapped nervously on the carpet as he said his usual "good morning" to the nation, and then I sat up straight, my pulse racing at his next words. "And now we go live to Sister Pamela Williams, who is on location for us today in New Temperance, where I understand there was a bit of trouble overnight?"

"That's right, Brother Jonathan." The anchorman disappeared from the screen, and I gasped when Sister Pamela came into focus in her purple robe, holding a microphone in her branded right hand. I recognized the building behind her. It was the administration building for the New Temperance Day School.

My school.

"Overnight, the citizens of New Temperance slept peacefully in their homes, unaware that the biggest threat to their safety lay not outside the town walls, in the badlands, but within the town itself. Within, in fact, one of their own children."

"Oh, the melodrama!" Devi rolled her eyes, but her jaw was tense and her forehead furrowed. She was almost as nervous as I was.

"Last night, police and other Church officials responding to an emergency on the east side of New Temperance found sixteen-year-old Nina Kane—a local high school senior—strangling her own mother with her bare hands."

"Oh no . . . ," I whispered.

My junior-year school picture appeared on the screen, in front of a national audience of *millions,* and though I was safe and hidden—at least temporarily—I suddenly felt more exposed and vulnerable than I ever had in my life.

As I stared at my own image, my heart pounding against my sternum, I wondered how it was possible that I'd looked so young less than a year before.

"Responding officers report that Kane seemed—quote—'gleeful and remorseless' as she stood over her mother's body. She refused to surrender to the authorities, and when they tried to arrest her, Kane produced a handgun and shot the lead officer in the chest. He was pronounced dead upon arrival at New Temperance General Hospital."

"They weren't police, they were exorcists!" I snapped at the television. *"Fake* exorcists, who were pointing guns at me! And I've never even *held* a gun!"

"They can't tell the truth," Grayson whispered, still staring at the screen. "I think they're allergic."

"They're scripting the news. That's what the Church does." Reese shrugged as if it were no big deal, but he looked just as angry as I was. "My dad said they recruit their reporters from college theater programs."

Devi huffed. "Well, that would certainly explain the melodrama."

I heard them, but none of it truly sank in. After years of hiding my home life from all forms of authority, I was wanted by the Church. Millions of people thought I'd strangled my mother and killed a cop, and now they all knew exactly what I looked like.

I couldn't turn away from the screen until my picture disappeared and Sister Pamela was back.

"Officers returned fire, but Kane fled the scene, and now the Church is asking for *your* help finding her."

My picture appeared again, this time in a little window next to Sister Pamela's head.

"Nina Elizabeth Kane has brown hair and light blue eyes. She is five feet six, approximately one hundred and twenty pounds." Which they knew from my latest physical. "Kane was last seen fleeing her east New Temperance neighborhood on foot, but police believe she is still in the area. If you see or hear from her, please call the number at the bottom of your screen, but *do not* attempt to contact her. Nina Kane is considered armed and dangerous, and Church officials have confirmed that she is, in fact, a victim of demonic possession."

I groaned, and the camera zoomed in on Sister Pamela's serious expression. "She may look and act like the girl many of you in New Temperance knew before yesterday, but the truth is that Nina Kane is dead, and the demon in control of her body will not hesitate to kill anyone in her path."

"Bullshit!" I stood, outraged, and Grayson shushed me with one finger over her lips, pointing at the wall our apartment shared with the neighbor. I sat again, but anger buzzed beneath my skin, setting me on edge.

"But there's more." Sister Pamela's faux confidential tone and the excitement in her eyes promised more juicy details about my public scandal. "Kane is suspected to have made contact with a group of teen fugitives known to be in the area, and Church officials believe she may, in fact, be the reason for their presence in and around New Temperance."

"Well, at least they got that right," Grayson said.

"While details about this itinerant group of young malefactors remain sketchy, the entire group is suspected of possession and was just this morning declared anathema by the Church."

"Oh shit. . . ." Maddock stared intently at the television.

"What's that?" Grayson's brown eyes were wide. "What does that mean?"

"We've been denounced by the Church." Reese took her hand.

Devi laughed. "'Bout time!"

"It means we're public enemy number one," Maddock explained. "The Church's top priority until we're caught or someone pisses them off worse."

Devi grinned. "It means they're scared of us. I say we own it."

"Own it?" Grayson frowned.

"Yeah. The Church says we're anathema? *I* say we're *Anathema*. With a capital *A*. We'll make it ours."

"I like it!" Reese declared. "We are Anathema."

The rest of them nodded, and it was official. Their gang of outlaws had a name.

I couldn't help wondering where I fit into that.

On television, Sister Pamela was still talking, and with every word she said, things got worse for us. "As the facts trickle in, the picture before us comes into sharper focus, and it is a grim picture indeed, Brother Jonathan. It's beginning to look like the demon known as Nina Kane could, in fact, be the founder of a subculture of possession and corruption here in New Temperance, running deeper than anyone knew, and that's why I'm on location today."

"What does that mean?" I said. "Why is she here?" But no one had an answer for me.

"When police began investigating the Nina Kane case last night, they discovered that Kane's fifteen-year-old sister, Melanie—who reportedly suffered a sudden breakdown at school yesterday—is, in fact, pregnant."

Sister Pamela paused for the inevitable shocked gasp from her viewing audience, and I could almost hear it, though none of us was surprised by the revelation.

"Church authorities are not yet ready to confirm

demonic possession in the younger Ms. Kane. Because of her condition, they're forced to examine her slowly and carefully." The very thought of which dumped fuel over the infant flames of fury simmering inside me. "But less than an hour ago, we got word that authorities have un- covered at least one other case of possession among the Kanes' known friends and neighbors."

"What?" I gaped at the reporter in shock. *Who?*

It could have been anyone. Demons were a much bigger presence in my hometown than the Church had any way of knowing. But one of my friends? Or neighbors?

"There's been no word yet on the identity of this sec- ond confirmed case of possession, but I'm told that we'll have a live update this afternoon, just in time for the eve- ning news. Make sure you all tune in then for the latest on this resurgence of the Unclean in the quiet town of New Temperance."

"I'm sure we all will, Sister Pamela," the national an- chor said as his image replaced hers on-screen. When he moved on with the rest of the headlines, Grayson turned off the TV and dropped the remote onto the coffee table next to her glass of water.

"I'm wanted for murder and possession." My voice sounded hollow with shock. Nothing felt real. "The whole damn country is looking for me."

"Welcome to the club." Grayson clinked her water glass against my bottle.

"Like you know anything about the most-wanted club."

Devi rolled her eyes at Grayson, then stood and stomped into the kitchen. "They don't have your picture. They don't even know you're with us."

"That doesn't put Grayson and me in any less danger, Dev," Maddock said.

"They haven't identified Grace and Maddy yet," Reese explained. "I don't think they even know for sure how many of us there are, but my picture and Devi's are out there too, if it makes you feel any better."

"Yeah, I saw them on the news." A lifetime ago, back when I'd thought my biggest problems were Melanie's pregnancy and coming up with something for dinner. My entire existence had shifted since then. The world had changed. "Why would they mention us but not the degenerates we killed?"

Reese shrugged, then let go of Grayson's hand and headed into the kitchen. "Because only the Church is allowed to save the day." He took a carton of eggs from the fridge and set a skillet on the stove. "If word got out that we were better at ridding the world of demons than the Unified Church is, people might start to realize they don't need the Church. The good brothers and sisters in charge aren't willing to let that happen, so they paint us as the bad guys in order to mobilize private citizens against us. Everyone knows bad guys don't kill monsters." He took a chopping knife from a drawer and gestured with it. "Bad guys *are* the monsters."

"Okay, I get that, but why are they leaving out the parts

that *don't* make us look good? Why don't they report on demons breeding their own hosts, or degenerates in New Temperance?"

"Because that makes them look like they can't protect the people," Maddock said. "It's a two-part propaganda technique. Make us look bad while making them look good. Make sense?"

I nodded reluctantly.

"Who wants an omelet?" Reese pulled vegetables from a drawer in the fridge and set them on a cutting board.

Everyone else called out requests for tomatoes and onions and cheese, the very prospect of which would have made my mouth water a day earlier. But now . . .

"Nina?" Reese called, and I looked up to see him holding a small block of cheddar.

"No thanks. I'm not really—"

"Shhh!" He cut me off and spun to face the door, knife wielded like a weapon. "Footsteps."

I couldn't hear them, and based on the wary but unsure expressions all around me, neither could any of the others.

Someone knocked, and we all froze. Then suddenly everyone was moving at once, silently and eerily fast.

Maddock stood and pulled a handgun from the end table drawer while Devi crossed into the kitchen and plucked two knives from the block. As she and Maddock headed for the front door, Devi pressed one of the knives into Grayson's hand and motioned her toward the bedroom.

It took me a second to realize she was hiding because she wasn't yet an exorcist, which meant she had no enhanced speed or strength to use against a demon.

"There's only one," Reese whispered from the kitchen, where he held a meat mallet in one hand and his chopping knife in the other. His gaze was focused on the front door.

"Not a degenerate," Grayson added as she backed through the doorway into one of the bedrooms, and I wondered how on earth she knew that. Then I realized she was right. I felt no urge to either flee or fight.

But degenerates weren't the only thing we had to fear.

I stood, my fists opening and closing at my sides, unsure what to do when no one offered me a weapon.

"It's me," someone called from outside.

Devi and Maddock frowned at each other from opposite sides of the front door. They obviously didn't recognize the voice.

"Look through the damn peephole!" the voice said.

They both hesitated. Then Devi started to step forward, but Maddock slid in front of her, shielding her from whatever stood beyond the door while he closed one eye and peered through the peephole with his other.

Maddock groaned and fumbled with first the deadbolt, then the chain, ignoring Devi's whispered demands to know what he'd seen. She backpedaled when he opened the door, then Maddock pulled the boy on the sidewalk into the apartment and slammed the door behind him.

Devi took one look at him and lowered her knife. "What the *hell* are you doing?"

Reese dropped his mallet into a kitchen drawer with a huff of exasperation.

"Relax. I come bearing gifts." The boy turned, lifting a brown bag with twisted-paper handles, and with a jolt of shock that resonated through my entire body, I realized I knew him. Jacob Gilbert was a senior at my school. I'd known him since we were five.

But how did he know Maddock and Devi and the rest?

It was unnerving to see him in our secret apartment surrounded by my new exorcist outlaw friends, when all my memories of him involved either school uniforms, teachers, and textbooks or . . . bare flesh, muffled sounds, and awkward touches disembodied by a dark room.

"Jacob?" Confusion echoed in my voice.

"Not exactly." He grinned at me, and I blinked. I'd never seen Jacob grin. Not even as he'd helped lower me from his bedroom window in the middle of the night, ending a single late-night encounter we hadn't so much as acknowledged since.

Then I noticed that his eyes were green, when they should have been brown.

They were Finn-green.

"What . . . ? What are you . . . ?" My tongue felt almost as sluggish as my thoughts. "Why are you *in* Jacob Gilbert?"

"Is that his name?" Finn looked down at his borrowed body. "I found him on his way to school and thought it might be easier for you to talk to me if I looked like someone you know."

"So you *kidnapped* one of my classmates?" That thought was too bizarre to truly comprehend.

Finn shrugged. "Then I took him shopping." He held out the bag, and I accepted it before I realized what I was doing, and once I held the bag, I opened it for the same reason.

Jeans. A couple of plain cotton T-shirts. And beneath that, I found underwear, still in the package, a bra, still tagged, and a new toothbrush. "What is this?"

Another shrug. "This guy's sister looked about your size. The rest is from the dollar store down the street from your school. Not top quality, obviously, but better than . . ." His focus wandered down from my face and I was suddenly hyperaware of the fact that I wasn't wearing a bra. ". . . whatever you're not wearing now."

"You stole this?"

"*I* didn't." Another indomitable grin. The boy had no shame, and I almost envied him that. "The assistant manager opening the store put them in a bag and set them just outside the back door for someone to pick up." He patted his borrowed chest, indicating that Jacob was that someone. "At least, that's what the cameras will show, if anyone ever realizes the store is missing a few pairs of underwear and the manager is missing a solid three and a half minutes from his morning routine."

"I . . . I don't know what to say." I'd always been the one who took care of Mellie, and it felt strange to let someone else take care of me. I wanted to return the favor. I wanted to be as much use to them as they'd been to me.

" 'Thanks' is the typical response when someone goes out of his way to supply you with new underwear so you can comfortably go into hiding because you're wanted on two counts of murder."

I found it hard to believe that particular scenario was common enough to have a typical response, but . . . "Thanks. And *wow*." No wonder they'd avoided getting caught for so long—securing food and supplies didn't represent much of a risk when they could have them delivered by one of the locals, who wouldn't rouse suspicion walking around town.

"Yeah." Devi slid the door chain home with an aggressive clank. "He knows a few clever party tricks. But he's not supposed to bring them *home* with him."

"Finn?" Grayson opened the bedroom door, and her eyes widened when she found him in a new form. She padded across the floor barefoot, then ran one hand over his chest and down one arm. "What on earth are you wearing?"

"Nina says his name is Jacob Gilbert. You like?"

She nodded solemnly. "Very pretty . . ." Grayson frowned up at him. "But you know you can't keep him."

"I know." He grinned. "I'll take him back right after I talk to Nina."

"Finn, man . . ." Reese frowned. "He's gonna be missed."

"He's probably *already* missed," Maddock said, but I could hear the confliction in his voice. He didn't want to deny Finn this outlet for expression—not to mention interaction with the physical world—but he understood the risk.

Even *I* understood the risk.

"Take him back." Devi slid her knife back into the block. "Now."

Finn's green eyes narrowed, and I recognized the stubborn set of his jaw—that expression had looked nearly the same on Maddock's features when Finn had occupied them. "Ten minutes." He turned to me. "Nina. Give me ten minutes." His gaze was solemn and intense. He really wanted this.

After a moment's hesitation, I nodded.

Devi ignored the pleading look Grayson threw her way. "If you haven't gotten that walking liability out of here in ten minutes, I swear I'll exorcise your ass right out of him."

"Devi!" Maddock sounded truly pissed for the first time since I'd met him. The real him, anyway.

Finn's expression hardened, but beneath his anger, his borrowed cheeks were pink with humiliation. He looked . . . bruised.

"Can she do that?" I didn't want to ask, but I had to know.

"No." Grayson glared at Devi. "Because he's not a demon. But *she* can be a real *bitch*."

Devi scowled, and when no apology came for what was obviously a huge personal insult to Finn, I tamped down my own misgivings, then boldly took his hand and pulled him toward one of the bedrooms.

"I'm sorry he's so sensitive, but we can't afford the kind of—"

I closed the door behind us, cutting off Devi's lukewarm attempt at damage control. Then I set the bag of clothing on the carpet and leaned against the door, studying the boy in front of me. Noting the differences between Finn and Jacob. The longer I stared, the more of them I found. It was like looking at a painting, picking out more intricate details with every passing second of study.

"That's amazing." I stepped closer, staring up at him, examining familiar features that suddenly seemed new. A mouth that looked softer. A brow that was less furrowed. Eyes that looked . . . smarter. Kinder. Greener.

"What's amazing?" His voice was a whisper, and though it was Jacob's voice, it was Finn's tone and resonance. Finn's words.

"The differences. You look just like Jacob, yet somehow you look *nothing* like Jacob. And it's not just your eye color."

He smiled—a real smile—and I knew I'd said something right. Fortunately, it was also something true. "You can see me?"

"Yeah, I can," I said, and his smile grew. "I can hear you too. The real you."

"Well then . . . mission accomplished." He sank onto the end of the twin bed, and I sat next to him, one leg folded beneath me, because there was nowhere else to sit. If Angela Reddy's daughter owned chairs, she'd taken them with her to college. "So, you know him? Jacob?"

My brows rose in surprise. "You can't tell? You can't . . . see his memories? Or whatever?"

"Nope. Whatever you don't want me to know about you and Jacob Gilbert is still unknown. I can't see any of his memories of you or anyone else. Because I'm not a demon."

"Of course not." I could feel myself flush, embarrassed both by the memory I didn't want him to access and by the fact that he'd seen through my question. "Sorry."

"No need." He took my hand, and I stared at his fingers folded around mine, fascinated to realize that Jacob's was the third of Finn's borrowed hands that I'd touched. They were each different. Yet they were each his. "Nina, I know that from the outside, what I do—what I *am*—looks a lot like demonic possession, but I swear it's not the same. I can't hear his thoughts. I'm not feeding from his soul. If I were to stay in here forever, his body wouldn't start to degenerate. Not that I have any plans to stay here."

"Glad to hear it. Jacob has a life and a family and a *consciousness*. You can't just . . . take his body."

"Obviously." He gave me a perfunctory nod. "Still, for potential future reference, this is the general look you go for, right?" He spread his arms, giving me a good look at Jacob's solid build, clear skin, and mass of thick, dark, wavy hair. "I picked him because he looks kind of like Maddy, and you seemed to like—"

"Finn!" I could feel my face flush. "Boundaries! You don't have to say *everything* you're thinking!"

He shrugged. "I have no body, Nina. Boundaries are kind of a difficult concept for me to grasp."

"Well, *try*," I insisted, but he only smiled. "So, now what? What happens when you . . . take Jacob back?"

"Nothing, really. He'll just wake up, with no memory of what happened while he wasn't in charge of his body."

"He'll be . . . okay? Will he know he was . . . possessed, for lack of a better term?" But Finn obviously didn't like that term, and I couldn't blame him.

"He'll be missing about an hour of his life with no explanation, and I'm sure that will scare him. Worst-case scenario? Someone else could see him looking disoriented and unable to account for the past hour and decide he's possessed. But I'll make sure no one else is around when I give him back his body, and there won't be any lasting side effects. He won't be an empty shell," Finn assured me. "Because I'm not a demon. You get that now, right?"

"Yes." I nodded decisively. "You've gone to a lot of trouble to show me that you may have no verbal filter, but you're not evil. Duly noted and appreciated."

He frowned. "That's the best I'm going to get, isn't it?"

"What else do you want?"

"Can I kiss you?"

I blinked, surprised. "You didn't ask last time."

"Last time I was trying to keep you from fleeing the building. This time I just want to kiss you."

I thought about that for a second and decided that one small indulgence wouldn't hurtle me toward death or damnation any faster than the course I was already on.

I nodded.

Then Finn kissed me, and I was pleased to discover that he made much better use of Jacob Gilbert's mouth than the original owner probably ever would.

FOURTEEN

"Hey." Someone shook my shoulder gently. "Nina. It's time to get up."

I opened my eyes to find Grayson staring at me from less than a foot away, kneeling next to the couch. When I sat up, fighting disorientation, she took the cushion next to mine and handed me a glass of orange juice.

Bacon sizzled in a skillet on the stove, and my stomach growled. Only Reese's lower half was visible while he dug in the fridge, but Maddock smiled at me as he stuffed cans from an upper cabinet into a worn backpack.

Grayson gestured for me to drink my juice. "You're a deep sleeper."

"I'm not normally." I took a sip, and my mouth puckered.

"It's your transition." Maddock zipped the backpack

and set it on a chair at the table. "I think you just slept off the last of it."

"Thank goodness." I drank more juice. The pulp was growing on me.

Devi came out of the nearest bedroom, carrying two more backpacks by their handles. "You snore, and you have bedhead."

"I don't snore." Bedhead was a definite possibility.

Grayson laughed. "Finn says you do but it's cute."

"It's not cute." Devi handed the bags to Maddock, then headed back into the bedroom.

I drained my glass and ran my hands through my morning hair. "Where is Finn?"

"Um . . ." Grayson's gaze trailed slowly back and forth across the living room. "He seems to be pacing." She turned back to me and took my empty glass. "Today he's more frustrated than usual by his inability to interact with the world. I think he wants to talk to you."

"Wait, you can hear him? How?" I stared at the empty living room, but I had no idea where I was supposed to be looking.

Grayson shrugged.

"She can hear things the rest of us can't." Devi crossed the living room with a stack of clothing. "Like degenerates. And Finn."

"I hear him like he's talking from inside my head," Grayson clarified. "Like I'm hearing his thoughts, but only the ones he *wants* me to hear. It's different with the

235

degenerates, though. I can *feel* them when they get close enough."

"Weird."

She stood with my empty glass. "Maddy can hear him too."

I turned to Maddock, fascinated.

He nodded. "Yeah, but not like Gray does. I actually *hear* Finn, like I hear you. As if he's standing right next to me." He frowned and dropped another can into a new bag. "Or shouting from the other room, as he's doing right now."

"Make yourself useful." Devi emerged from the bathroom and shoved a toiletry bag at me. It was nearly full of half-used tubes of toothpaste, rolls of floss, and sticks of deodorant. "Take everything we could possibly use in the badlands. We can't risk breaching another town until we're no longer a national headline."

I stood, suddenly relieved to realize I'd slept fully clothed. "Wait, you're leaving? Today?"

"*We're* leaving," Maddock corrected. "You have to come with us, Nina. If you stay here, they'll find you. They've locked down the town and they're patrolling the wall. Our only chance to get out is during the press conference."

"Which is where these come in," Devi added from the bedroom doorway, where she held a white school blouse in one hand and a pair of navy slacks in the other. "The daughter's closet is full of old school clothes, which should help us blend into the crowd on the way to the south gate."

"What crowd?" I set the toiletry bag on the bathroom counter and dropped a bottle of acetaminophen into it.

"The press conference is shaping up to be a public spectacle." Reese set a platter of bacon on the table. "They're going to reveal the identity of whatever demon they claim to have found hiding among your friends and neighbors. The Church is ramping up the drama with the 'monsters among you' angle, and they've set the press conference for five o'clock so they'll catch parents on their way home from work and kids lingering after school for the drama."

"They're expecting a turnout of a couple thousand." Grayson snagged a slice of bacon. "It's our best chance to blend in. Thus the school clothes."

"How do you know all that?"

"You slept through the news," Maddock said around a slice of bacon.

"You *snored* through the news," Devi corrected.

"Five o'clock . . ." My thoughts raced. We had less than an hour. "I'm not going without my sister." I said it softly, but everyone heard. All sound ceased, except for the sizzle of eggs frying in the kitchen. "How hard could it be for Finn to jump inside some Church official and unlock her cell? We'll take a set of those for Mellie too"—I pointed at the uniform hanging on the bedroom door—"and we'll leave as soon as we have her. She'll fit right into your plan."

Devi was the first to break the near silence. "I *told you* she'd be a pain in the ass. I knew the minute I saw her with her mouth all over my boyfriend that she'd be nothing but—"

"Devi, *shut up!*" Grayson snapped, and we all turned to her in surprise. "That was from Finn," she clarified. "But I second the motion."

"Nina." Maddock set the second full backpack next to the first, practically begging me with his gaze to cooperate. "I'm sorry, but your sister's beyond our reach. Even if we could get her out of Church custody—and we can't—the whole world has seen Devi, Reese, Melanie, and you on the news. If any one of you is recognized, we're screwed."

Devi squeezed her arms crossed over her chest. "Which is why we're going to skirt the edge of the crowd on our way out of town, not march through the heart of the assembly and into the courthouse, where we're most likely to be recognized, then arrested."

"Then executed," Reese added.

"So you're going to run," I said flatly.

"No." Devi spread her arms to take in the entire room and everyone in it. "This is regrouping, so we can come at them again. That's not the same as running. April ran."

"April?" And suddenly I understood. "April Walden?"

The girl from Solace who'd died in the badlands. "She was an exorcist?"

"She would have been. When the degenerates started flocking north, we followed them, but they weren't leading us to New Temperance. First they led us to Solace." Which would have been between them and my hometown, coming from the south. "Finn and Reese found her, and she hadn't been triggered yet, which should have been good, except that she didn't know what she was. When they told her, she didn't believe them. Until the degenerates found her. Finn and Reese tried to get her to fight—she had to kill a demon to trigger the rest of the transition—but she ran."

"Into the badlands? How is that any better than fighting degenerates? The badlands are crawling with them, right?"

Grayson nodded. "I think she panicked. She was terrified, but she knew a way out of the town. Reese held off the degenerates so Finn could follow her. She made it through the wall before he caught up with her, but when he did, he had no way to talk to her. So he took over her body. He was just going to bring her back to us so we could help her, but . . ."

"But more degenerates found us before I could get her back inside the town," Reese said, and I glanced into the kitchen to see him leaning against the counter while the eggs sizzled behind him. Only it wasn't really Reese. "I fought them, in her body, but there were too many of them, and I'd never been in her before, so . . ."

"There's nothing else you could have done," Grayson said when his voice faded.

"If I had a body . . ."

Grayson actually rolled her eyes and managed to make the gesture look comforting. "If you had a body of your own, things would have been different from the start, but we work with what we have. That's the best we can do."

"Right now the best we can do is get the hell out of dodge and regroup, then come back for your sister when we've faded from the headlines," Devi insisted. "We can't get to her now."

I set the case on the bathroom counter, frustration raging deep inside me. "We're faster and stronger than anyone I've ever met. We *can* get to Melanie. We're the *only* ones who can. But if you badass, super-strong demon hunters are too scared of a handful of human jailers to help me, I'll damn well do it myself."

For a moment, silence reigned. Even the eggs were quiet, draining on a paper towel–covered plate, where Reese had put them now that he was back in his own body. Then Grayson whispered from the couch, "I love her fight." When everyone turned to her, she gave us a sheepish shrug. "That was from Finn. Also, he says he's in. And so am I."

Maddock shrugged. "If Finn's in, I'm in."

"No!" Devi shouted, and I hoped everyone in the apartment next door was still at work. "Your bullshit plan is tantamount to suicide, and that's one sin I'm not eager to try out."

Maddock covered his ears with both hands. "I can't think with you both shouting at once." Grayson looked uncomfortable too, and I realized that Finn was trying to be heard. "Finn says he's staying to help Nina, and that if the rest of us leave her, he'll . . . never forgive us."

"Only his version was slightly more profane and much more entertaining," Grayson added.

"Fine. He's made his decision. We're leaving." Devi reached past me to scoop an armful of pill bottles into the toiletry bag from the open medicine cabinet.

"No." Maddock scowled at her. "We stick together. All of us. Including Nina. We need her, and she needs us." Maddock turned to me then. "You know how you get stronger and faster when degenerates are near? We call that 'proximity strength,' and it's amplified in the presence of your fellow exorcists, which means we need every exorcist we can find."

I stared at him, trying to take it all in. If they'd be gaining speed and strength from the presence of one extra exorcist, I could only imagine how much I'd be gaining from the addition of *three*. Four, if and when Grayson transitioned.

"If we help you get Melanie, we need to be sure you

and your sister aren't just going to disappear into the badlands," Maddy continued. "We need to know you're willing to risk as much for us as we are for you."

I hadn't actually thought out my next move, beyond stealing my sister back from the Church, but disappearing into the badlands by ourselves was *not* on the list of possibilities.

"Yes. We're with you." We had no one else in the world, and even with the bickering, they were already more of a family to me than my mother had ever been. "So . . . now what? I've never organized a prison break."

We gathered around the small breakfast table—Devi stood as far from me as possible—and ate Reese's bacon and eggs while we developed a plan.

"The uniforms will work as well for a rescue as for an escape," Maddock said around a mouthful of bacon. "They won't be looking for us in school clothes or at the press conference."

"That's because we'd have to be stupid to show up at the courthouse, where every cop in New Temperance is waiting to arrest us."

I ignored Devi, and that was so much fun I decided to try it more often.

"They're holding the press conference in the square outside the courthouse," Reese said. "What can you tell us about the layout?"

The town square was almost identical to the courtyard

242

at my school, but on a larger scale. "Um . . . There're buildings on three sides—one is the courthouse—and at the center there's a stone dais with leg irons for three, and room for hundreds to congregate in front." And, of course, there was a giant television screen that could be set to show a news feed or a local feed, such as when they announced new Church positions or broadcast school ceremonies, like my third-grade Church creed recital.

"Any idea where they'll be keeping your sister?" Devi asked as yolk dripped from her forkful of egg onto her plate.

"The police are headquartered in the courthouse, but I've only been in there once. Maybe Finn could do some recon and find out where the jail section is?"

Maddock stabbed his fried egg with his fork, and bright yellow yolk bled all over his plate like a sunshine hemorrhage. "He says he's up for that."

"There's probably an entrance on the other side of the building, out of sight from the square. Fewer people would see us if we go in that way."

Devi snorted in contempt and Reese dipped a strip of bacon in his yolk. "We'd draw more suspicion if we avoid the crowd than if we hide within it."

"Oh." I took a big drink of juice to cover my embarrassed flush.

Grayson gave me a sympathetic smile. "If the turnout is big enough"—and it would be; nothing this sensational

had happened in New Temperance since the war itself—
"we should be able to slip into the courthouse through an
entrance in the square without being noticed. But it'll be
harder to blend once we're inside."

"We can't all go," Devi said, and I had to remind myself that she wanted to survive this just as badly as I did,
and that she had more experience avoiding arrest than I
probably—hopefully—ever would. "The more of us there
are, the more attention we'll draw."

"The fewer of us there are, the harder it'll be to fight
our way out if necessary," I pointed out.

Devi snorted again. "They have guns. If we have to
fight, we're already screwed."

"Don't *we* have guns?" Not that I wanted to shoot anyone, but guns make for a very effective threat. "Finn had—"

"That's our only one," Maddock said. "It stays here
with Grayson. The rest of us will go in pairs. That way, if
one pair is caught and forced to run, the other can keep
going. Finn's on his own."

Something told me Finn was usually on his own.

Devi pushed her empty, grease-smeared plate back.
"Maddy and I will approach the square from one direction, and Reese and Nina can go in from the other."

Grayson shook her head. "You're either going to have
to pair Maddock with Nina or take me, so Finn can com-
municate with her."

"We've been over this." Reese plucked an uneaten strip

of bacon from her plate. "You're not strong or fast enough to get away if this goes badly."

"I know. I'm a liability." She looked distinctly unhappy about that. "I'll stay here and finish packing."

"That's it, then," Maddock said. "I'll go with Nina. Devi, you and Reese find a spot within view of the side entrance of the square. Stay near the back of the crowd and try to blend, but if someone recognizes you, run. Don't hesitate."

That was when I truly realized how hard it would be for either of them to disappear into the hometown crowd. Even if their pictures hadn't been flashed on the news, along with my own, Devi's distinctive beauty would stand out in a sea of mostly pale faces, and Reese was several inches taller than the tallest student at my school.

Together, they would *certainly* stand out.

"What's Reese going to wear?" I studied his build critically. "I don't think we have any school clothes to fit him."

Grayson jumped up from her chair, her brown eyes flashing with excitement. "Finn picked this up for him." She threw open the coat closet and pulled out a long navy garment. At first I thought it was some kind of a coat. Then . . .

I turned to Reese. "You're going as a cop?" As a pledge, since there was no embroidery on the fitted cassock.

He only grinned and chewed, while Grayson hooked the hanger over the closet door.

Maddock swallowed a bite of bacon, then cleared his throat. "Finn got it from a dry cleaner this afternoon. He says that's the only one that would fit."

"That's either truly brilliant or profoundly idiotic." Reese would be more visible than ever as a cop—but people wouldn't be looking at his face. They'd notice the authority his navy robes granted, then dismiss him without further thought.

Hopefully.

"Okay, this might work." It *had* to. "But Reese and Devi probably shouldn't be obviously together."

"Agreed," Maddock's focus found them both. "Go separately, but stay in sight of each other and of the courthouse side entrance. Got it?"

"Sounds complicated, but I think I can manage." She pushed her chair back and stood. "Let's get moving." Devi grabbed the school uniform hanging from the bedroom doorknob and slammed the door behind her, leaving her dirty plate on the table.

"I don't think she likes me."

Grayson started stacking the used plates. "Devi doesn't like anyone but Maddy. I don't think she even likes herself most days."

Well, at least that gave us *something* in common.

FIFTEEN

"You okay?" Maddock's sneakers crunched on loose gravel as we crossed the apartment parking lot, headed for the center of town. I kept walking forward, even though every instinct I had was telling me to put as much distance as possible between me and whatever spectacle was about to unfold at the courthouse.

Reese and Devi had left separately ten minutes earlier so they could arrive alone from different directions.

Finn had gone even earlier than that, promising to meet us there with whatever information he managed to dig up.

"I'm . . ." I stared at the gray sky and hunched deeper into my borrowed coat. "Well, I'm alive, and right now that feels like a pretty big accomplishment."

Twenty minutes earlier, the national news had showed footage of Church investigators crawling all over my house. I'd fought tears, watching them paw through my medicine cabinet, examine the sheets on my bed, and assess the modesty of the underwear in my top drawer, in search of proof that I was possessed or lecherous or just generally evil. They'd found the clothes I'd "stolen" from the Turners and the makeup Mellie and I purportedly wore. They'd also aired images of a closet full of "immodest" clothing I'd never seen in my life, which we were supposed to have worn in order to lure the devout youth of New Temperance into our demonic embrace.

They were even linking us to the death of April Walden, the dead girl from Solace, though they probably had no idea how close to the truth that particular lie was.

However, the rest of it was beyond ridiculous. But with the misleading facts, half-truths, and outright lies rearranged, compiled, edited, and commented on by newscasters—familiar faces lent authority by embroidered Church cassocks and their very presence on the air—even I had to concentrate to remember that none of it was real.

But the worst bit of all was the fifteen-second clip of my sister, tears staining her cheeks and standing in her eyes. "She was a demon," Mellie had sobbed in front of the camera. "I didn't want to believe it, but she was *so* fast and *so* strong, and she *admitted* it. She said she was going to sell me as a host—" The footage cut off so abruptly that anyone with half a brain could tell she'd had more to say, but only Anathema and I knew that Mellie wasn't really talking about me—she was talking about our mother.

The news anchor was careful to remind the world that Melanie's tears could merely be manipulation on the part of the demon possessing her—the Church hadn't yet finished its examination of the younger Kane sister—but anyone who watched the overplayed clip with a slightly more critical eye would notice that the close camera focus seemed designed to hide her whereabouts as well as the circumstances of her incarceration.

I couldn't even imagine what kind of incendiary revelation the Church had saved for the national press conference, or which of my friends and neighbors they would declare possessed and in league with me and the rest of Anathema.

"So, how did you meet Finn?" I asked as we turned the first corner, desperate to think about anything other than the disaster my life had become and the incredibly slim chance that we'd actually be able to snatch Melanie from Church custody.

"We grew up together." Maddock stuffed his hands into the pockets of the navy slacks he'd borrowed from Angela Reddy's daughter; hopefully no one would notice they were too short. "He's just always been there."

"How is that possible?" I couldn't quite picture a toddler with an invisible playmate.

Maddock shrugged. "Finn's in my earliest memories." He kicked a bit of gravel down the cracked sidewalk as we passed the peeling paint and chipped brick facades of some of the oldest houses in town. They were old even before the war, back when New Temperance had another name and no wall, and looked just like thousands of other towns in hundreds of other counties around the nation.

"Everyone thought he was my imaginary friend," Maddock continued. "But the only part I could say at the time was 'friend.' It came out as 'Finn.' "

"You named him!" I couldn't resist a smile at the thought. "So . . . how did you play with someone you couldn't see?"

He shrugged again, and his pocketed hands pulled his pants up briefly to expose more of his socks. "We were about five when he figured out he could step into my body." Maddock chuckled at the memory, and I glanced around to make sure we were the only ones on the street. A boy and girl walking alone together would be noticed unless they looked and acted like brother and sister.

Fortunately, the neighborhood looked deserted. We were still at least a mile from the center of town.

"Finn used to get me in so much trouble! For a while, every time he got a turn in my body, he'd take a bite out of everything he could reach in the fridge, to see what it tasted like. A couple of times I got sick."

We turned another corner, and storefronts came into

view on either side of the street, forming a redbrick canyon. I wrapped my coat tighter; the temperature seemed to be dropping by the minute. "I wish I could hear him like you and Grayson can."

"He wishes that too." Maddock's blue-eyed gaze caught mine and held it. "He really likes you, Nina."

"He's been very candid about that." And his candor had caught me by surprise. I shrugged. "It's not like kids in New Temperance don't sin. We just don't flaunt it."

Maddock nodded. "I think it's the same way everywhere. And maybe that's how it should be. Maybe we *are* sinning, and maybe we *do* deserve to be tortured in hell by demons. But then again, if the Church knew what we know—that demons are already delivering hell right here on earth—maybe they'd be a little less eager to judge us for enjoying whatever life we have left. Real exorcists rarely live long enough to donate their souls, you know."

I hadn't thought about that, but I wasn't surprised.

Ahead, the school came into view, its tall, postwar fence punctuated with sharp wrought-iron points, and my heart began to pound. We were four blocks from the courthouse, and the crowd had grown denser. People were *everywhere*.

I glanced at Maddock, but if he was anxious, I couldn't tell. I'd put my hood up and tucked my hair into it, fighting not to stare at the ground, certain I'd be recognized any second, but he walked next to me like he belonged in New Temperance. As if he'd been born here. And that was when I realized what he was doing.

If he didn't look out of place, people would have no reason to notice him. Maddock was hiding in plain sight. But that was easier for him than it could possibly be for me, because his picture hadn't been broadcast to millions of people who were eager to hunt him down and turn him in. His face wasn't . . .

. . . on a giant Wanted poster plastered in the front window of the Grab-n-Go.

I sucked in a sharp breath and Maddock followed my gaze to the poster, where my face stared out at us both, literally larger than life. My name was right under it in huge block letters, along with details about the reward for information leading to my capture.

Below that were smaller school pictures of Reese and Devi, side by side, looking younger and more innocent than the exorcists I knew them to be.

"Don't stop," Maddock hissed when my steps lagged.

I matched his pace but couldn't slow my racing pulse or the wave of dizziness that rolled over me. My plan wasn't going to work. Someone would recognize me. I was going to get us all arrested, or worse.

"Calm down," Maddy whispered. "It's too late to back out now. We'd draw more attention by turning around."

I had no intention of backing out, but . . . "You should find Reese and Devi and get out of here. There's no reason for us all to get caught." I'd never forgive myself if I got them hurt or captured.

"No way," he breathed, and I could hardly hear him over the footsteps and whispered conversations all around us. "We don't abandon our own."

I wanted to argue, but by then we were part of the flow of traffic, carried by its current toward the town square, and so tightly surrounded by other spectators that if I reached out, I could touch at least three other people.

We were trapped within the mob gathering to hang us. Figuratively speaking.

At least, I hoped that part was figurative.

The crowd buzzed around us, and my name was on every tongue. People who'd never even said hi to me were suddenly experts on my early life, my school records, and my state of mind. They argued about how long I'd been possessed and whether or not my "deviant proclivities" had brought me to the attention of my demonic parasite or somehow made me more susceptible to possession. They mourned the loss of my mother, who should have been able to see what was going on in her own home but surely didn't deserve the death she'd been dealt.

I bit my tongue and shuffled forward with Maddock while indignation raged inside me.

Through the crowd, I saw Wanted posters bearing my picture in the front windows of two more stores, and when we got close enough to see the courthouse, with its white pillars and modest rotunda, I found my face on the big screen towering over the town square.

The giant television monitor—the only technological upgrade New Temperance had approved in my lifetime— was used to air public assemblies and school ceremonies, and to broadcast the national news feed during any large-scale emergency.

Earthquakes. Tsunamis. And me.

Hurricane Nina. I was an unnatural disaster.

I barely recognized the town square. I could hardly even see it through the throng trampling the grass as people flocked toward the dais.

In the past twenty-four hours, while I'd hidden from the world and from the degenerates tuned in to my heartbeat, national public interest had turned New Temperance into a circus of stage lights, news cameras, and preening public officials wearing pressed cassocks and identical grave expressions. As Maddock and I entered the crowded courtyard, carried along by the relentless flow of pedestrian traffic, I suddenly understood how, during past public crises in other cities, the news had managed to capture every aspect of the unfolding drama as it happened.

There were cameras everywhere.

I counted three aimed at the dais alone and two slowly panning the crowd from courthouse balconies, providing broad shots from above to showcase the sheer size of the throng. Two more cameras were carried on the shoulders of big men following familiar news correspondents through the crowd. The journalists stopped every few feet to shove a microphone at someone, and I realized they were in search of local flavor—a ten-second news clip of a New Temperance native willing to comment on the spectacle, live from the scene.

On the huge screen overhead, broadcasting the national news feed, a small inset window showed the crowd as the cameras panned, while in the main window, Sister Florence Bennett, deacon of New Temperance, was being interviewed in her office by a national correspondent, looking polished and composed in her steel-gray cassock with elaborate green embroidery.

I couldn't hear what the deacon was saying over the din of the crowd, but she looked poised and solemn, projecting the perfect combination of concern over the danger Anathema represented for New Temperance and steadfast confidence that we *would* be caught.

For a moment, as the balcony cameras panned the crowd, I panicked, sure one of them would catch me. Then I realized that no individual face would be recognizable among so many, all eager, as far as I could tell, to witness whatever spectacle Deacon Bennett had planned.

I prayed with all my heart that that spectacle wouldn't involve my sister. We couldn't rescue Melanie if she was on display in front of millions of at-home viewers, not to mention the live crowd.

Something touched my arm and I jumped, sure I'd been caught, until Maddock's gaze met mine. "Over here," he mouthed, and I followed him, elbowing my way through the crowd with my head down.

He found a spot for us near the courthouse wall, next to a giant speaker spewing the audio from the deacon's interview. Because of the noise and the distance from the dais, the crowd was thinner there, and I felt like I could breathe for the first time since we'd passed the Grab-n-Go.

"Do you see the others?" Maddock shouted into my ear, competing with the audio from the news broadcast, and I shook my head, scanning the faces and clothes of those closest to us. But I couldn't distinguish individual faces in the crowd. Fortunately, the same was evidently true for everyone else. No one was looking at us. No one even seemed to be looking *for* us. They didn't expect us to show up where, in theory, we were mostly likely to get caught.

After the interviewer's last question for Deacon Bennett, the giant speaker on my right played a three-beat chord and the image on the big screen changed. My breath caught in my throat when Dale's face appeared, staring out at me from behind the counter of the Grab-n-Go. The reporter introduced him and asked him to share what he knew about the demon known as Nina Kane.

"You know, everyone acts so surprised, like she's the last person they'd ever expect to host a demon, but that's only 'cause they don't know Nina like *I* do."

I groaned, and Maddock glanced at me for a second, then turned back to the screen.

"I don't know when she got possessed, but I can tell you right now she's *always* been a thief. I caught her several times, here in the store, and she always tried to buy her way out of trouble, if you know what I mean. You know, with the only kind of payment a girl like that understands."

My face flamed, as much in anger as in humiliation, and when Maddock looked my way again, I couldn't meet his gaze.

"I turned her down, of course, 'cause that's the right thing to do, but I'm not gonna say it was easy." He rubbed the stubble on his jaw and frowned solemnly at the reporter. "But I have to set an example for the younger generation, ya know? I have to rise above that sort of vulgar temptation."

The reporter nodded sagely and congratulated Dale on his prudence and self-control in the face of such corrupted morals, and I wanted to rip their heads from their bodies.

The scene on the giant monitor changed again just as a ripple of sound and movement worked its way through the crowd. On-screen, the camera zoomed in on Sister Pamela Williams as she emerged from a door in the courthouse, and when I turned to my left, there she was in her purple journalist's cassock, just twenty feet away. She smiled and waved as two men walked ahead of her, clearing a path for her and for the cameraman walking backward in front of her, following her progress toward the dais.

I didn't release the breath I'd been holding until the whole procession passed us without incident and Maddock and I could go back to scanning faces for Devi and Reese, which was even harder now that everyone was staring at the screen overhead and all we could see were the backs of their heads.

Then a man at the rear of the crowd turned, just feet from where I stood, and my heart thumped painfully while his gaze roamed the courthouse wall. His attention lingered for a moment on the speaker to my right, and I assumed he'd found what he was looking for.

Then he looked directly at me, and as his eyes widened in recognition, the last of my hope was swallowed by a wave of fear and determination unlike anything I'd ever felt.

The man opened his mouth to shout.

I raised my fists to stop him, and panic dumped adrenaline into my bloodstream, like fuel on the fire.

If I was going down, I would go down fighting.

SIXTEEN

I darted forward, fire surging through my veins, wondering how many of them I'd have to disable to clear a path of escape. Maddock grabbed me from behind. And that was when I noticed the stranger's eyes.

They were Finn-green.

Maddock let me go and Finn and I squeezed between the wall and the huge speaker. With its sound projected in the opposite direction, we might actually be able to hear one another behind it.

"I found your sister," Finn said, and before I could respond, he rushed on, and I realized he couldn't spend more than a few minutes in the stranger's body before someone would notice it was missing. "They have her locked in a cell, bound in the posture of penitence."

My chest ached at the thought. How long had she been there? Did they let her up to rest? To eat? To use the restroom? "How does she look?"

"Tired and scared, but whole. The cells are opened by electronic locks, and I've figured out how to get hers open, but the leg irons require an actual key. Even once we find that and unlock her, we'll have to get her past at least half a dozen cops and courthouse employees just to get out of the building. Then, of course, there's getting us all out of town."

"Okay. We'll deal with the courthouse first." I took a deep breath and looked around to make sure no one was watching. "Are there limits to your . . . ability? Can you take over anyone you want?" Seizing strangers' bodies without permission felt like a fundamental violation, but there was no line I wouldn't cross to get Mellie back.

Finn shrugged. "Anyone human. As far as I know, anyway. But I can't get into someone who's possessed."

"Okay. Can you get inside someone who has the authority to just walk out with her? Like . . . fake a transfer or an appointment or something?"

"I think so," he said. "They'll probably send a security escort, but if I can get them out the back door, you guys can help get rid of the extra security, right?"

"Yeah." I almost felt bad for anyone willing to stand between me and my sister. Almost.

"You might even be able to get a car," Maddock added, and I could hear the excitement in his voice, even over the speaker and the buzz of the crowd. "I mean, if she has an appointment somewhere—like with a doctor, for the baby—they'd expect someone to drive her there, right?"

Finn nodded. "Okay, I'll be back once I've lined up a body and a car. You two find Reese and Devi, and be ready to go when I have details." Then Finn walked his borrowed body back to the edge of the crowd. I could tell when he was gone because the man whose body he'd hijacked stiffened, then glanced around in confusion, no doubt wondering how he'd managed to fall asleep on his feet and miss half the press conference.

We'd missed the first part too, but when I looked up at the screen, Sister Pamela was still recapping what everyone already knew about the "crisis in New Temperance," along with the latest suspicions from investigators about where the outlaws might be hiding.

They'd found the remains of our refuge in the abandoned warehouse and were currently searching that same area for something similar in another unoccupied building.

They were way off base. Thank goodness.

"We're going to have to go deeper to find Devi and Reese," Maddock said into my ear, and I followed his gaze to a clique of four policemen at the edge of the crowd. Reese and Devi would have moved as far from them as possible, especially Reese, who couldn't afford for members of the New Temperance police department to realize they didn't know this particular brother in blue.

We slowly began to move up through the crowd, sticking close to the wall of the courthouse so Finn would be able to find us once he'd selected a police officer's identity to assume.

While Deacon Bennett spoke to the cameras, detailing the town's efforts to catch me and the rest of Anathema, my focus volleyed between the huge screen and the crowd. My nerves were raw, my concentration shot from the knowledge that any second someone could turn and get a good look at me. There was no quick way out of the courtyard from our position, and since they actually believed I was a demon, the crowd could morph into a mob in seconds.

We'd only moved forward about fifty feet when a rumble began at the front of the crowd. I couldn't tell what people were whispering, but one glance at the big screen made my heart drop into my stomach.

Sister Pamela stood in front of the dais. Deacon Bennett stood next to her, having just finished her short update. In a smaller, inset screen, Brother Jonathan Sayers sat behind the anchor's desk in a studio thousands of miles away, courtesy of a technology our ancestors had developed and the Church had long ago seized.

"Thank you so much for that update, Deacon," Brother Sayers said. "Thoughts and minds all over the country are with those of you in New Temperance as you struggle with this horrific demonic uprising."

Someone was moving around on the dais behind Sister Pamela, but both the light and the camera were tightly focused on her and on Deacon Bennett, so we couldn't see much beyond that blur of movement in the artificially lit courtyard.

"Brother Jonathan, as you'll soon see behind me, Church officials here in New Temperance are acting soundly and swiftly in the face of this rising threat," Sister Pamela said straight into the camera. "As you well know, only the hammer of true faith can beat back the surge of evil in our midst."

"I couldn't agree more," Brother Jonathan said from his inset box near her head, and when I heard the familiar heavy clink of metal in the background, my heart began to thud in my ears. "What's that going on behind you, Sister Pamela?"

She turned to her right and the shot widened so that the dais was in full view, brightly illuminated by the network's lights. "Brother Jonathan, *this* is how the fine people of New Temperance deal with the Unclean."

An "exorcist" in his black cassock was bent over the center set of calf manacles, checking the hinges for rust or weakness. A second was sweeping dust and fallen leaves from the stone platform, his silver buttons shining in the bright light.

Sister Pamela was careful not to block the view of the dais. "Deacon Bennett has gone into the courthouse to bring out the demon uncovered in the continuing investigation of the Kane sisters and the demonic subculture recently unearthed here in New Temperance. The identity of the human host of this demon has not yet been released to the public, but just minutes from now both his body and his soul will be purified by the only means we know to be effective against the Unclean."

Oh shit. I stumbled, and Maddock caught me before I could bump into anyone and expose us both. *Oh shitshitshit.*

Sister Pamela stared solemnly into the camera. "As I'm sure you've guessed, Brother Jonathan, the demon's stolen soul must be purified by the holy flame."

A ripple of whispers rolled over the crowd. Some people were excited, some were obviously horrified, and yet more were curious, anxiously glancing between the screen and what little they could actually see of the front of the courthouse, from which this alleged demon would soon emerge.

"His soul?" Maddock mouthed silently to me in question, but I could only shake my head, my gaze glued to the screen, my hands gripping the sides of my school slacks so tightly my fingers had gone numb. I had no idea who they were about to burn, and—as horrible as the thought was—in that moment all I cared about was that it wasn't Mellie.

Not yet, anyway.

Sister Pamela laid one hand over her heart and looked thoughtfully, somberly into the camera. "I'm so grateful to the citizens of New Temperance for the honor of being a witness to this glorious moment."

"I know *I* have chills." Brother Jonathan's sincerity echoed across the crowd.

I had chills too. I'd seen Clare Parker's soul "cleansed." I'd heard her scream. I'd smelled her flesh roasting.

It was not an honor.

"Oh, here they come!" Sister Pamela pivoted to her right, and while the crowd turned, the camera focused on a procession coming from the front of the courthouse. Half a dozen fake exorcists escorted a man with his arms cuffed at his back, his head covered by a burlap hood. His feet were bare, and he wore a white school shirt, ripped in places and stained with blood.

He was a student.

My heart beat too hard. My chest ached. My vision started to blur until I realized I needed to blink. My gaze was glued to the screen. To the man—the *boy*—being paraded toward the dais, stumbling, tripping, and ultimately pulled along by the "exorcists" who held his arms.

They marched him up onto the stone platform, then forced him to kneel like Matthew Mercer had knelt two days before. Like my sister was kneeling even then, in her cell in the courthouse. They slapped the metal cuffs over his legs, just below his knees, and we could hear him now, his breath hitching as if he couldn't get enough air. Or couldn't get it fast enough.

We watched in near silence, at least two thousand of us in person and millions at home, waiting to see his face. To see who among us knew the "demon" the Church claimed to have found. Was he a real demon, like the woman whose apartment Anathema had seized? Or was he like us—unlucky enough to have pissed off the Church, and now paying with a fabricated charge?

Could Mellie see this? Were they making her watch from her cell? Did she know how close she was to sharing this poor boy's fate?

Deacon Bennett directed the last two exorcists in the procession to set large black plastic canisters on the edge of the dais, just feet from where the boy was locked into place, his hands still at his back, his chest heaving with each labored breath.

I felt like I could throw up.

"It turns out the demon is actually . . . ," Sister Pamela said as the lead "exorcist" pulled the hood from the doomed boy's head, ". . . the father of Melanie Kane's unborn child."

Oh no, no, no . . . Please, no.

The camera zoomed in on Adam Yung's face, bruised and bloody. His left eye was swollen shut. He'd fought someone and lost. Had he fought for himself or for Mellie?

I'd stopped searching the crowd entirely. Sister Pamela

was still talking, but I couldn't process anything in that moment. All I could see was Adam's puffy face. All I could hear was the word he wasn't truly saying. The word I recognized on his lips, even though it carried no real sound.

Melanie.

He was calling for Melanie.

Deacon Bennett demanded that he confess to having a demon inside him, but Adam only murmured my sister's name into the microphone shoved in front of his face. The exorcists threw holy water over him, and he screamed as if it burned. The crowd gasped and my heart stopped beating for just a second until I realized that didn't mean anything.

Demons aren't hurt by holy water. Finn had said so. Because demons aren't "unholy." They were just plain evil.

"He's not possessed," I whispered into Maddock's ear, our gazes glued to the farce of an exorcism being broadcast all over the country, live from my hometown.

"I know." His words were so soft I could hardly hear them.

"So why does holy water hurt him?" We were taking a risk in the middle of the crowd, but no one was looking at us. They were all staring at the screen, engrossed, listening to Deacon Bennett explain that Adam was no longer the Adam Yung many of us knew. Adam was dead, and a demon had control of his body, and that demon must be cleansed from Adam's body and his soul so he could find eternal peace.

"It's saltwater," Maddock said. "Burns in every open wound. That's why they beat him first."

"This can't be happening." I shook my head. "This isn't real." I couldn't stop thinking it. I couldn't stop saying it, though any minute my whispered denials could get us caught.

On-screen, the lead exorcist signaled to two others, who each picked up one of the plastic canisters. Adam's chest rose and fell rapidly, and my heart raced in sympathy with his. The exorcist in charge stood in front of the dais, facing the crowd, and though I could only see the top of his black hooded robe from my position halfway through the enormous crowd, my view of the screen was miserably unimpeded.

"Citizens of New Temperance," the exorcist called in a commanding voice, "please understand that Adam Yung has been absolved of the crimes of fornication and unlicensed procreation; Church authorities believe it was actually the demon inside him who committed such egregious sins. Now, those of us who love him—who failed to protect him from this monstrous evil—we must not fail him again!" The exorcist's silver embroidery glittered in the bright lights when he raised one fist. "We *must not* allow his soul to be tarnished by the same demon that has claimed and defiled his body."

"Make it right!" someone called from the crowd, and the exorcist nodded approvingly.

"Save his soul!" a woman cried, and on the tail of that, another shouted, "Cleanse him!"

I groaned as similar cries broke out all around me and Adam slumped on the dais. The camera zoomed in on his face, and I read defeat in his eyes as surely as I'd ever read his incomprehension of decimals or his affection for my sister.

The exorcist turned to face him and asked the "demon" if he had any final words before the soul he'd "stolen" was commended back into the well for the common good, purified by holy flames.

Adam took a deep breath. Then he shouted my sister's name.

Chills raced up my spine and the world tilted around me; I was knocked off balance by the desperation in his plea.

The exorcist nodded, and two others stepped forward, unscrewing the lids from their canisters. The crowd gasped, then went virtually silent, determined not to miss a moment of the brutal spectacle.

Outrage seethed within me, demanding action. I could *not* just stand there while they set my friend and neighbor— the father of my unborn niece or nephew—on fire.

But there was nothing I could do or say without putting even more people in danger. Including Mellie and her baby.

The fake exorcists dumped both canisters of gasoline over Adam, and several people in the crowd gasped, as if they hadn't expected that to actually happen. As if they'd thought the whole thing was a warning, or a prank that had finally gone too far.

Adam screamed as gasoline ran into his eyes and his mouth and every open cut on his body.

On the inside, I screamed with him. On the outside, I clutched handfuls of my uniform pants and clenched my jaw shut with staggering effort.

Then the screen shifted to a new angle to show the lead exorcist kneeling next to a little girl at the front of the crowd, still dressed in her school uniform, blond pigtails brushing her shoulders.

With a jolt of shock, I recognized Elena, from my kindergarten class, just an instant before the exorcist put a match in her small hand. He helped her strike the tip against the side of the box, and for a moment, like the rest of the live audience, I was transfixed by the glow of that tiny flame.

Then the exorcist stood and demonstrated a tossing motion for Elena. The men with the canisters stepped down from the dais and onto the sidewalk. And five-year-old Elena Phillips threw the lit match onto the gas-drenched stones.

SEVENTEEN

Fire consumed Adam and most of the dais in the span of a single heartbeat. Flames masked his ruined face, but could not mute his screams or the crackle of his crisping skin, captured by multiple microphones and broadcast all over the country. He hunched forward, futilely trying to protect the most vulnerable parts of his body as smoke rose and disappeared into the rapidly darkening sky.

I choked on the scent of burning flesh and hair. Fresh horror melded with the memory of Clare Parker's gruesome death, and together they obscured the courtyard around me, the crowd hiding me, and the trampled grass beneath my feet until I could see and hear nothing but the steady roar of a martyr's flames.

My mouth dropped open beneath the force of shock and outrage I could no longer hold back, and I didn't realize I'd intended to scream until a hand closed over my mouth, trapping my terror inside me. I bit one of the fingers and shoved the man off me, but didn't notice his bright green eyes until he'd already stumbled into two other people.

They twisted to look, and he apologized. I pulled my hood as low on my face as it would go and turned just as Maddock took my arm. A second later, Finn had the other one, and I didn't recognize the face he wore this time, because the man he'd been a second earlier was still trying to figure out how he'd stumbled backward into several people when he couldn't even remember looking away from the screen.

"We have a problem," Finn said as we pushed our way toward the back of the crowd. We weren't trying to hide my face anymore because our withdrawal didn't stand out. Everyone with a weak stomach—or a strong conscience— was retreating from the human torch who used to be one of my friends and classmates.

"Understatement of the century," Maddock mumbled from my right as they guided me through the crowd without any spoken plan or direction, as if they could read each other's minds. "They just lit a kid on fire, and I'm betting there's more gasoline where that came from."

Finn exhaled heavily. "That's not the problem."

"Wait!" I pulled away from them both and turned

toward the side entrance of the courthouse, prepared to push my way back through the crowd, which had thinned but not dispersed. "I'm not leaving her."

"Shhh, Nina, please." Strong hands turned me, and I found myself staring at a dark, middle-aged face eyeing me with concern—through bright green eyes. Finn's rapid body switches were making me dizzy. "I'm so sorry about your friend. But getting us caught won't help him *or* your sister. Okay? It's not safe for us here. It's less safe than you can possibly imagine."

"Why? What happened?"

"I'll explain once we're out of the crowd." His voice was as loud as it could possibly be and still qualify as a whisper. "We'll have to find another way to get to Melanie."

We were two-thirds of the way through the crowd when a shrill scream pierced the steady crackle of flames, then was cut off abruptly.

At first I thought it was Adam. Then I realized he'd passed out from either the smoke or the pain almost a minute earlier. Or maybe—mercifully—he was already dead. People were looking around, craning their necks, but no one seemed to know where the scream had come from.

When a second person screamed, I stopped walking. Something was wrong.

I turned when several more voices joined the chorus of horror, shrieking in pain and fear, and both Maddock and Finn turned with me, but we couldn't see the source through the throng.

On-screen, the camera panned the now-skittish crowd while an obviously startled Sister Pamela spoke in an inset window, demanding an answer to the question we were each asking ourselves. And finally the camera zoomed in on a rapidly expanding gap in the crowd, widening like the eye of a hurricane. We couldn't see what was happening, but people were trying to get away, and as some ran, others fell and were trampled.

"Shit!" Maddock shouted, and I turned away from the screen to follow his gaze just as an inhuman snarl ripped through the crowd on my left. A new chorus of screams followed, and the horror was closer now. People were panicking. Fleeing. Falling. Some pulled their friends up, and others left them behind. Yet I still couldn't see the source of the panic.

But I could smell it.

Rot. Filth. Fetid bodily fluids.

Degenerates. My transitional period was over; I hadn't felt their approach.

I'd hardly processed that realization when another series of shrieks echoed from my right. I turned just as a male degenerate in tattered mechanic's coveralls dropped from a courthouse balcony onto a man in a suit, driving him to the ground. People scrambled in all directions. Two of them ran into me, pushing me backward, but I ducked, then squeezed between the next two while the man in the suit screamed.

My hand was already glowing when I stepped into the ever-widening opening in the crowd, but no one stopped running long enough to notice.

The man was dead before I got to him, so instead of pulling the degenerate off him, I slammed my burning hand down on the demon's back and pressed as hard as I could. The monster thrashed between me and the corpse of his own making, but I held my ground. This time I could *feel* the empty chill of his hunger—a maddening, ravenous existence—and I let the heat in my palm burn him up until there was nothing left in his mutated body but a charred, smoking hole the diameter of my hand.

The dead degenerate collapsed on top of his victim, and I stood, ready to run, certain that someone had seen what I'd done and that the fake exorcists were already closing in on me with guns drawn.

And people *had* seen, surely, but in their panic they'd had time for nothing but their own escape. No one was staring at me. No guns were aimed at me. People didn't care who I was or what I was wanted for, as long as I stood between them and the monsters.

A flash of bright light exploded on my right and I turned, expecting to find Maddock exorcising another demon, but instead I found Reese, badass and scary in his police cassock, his navy blue hat half trampled on the ground at his feet.

Maddock was several yards away, pulling a degenerate off a screaming, bleeding woman, and from deeper within the crowd came another flash of light, and a shout of triumph that could only have come from Devi.

"Nina, look out!" Reese shouted, and I turned as another degenerate pounced on a child in school clothes—eight years old, at the most—shoving him into me. I pulled the kid from the demon and accidentally hurled him ten feet away, where Reese lunged and caught him, then set the terrified child on his feet.

The degenerate was on me in a second. He drove me to the ground, snapping at my face, but my hand was already warmed up. I shoved my left palm into his chest and the monster screamed. He tried to scramble off me, but the fire in my hand had captured him, and the demon was stuck there, convulsing in the throes of death as his rotting flesh fried.

When my light faded, I wedged my bent legs between me and the demon and kicked the body as far as I could. It flew over the crowd as I jumped to my feet. I didn't see where it hit, but I heard the grotesque thud of its impact with the ground and the screams of those near where it landed.

When I turned back to Reese, he had one degenerate pinned to the ground, his fiery hand burning a hole in the monster's ripped shirt, and he held a second at arm's length by its neck, while it clawed and snapped at his arm.

"Reese, I'm open!" I shouted. He looked up, then shoved the second degenerate at me. I ran forward to meet it, and the moment my hand touched its back, that fire exploded between us. When the monster fell with a blackened hole smoldering in its chest, I stood and took a deep breath. People still screamed and ran all around me, but I felt . . . focused. Driven. My hand burned, my head rang with the cacophony of terror en masse, and my nostrils were flared from the stench, but for the first time in my life, I knew where I belonged.

I knew what I was supposed to do.

And I knew exactly how this was destined to end— with a pile of dead degenerates, hopefully much bigger than the pile of their victims.

"Why aren't they shooting?" I called to Reese as I dodged fleeing civilians, then lunged for another degenerate. "The Church's 'exorcists'?" Why were they willing to shoot me in my own home, but not these monsters tearing into the civilian congregation?

"They don't shoot demons," he called back, pulling another monster off its feet. "Not in public, anyway. They pretend to exorcise them with holy water and pointless Latin chanting. Shooting these degenerates without all the pomp and circumstance would expose them as fakes."

"So they're just going to let us do all the work?" Claws ripped through my coat sleeve and drew blood from my arm. My hand blazed to life, and then another monster fell dead beneath me. "Won't *that* expose them as fakes?"

Reese shrugged and tossed another dead demon aside. "My dad always said the Church does its best work covering up its own crimes. . . ."

For several minutes, the monsters kept coming and we kept burning them out. Two managed to pin me, and a third ripped right through my hood and pulled out a chunk of my hair, but that proximity strength—as Maddock called it—was in full effect with this many degenerates around. I'd never been stronger or faster. My reflexes had never been sharper.

After each exorcism, I scanned the rapidly thinning crowd for other points of light, and twice, a stranger with familiar green eyes shoved terrified onlookers out of my way or pushed degenerates into my path, away from fleeing groups of civilians. Without an exorcist's body to inhabit, Finn lacked super strength and speed, and he couldn't banish any of the demons, but he was there every time I turned around, in a different large, capable body, pulling demons off of women and children and shouting for them to run. Then shoving them in the safest direction.

Finn made heroes out of a dozen different men in less than ten minutes.

The whole thing was over almost as soon as it had begun, and only when the last of the degenerates were lying dead on the grass or fleeing into the night—we couldn't get them *all*—did I begin to feel the toll the night's battle would take on my exhausted body. But there was only time for a single deep breath before more yelling began.

This was angry shouting, not terrified screaming, and when I turned toward it, I found the Church's fake exorcists pouring from the nearest courthouse exit, confidently aiming guns at us now that the demons were all gone.

Not one of the casualties wore a black cassock.

"Down on the ground!" the closest of the exorcists yelled, and what few civilians still remained—most injured and bleeding—dropped onto the cold grass, some just feet from the putrefying degenerate corpses.

Reese, Devi, Maddock, and I froze. I glanced at each of them, spread out across the courtyard, hoping for some sign of what I should do, but I wasn't yet tapped into whatever strange connection—experience?—made them such great silent communicators.

I'd lost sight of Finn. Several of the bodies he'd confiscated, then abandoned, sat on the ground, staring around in confusion.

"Get down!" the fake exorcist repeated, and I counted six of them, all aiming guns at us while Deacon Bennett and Sister Pamela watched in shock from near the dais, where the last of the gasoline was now burning out over Adam's charred corpse.

The huge screen overhead was blank except for a slowly scrolling message alerting viewers to "technical difficulties," which the network promised would be resolved very soon.

Now that the crowd had cleared, I could count the television cameras. Two on huge mounted tripods had been abandoned entirely. On a courthouse balcony, a dead cameraman was slumped over the railing behind a third camera, still aimed at the ground. A fourth, shoulder-mounted camera was still rolling, focused on us, though nothing was currently being broadcast on the news.

"Last warning!" the lead exorcist shouted, adjusting his aim at me. "We don't want to shoot you, but we will."

If they didn't want to shoot us, why were they pointing guns at us?

No one seemed to know what to do. We couldn't let them take us into custody, but being shot in the back as we fled didn't seem like much of a viable alternative. So I tried something rash.

"Wait!" I shouted when the fake exorcist aiming at me cocked his gun. "We're not demons. We—"

"Nina, shhh!" Maddock hissed from ten feet away, and people on the ground all around me murmured my name, just then realizing who I was. "That won't help."

"It has to!" I turned back to the Church officials, then

glanced around at the civilians staring up at me in shock and fear. "We weren't fighting *against* you, we were fighting *for* you! We were protecting you. We're not demons, we're—"

The deafening crack of gunfire came half an instant before a man threw himself in front of me, facing the guns. The bullet hit his left shoulder, and I gasped as he stumbled backward, off balance but still upright. For a moment, no one moved. I forgot how to breathe. Then the man turned to look at me as more gunfire thundered into the quiet night. He jerked with each impact, and I flinched, tears rolling down my face, but I was too stunned and terrified to move.

The man's hands landed heavily on my shoulders. Shock froze my feet in place. His eyes were Finn-green.

Finn had thrown an innocent man's body between me and certain death.

"Nina . . . *run*." His whole body jerked again, then fell toward me as bullet after bullet tried to punch through him to get to me.

Eyes wide, heart pounding, I caught him beneath his arms as he fell, and though the degenerates were all dead, I didn't even stagger beneath his weight. Tears blurred my vision, and wordless rage shrieked inside me. Then someone grabbed my arm and nearly pulled me off my feet.

Maddock ran, hauling me with him, and now *he* had Finn's green eyes. I couldn't keep up with all the body hopping and flying bullets. "Run, Nina!" Finn shouted in Maddock's voice, and I made my legs move, yet I could hardly keep up with him.

More gunfire and footsteps echoed behind us, and Reese and Devi raced ahead of us. Finn tugged me left, then right, and as I stumbled after him, faster than I could have imagined running two days earlier, I realized that our enhanced speed and crazy zigzagging made us difficult targets to hit. Bullets flew past us on either side, chipping chunks of brick from the courthouse wall, and Finn seemed to know just how to avoid them.

Why were we still so fast and strong if we'd killed all the degenerates?

As we fled around the corner of the courthouse, I turned to glance at the square, convinced we'd missed at least one of the monsters. How else could our proximity strength still be active? In the second before Finn pulled me out of sight, I noticed three things.

First, the square was still littered with shocked, innocent civilians, most injured, many dead.

Second, the fake exorcists were racing after us now, two of them trying to slide fresh clips into the grips of their guns, and they weren't alone. Sister Pamela and Deacon Bennett were running as well, along with several other, older Church officials, and none of them looked the least bit winded from the sprint.

Third—and most terrifying of all—every single one

of the Church officials chasing us stared back at me with eyes that shone in the dark like a cat's. And suddenly I understood why our proximity strength hadn't faded. The surviving degenerates may have fled, but there was no shortage of the Unclean in the town square.

The town of New Temperance—my hometown—was being run by demons.

EIGHTEEN

"Did you guys *see* that?" Each grinding thump of my shoes against pavement bounced back at me from the brick walls of yet another dark alley, and I wondered if I'd ever walk on Main Street again. Why hadn't anyone told me that claiming my exorcist birthright and being declared anathema meant giving up daylight and sidewalks forever?

"See what?" Devi snapped. Finn was hanging back for me—I didn't yet have their stamina—and since he was in Maddock's body, she was hanging back for him, shooting us angry glances every couple of seconds while Reese maintained the lead she clearly wanted. "The part where a pack of degenerates attacked a large congregation on live television for the first time since the end of the war, or the part where you called the Church out in front of all those innocent people, further pissing them off and endangering yet more innocent lives?"

"I didn't call anyone out!" I was huffing, though the rest of them sounded fine, and a glance back told me we'd finally zigged down enough alleys and zagged across enough open lots to lose our fake-exorcist pursuers.

"Bullshit!" Devi grabbed my arm, trying to haul me forward at her pace while she yelled at me, but my legs couldn't go any faster. I jerked free from her grip and Finn moved between us in the tight space. He shot a warning glance at her, but he couldn't stop her mouth from moving even faster than her feet. "They were trying to take us alive—"

"They were . . . *shooting* . . . at us!" My words were disjointed, punctuated with short gasps for air. My lungs burned.

"They would have shot to wound," she insisted as one alley faded into the next, broken only by short sprints across deserted streets. "To slow us down. They took Carey alive, and he wasn't the first exorcist they've plucked off the street, which seems to suggest that they wanted us alive too. At least, they did until you tried to tell two dozen civilians that *their* exorcists are fake and *we're* the real thing. To the Church, the truth is like a disease—they can't let you infect anyone else. You practically dared them to kill us!"

"It was worth it," I said as Reese finally slowed when the town wall came into view. We were approaching the apartment complex from the back and couldn't afford to draw attention, so I lowered my voice to an angry, huffing whisper. "We got away, and now two dozen people know the truth. Or at least they know the Church is lying about us." I sucked in another cold breath, trying to put out the fire in my chest, but oxygen seemed to feed the flames. "If the truth is like a disease, let's hope it spreads."

Devi glanced at Finn while I bent with my hands on my knees, trying to catch my breath. "Can she really be that stupid?"

He scowled at her with Maddock's furrowed brow. "She's not stupid."

"Colossally naive, maybe." Reese stared down the length of the town wall in one direction, looking for police or exorcists or whoever the Church had patrolling for us. "Recklessly optimistic, definitely. But not stupid." He turned in the other direction, and I saw the sweep of several broad flashlight beams just as he did.

My heart jumped into my throat. They were so close. Too close. But they seemed to think we'd made it over the wall.

Reese held out both arms, herding us toward the seized apartment while Devi warned us to be quiet with one finger pressed to her lips. As if we needed a reminder.

Finn let us in with Maddock's key, in Maddock's hand,

and the moment Grayson saw us, she threw herself at Reese. He shushed her even as he caught her in both arms.

"I saw the news until everything went crazy and the picture cut out! I was afraid they got you!"

"We're fine, but they're close," he said while I closed and locked the door.

"Thanks to Nina. If I didn't know any better, I'd say she was working for the other side." Devi grabbed a bottle of water from the stack Grayson had been packing, then tossed one to Finn. "Don't let Maddock dehydrate."

"Hey, I'm not the one who exposed us." I grabbed a bottle for myself and opened it with so much force I nearly cracked the plastic. "We *all* did that, because our only other option was to let degenerates shred those poor people like beef through a grinder."

Devi wagged one pointed finger at me, scolding me like a naughty child. "It's *your* fault we're still in this miserable little town, and it's *your* fault we were at the courthouse, and—"

"And if we hadn't been, instead of losing ten or twelve lives, New Temperance could have lost fifty. A hundred, maybe. Who knows how long it would have taken the fake exorcists and their stupid guns to do what we did in minutes?"

Devi stomped closer, speaking through clenched teeth, her nose inches from mine when I refused to back away. "I don't *care* how many people your backward-ass town would have lost. I don't care about anyone but the people in this room, and *you* keep dragging them all into serious trouble, which means I care less and less about *your* well-being with every passing second."

"Fighting each other is doing their work for them." Finn pulled her away from me before my temper could snap or hers could boil over. "Don't do their work. Do *our* work."

Devi didn't even glance at him. She was too busy glaring at me.

"I'm done apologizing for my existence, Devi. I'm not sorry that I'm here, and I'm not sorry that I'm one of you, and I'm not sorry that we saved hundreds of innocent people today. Hell, you saved way more than I did."

She looked only slightly mollified by my admission. "Those 'innocent people' were chanting for them to burn your friend alive. What *century* is this, anyway?" Devi slammed her bottle down on the table and water sloshed over her hand. "That was barbaric. Beyond that, it's asinine. Souls have no physical form—Finn's proof of that—but fire is the *physical* expense of energy, right? So why on earth would fire have any effect whatsoever on a soul? That wouldn't make sense even if your friend *was* possessed."

"And they know that." I tried not to think about what I'd seen. About the friend I'd just lost. About the horrifying stench of burning flesh still clinging to our clothes.

Look forward, Nina. Focus on what can still be dealt with. "Which brings me back to my original question. Did anyone else see their eyes?"

"I saw them," Finn said with Maddock's voice. "That's what I was coming back to tell you."

Ohhh. The problem he'd mentioned hadn't been the incoming degenerates. He'd been talking about the demons in Church robes.

"Whose eyes?" Reese twisted the cap from his own bottle of water and accepted a cellophane-wrapped muffin from Grayson with his other hand.

"All of them." I glanced at Finn, and he held up one finger, asking for me to wait. Then he closed his eyes, and when they opened again, Maddock looked out at me from his own body. He stiffened and blinked in momentary confusion, then relaxed a little when he saw the familiar surroundings and faces he knew.

When his gaze lost focus, I realized Finn was filling Maddock in on the parts he'd missed. Then Maddock frowned at me. "They were demons? All of them?"

"All of *who*?" Devi said.

"The Church." Grayson sank into her chair, stunned by what she'd obviously heard from Finn.

I nodded. "Every single cassock-wearing son of a bitch out there chasing us today had shiny demon eyes. The cops. The deacon. The fake exorcists. Even the cameramen. They were all possessed."

"*All* of them?" Reese froze in the middle of unwrapping his muffin. "Are you sure?"

I shrugged. "All the ones I saw."

"Finn says, 'Me too.'" Grayson relayed the information in a flat, shocked voice. "That's why he couldn't get Melanie out. He couldn't get inside anyone with the authority to unlock her cell, because everyone who qualified was already possessed."

"Of course they were." Devi glared at me, hands propped on the generous curves of her hips. "Naturally, Nina's the product of a town being run by demons!"

"That's a recent development. It has to be." Didn't it? I couldn't possibly have been living in demon central my whole life without knowing about it.

But then, how was I supposed to know? How was *anyone* supposed to know? Only exorcists could see the demonic gleam in a possessed person's eyes, and I'd only transitioned a day ago. There was no way I could have known about the deacon and the school officials and . . .

How many were there? How many had I seen every day of my life, and spoken to and been taught by?

Anabelle.

Anabelle was an ordained Church pledge. But she wasn't possessed. She couldn't be. I'd known her all my life, and she was still the same kind, friendly girl she'd always been. Anabelle wasn't a demon. Surely they weren't *all* demons. Right?

I sank onto the couch, half-crushed by the enormity of the possibilities coming into focus in my head. My lungs wouldn't expand. The truth was heavier than the air I needed, and it filled me, leaving no room for me to draw breath.

I shivered. I shook so hard the room seemed to tremble around me. The truth was cold and sharp like the October wind, and bitter like ashes on my tongue.

The truth . . . made no sense.

"It can't be *all* the Church members in my town, and it can't be *just* my town." I wasn't sure whether to hope I was right or pray that I was wrong about that last part. "Sister Pamela isn't from here. Neither are the cameramen. But they're all possessed."

"Could they have gotten possessed since coming to town?" Reese asked, and they all turned to Maddock for the answer, presumably because he'd seen more of the country than the rest of us.

He shrugged and seemed to be listening to something we couldn't hear—Finn, of course. "Anything's possible, but I haven't noticed any higher percentage of demons among the private citizens here than in half the towns we've been in this year. Finn agrees. In fact, there's a *lower* percentage in New Temperance than in some of the bigger cities, like Constance and Verity."

"So, are those cities run by demons too? I mean, it can't be just New Temperance and the TV people the news station sent, can it?" Reese said. "That's too much of a co-incidence, and my dad always said that coincidence is just conspiracy dressed up for show."

Devi huffed. "Your dad was a heretic and an idiot. There's no way two of the largest postwar cities in the world are being run by demons."

"My dad was a patriot and an advocate for free access to the true history of the world." Reese clutched his muffin so tightly it crumbled between his fingers. "And at least I know who my dad was."

I was surprised by such a juvenile, spiteful jab from Reese until I saw his face and understood the truth behind his words—he was still mourning his father.

Devi's eyes narrowed, and I spoke before she could return fire. "But if it was the whole Church, wouldn't you guys already know that? I mean, you've been all over the country looking for other exorcists, right?"

No one seemed to have an answer. Finally, Maddock shrugged. "We've been around, and I've seen the occasional demon wearing a police cassock or hospital whites, but I never really thought about it because I've never seen them in large numbers."

"Most of the cassocks we see these days are on TV," Devi added. "And that demonic eye gleam obviously doesn't show through the camera."

And, of course, they'd had to leave their own homes as soon as their exorcist skills—including the ability to identify demons—manifested, just as I would have if not for Melanie.

"Okay, so New Temperance probably isn't the only town being run by the Unclean." Maddock sat on the arm of the couch, from which he could see the rest of us. Except Finn. "So, we have several unanswered questions. First, how many of New Temperance's Church officials have been possessed? Second"—he ticked his points off on the fingers of his left hand—"how many other cities and towns are being run by demons?"

"Third, how the hell did this *happen*?" Devi interrupted. "How can a town's entire governing body—even one as small as this civil infection of a settlement—get possessed without anyone noticing? I mean, it had to start somewhere, right? With one teacher or cop or doctor? I get how Nina didn't notice her mother was a demon, because she'd been a demon all along, but *the deacon*? Are we seriously supposed to believe no one noticed that the deacon of New Temperance was suddenly evil one day?"

Grayson shrugged. "Maybe there wasn't much of a change to notice. Demons killed Nina's mom, and the Church killed Reese's dad. Demons hunted all of us, and now the Church is hunting us. If you think about it, demons and the Church are kind of like matching bookends. They're both cruel and evil and homicidal, and stuck in between them you have—"

"Us," Reese finished for her. "Both us, exorcists, and us, the general public."

Devi looked more bewildered than angry. "So, what do you have when the demons *are* the Church?"

They stared at one another, at the table, and at the ceiling, trying to come up with an answer, but all I could think about was my mother. The demon I'd known all my life, yet had learned nothing from. Even after I'd found out she was Unclean, my mother had spoken in riddles and nonsense, and I could hardly tell one from the other. . . .

And suddenly the answer was there, staring me in the face. *Laughing* in my face.

"New Temperance. That's what you have when the demons *are* the Church."

"What?" Reese frowned.

"Finn's making weird noises," Grayson said. "He's kind of . . . groaning."

Because he'd figured out what I finally understood. What none of the rest of them could see yet.

"You get New Temperance," I repeated. "And Verity. And Constance. And Solace. And Caridad. And every other town that survived the war, if I'm even *close* to right about this. My mom told me, but I didn't listen. I couldn't understand."

"She told you what?" Maddock's brows were furrowed in confusion.

I'd said, *The war is over. We won.*

Yes, we did, she'd answered, and I could still see her smug expression in my mind.

I turned to Devi. "There was no first postwar possession in New Temperance, or anywhere else. No one noticed Church officials suddenly getting possessed, because they *didn't* suddenly get possessed. The demons have been here all along, just like my mom, only on a larger scale. *That's* why they're hunting us. *That's* why their exorcists are fake."

"What the hell is she talking about?" Devi said to Maddock, who was still frowning, and I wondered if Finn was explaining it to him at the same time.

"I'm talking about the war." I stood. I couldn't sit still anymore. "It didn't happen like they say it did. They've been lying all this time, and we've been eating it up like gravy because they look like us and they sound like us and they act like us—at least when people are watching—but they're *not* us. They never were. We were just too stupid to see it."

Devi glanced around the room in exaggerated frustration. "Can someone please translate? I don't speak lunatic."

"Okay." I cleared my throat. "It sounds crazy because it *is* crazy, but that doesn't mean it's not true. Demons didn't lose the war; they just stopped fighting where we could see them. They *became* the people we trusted most—the Church—and told us they could save us. And we believed them. We were scared and desperate and facing the extinction of our species, so we gave them everything we had. We gave them our money, our service, our government, our children, and our freedom, and when the war was 'over,' we celebrated, like *fools*! We praised the Church and pledged our loyalty, and we were *grateful to be alive,* but the joke was on us."

They stared at me, stunned, and I was dimly aware that my voice was gradually rising with every word, but I couldn't make it stop. The dam had broken and the words *would flow.* "The joke is *still* on us. We didn't win the war; we gave away the victory. The Church didn't save us. It *enslaved* us." I gestured frantically to each one of them. To Anathema as a whole. "And they're going to hunt every single one of us down and burn us alive, because we're the only ones who know the truth."

NINETEEN

"I have to get to Melanie." I stood, and Reese stood with me, reaching for a half-packed bag.

"Nina, we have to get out of here," he said as Maddock turned on the television, then muted Brother Jonathan's voice. "With that as the goal, walking into a building full of demons sounds a little counterproductive."

"Oh shit!" Maddock said, and we all turned to see what he was staring at. "According to the headlines, the Church is blaming thirty-eight civilian casualties on us!"

But the degenerates hadn't killed anywhere near that many.

Devi was right. The Church had executed the survivors who'd heard my plea. I'd singlehandedly raised the death toll by at least sixteen.

"Your sister doesn't know the Church is being run by demons, so she's safer than any of us," Reese said gently.

"They just burned Melanie's boyfriend alive. She is *not* safe," I insisted.

"I have to agree with Spawn on this one," Devi said, and I glanced at her in surprise. "They burned the boyfriend for a reason."

"Yeah. He embarrassed the entire town by getting a fifteen-year-old pregnant. Not the kind of press the deacon wanted."

Devi rolled her eyes at Reese. "Seriously? They've just told the world there are demons on the loose, yet they have nothing better to do with the national spotlight than punish a teenager for making a baby without a license?"

"Enlighten us," Maddock said, and I turned to find Finn's green eyes staring out of his best friend's face once again. "We're not all gifted with your insight into the world's spiritual authority."

"What?" I glanced from Finn to Devi, but neither elaborated.

"Devi was raised as an ecclesiastical dedication. Her parents gave her to the Church," Grayson said finally, accepting the packed bag Reese handed her.

"Really?" Other than a soulless death, my worst fear for Melanie's baby was that the Church's price for providing the infant's soul would be both Mellie's and her child's service, for life.

"Yeah, well, the joke was on them." Devi threw her long black braid over one shoulder and sat straighter on the edge of the coffee table, her dark eyes glistening. "I was conceived in sin and chose to honor the lifestyle. But what my unfortunate upbringing has taught me is that the Church does nothing without a reason. They burned Adam to send a message. To Nina. And that message was . . . ?" She turned to me expectantly.

"They're willing to kill people I care about. People who have nothing to do with my being an exorcist. Including Melanie." I sank onto the couch again, weighed down by the grim understanding. "If I don't turn myself in, they'll douse my sister in gasoline and burn her alive on national television."

Reese set his bag next to his feet. "How long do you think she has?"

Devi shrugged. "Another day or so. They have no way of knowing whether or not Nina understood their message—she's not the sharpest knife in the drawer—so I'd guess they'll replay the footage a few times or torch another one of her friends before they trot out the pregnant sister."

Who else could they hurt? Anabelle? Ironically, if she were a demon, she'd probably be safe from their "purifying" flames, but if she was human . . .

"Either way," Devi continued, "I think they'll give you until tomorrow to turn yourself in."

"Good. I'll make my move tonight."

"I'm sorry, Nina." Reese shoved the last two bottles of water into his bag. "I'd help if I could, but I have to get Grayson out of town. She's defenseless until she transitions."

"*If* I transition . . . ," Grayson mumbled, obviously frustrated by her own vulnerability.

"No, I get it," I assured them both, the gears in my head grinding around the beginnings of a risky new jailbreak possibility. "I don't want Gray hurt either, and part of my plan depends on you guys getting out of here—with as much noise and demon bloodshed as possible."

"You're going to use us as a distraction?" Devi sounded impressed, and a tiny flame of pride flickered inside me.

"Yeah. I'm counting on your escape to occupy most of the cops in town—and hopefully *all* the fake exorcists— while I break Mellie out of jail."

"I'm going with you," Finn said, and I smiled, trying not to let him see how relieved I was by the offer.

"Not in Maddy's body, you're not," Devi insisted, and I spoke up before he could argue.

"She's right. And anyway, I need you in your natural state." Finn's brows rose, and my cheeks burned. "I mean, you'll be more help to me if you're not restricted to one body."

"Fair enough." His green-eyed gaze held mine. "So, how do we get out with your sister if we've already spent our distraction getting to her in the first place?"

"I'm kind of hoping you'll be able to open the right doors and push the right buttons when the time comes. I mean, the ordained can't *all* be possessed, right?" But no one seemed to have an answer to that.

"So, when do we go?" Reese was already peeking through the curtains, edgy and on alert.

"We wait until the search dies down and we can get closer to the wall before we're spotted, or until the search comes to our door and we *have* to run," Devi said, headed for one of the bedrooms. "Until then, we rest up for the big moment."

But I was too scared and exhilarated to sleep. While they settled into the bedrooms to nap in pairs, I sank onto the couch alone, staring at the silent headlines scrolling on the TV. I watched misleading footage and read blatant lies.

And I directed all my fear and fury into outlining a plan that would hopefully put us all well beyond the Church's reach. . . .

* * *

"I think you've seen enough of that." Reese dropped onto the couch next to me and plucked the remote from my grip. He turned off the TV and set the controller on the coffee table.

"More than enough," I agreed, studying Finn's latest face. "What about Grayson?"

"Reese convinced her to rest up before tonight and gave

me an hour in the driver's seat." Finn stretched his arms, one of them behind me, as if he were checking the fit of a new shirt.

Maddock and Devi had retreated into the other bedroom, and I was on watch. "Well, I won't turn down the company," I said as Finn leaned down for a kiss. "Mmm . . . ," I murmured when I finally pulled away for a breath. "You taste minty."

"I like brushing my teeth." His grin was all Finn, even with Reese's mouth. "I like having teeth to brush." His thumb rubbed over my knuckles while he examined my eyes. "Still working on the plan?"

"Thinking about after. Assuming we actually make it out with my sister, she'll still be pregnant. In the badlands. There aren't a lot of happy ways for that to play out."

Mellie would carry her baby for at least seven more months. She would feel it kick, and she would deliver it, and she would love it.

Then she would watch it die.

"Unless you happen to have an extra soul in your back pocket," I finished, unable to disguise the grim note in my voice.

"Well, the pants are Reese's, but I doubt it." Finn squeezed my hand. "People die unexpectedly, right? Accidents. Heart attacks. Shot in the chest by an outlaw." I remembered the fake exorcist he'd killed in my living room to protect me. "I mean, look how many people the

Church killed tonight just to protect their secret! So there have to be *some* souls in the well at any given time. Not enough to make the world go round, but maybe enough for one baby born on the run in the badlands without a donor. Right?"

I nodded slowly. "But how do we know there will be at the time her baby's born? How can we know for sure?"

"We can't. Your sister is in the unenviable position of giving birth with no guarantee. Just like women a hundred years ago."

"Okay, but even if she and the baby both survive the delivery, infants are like helpless little police sirens, going off with no warning. Noise attracts degenerates, Finn. Beyond that, he'll need diapers and clothes. And what if he gets sick? We can't—"

Finn laid his finger across my lips. "Yes, there's a lot to figure out. But what's your other option? We'll make it work because we have no other choice. You don't have to do everything on your own. You're not alone anymore, Nina."

His hand moved over my jaw, his fingers sliding slowly into my hair, and I closed my eyes. His mouth met mine again, and this kiss was deeper. Slower. The novel feel and shape of Finn's new lips was more obvious under such thorough attention, and I shoved my reservations away. I'd realized that every physical moment we shared would be precious because it would be short-lived. It would be borrowed.

Finn's existence was a miracle defined by impossibilities, and to be with him, I would not only have to accept those impossibilities, I would have to embrace them.

When he tried to pull away, I slid my hand into his hair, holding him close. I wanted more.

A door flew open in the short hallway and I pulled away from Finn, my cheeks flaming, as if we'd been caught. Devi stormed across the living room, tugging her shirt into place over the waist of her pants. "Someone's outside."

Finn stood, and I stood with him, instantly on edge. "Gotta go." He blinked, and then Reese's brown eyes were back and he glanced around the room in confusion as Grayson and Maddock both emerged from the bedrooms.

"Company," Devi explained, headed for one of the windows. "Reese, whatcha got? Degenerates?"

He stared at the front wall, and I realized he was hearing something from beyond it. "Degenerates don't wear boots," he mumbled on his way across the room.

Devi and I froze when a beam of light flashed through a gap in the drapes, shining in our eyes for a second. Then it was gone.

"What the hell was that?" Grayson stared at the window from the kitchen.

"Boots, flashlights, commands," Reese whispered, rounding the end table. "Could only be cops."

"Or fake exorcists," Grayson said.

Reese pulled the edge of the curtain away from the wall and peeked onto the covered portico shared by our apartment and three others. "This is still the door-to-door. They won't send in the big guns until they've actually found us."

Devi grabbed two knives from the block on the counter.

Someone banged on the door of the apartment next to ours and I jumped. "This is the police. We have reason to believe certain fugitives may be hiding in this area. Open the door so we can search the premises."

A second later, another cop repeated the same speech in front of the apartment across from ours.

"We're next." Reese held up a one-minute finger, still peering through the window. Then he turned, crossed into the dining room in three huge steps, and threw his duffel over one shoulder. "They're all inside. We have to go now, before they come back out."

I took the backpack Grayson handed me. It was light because I'd have to move quickly. "Finn says he'll be right next to you the whole time. He'll open any doors he can."

Devi picked up a pack and her sleeping bag. "We'll ram the gate, then head south and wait for you in Faireview. Do you know it?"

"Yeah. Ghost town about an hour south of New Temperance, not quite halfway to Solace." I'd been there on a field trip once. "I guess I'll have to . . . steal a car?"

"Finn can help with that," Reese said. "Can you drive?"

"I don't have much practice, but yes."

"All right. Now or never." Maddock unlocked the door, weighed down by both a duffel and a pack. Reese peered through the window again, then nodded, and Maddock opened the door.

We filed out one at a time, and as we walked, the cold seeped beneath the hem of my jeans and the cuffs of my coat, raising goose bumps all over my skin. The bitter wind stabbed my cheeks as if it were raining icicles, and the first breath I inhaled nearly froze me from the inside out.

We stepped silently, carefully, as if the sidewalk were rigged to explode upon contact. From inside the adjacent apartment, I heard doors being slammed and furniture being shoved across the floor, and every few seconds a cop shouted, "Clear!" but there were no protests or objections. The neighbors were cooperating, and I couldn't blame them, with Adam's ashes still blowing all over town.

We turned the corner of the building, sticking to the shadows, and my heart thumped harder when I saw two more teams of cops, the ends of their navy cassocks flapping in the cold wind. They had their backs to us, and they turned left into the next section of the complex without seeing us. But there would be more of them. We could hear them all around us, knocking on doors and demanding entry.

"Finn says this way!" Maddock shout-whispered as I fell into line with them. Then he did an about-face and led us back the way we'd come. We tiptoed past the cluster of apartments we'd been staying in, then followed Maddy into the portico of the next bunch just as a man threw open his door and stepped onto a worn welcome mat.

Devi brandished the knife I hadn't realized she was still carrying, and the man gave her a big smile. And winked one bright green eye. Then he tossed a set of keys at Maddock, who caught them.

"Parking spot C40, around the corner and to the right." Then the man stepped back into his apartment and closed the door. And suddenly I understood how Finn could help me steal a car.

"Damn, he's handy!" I whispered to Grayson as we jogged toward the lot as quietly as we could.

"Yeah." Her bright white smile shone in the parking lot lights as we followed Maddock down the center aisle, past mostly empty parking spaces. "He scouted out two of them a few days ago, in case we needed a quick escape."

The vehicle in space C40 was a massive, dented, rusted thing with three rows of seats, a hatchback, and plenty of cargo space in the rear. I couldn't tell what color it was in the yellowish lights, but the paint was dark. Maddock unlocked and opened the cargo area, and everyone threw their bags in, while I clutched the strap of my backpack tighter. Then Maddy slid into the front seat behind the wheel and Devi climbed in next to him while Grayson and Reese piled into the middle row.

"What's your plan for getting through the wall?" I asked.

Maddock met my gaze as he shifted into reverse. "How many guards work the gate at night?"

"Two on a normal night." However, I'd already counted more than a dozen points of light bobbing on the grounds as cops went from door to door looking for us. "But with the town on lockdown, there could be two or three times that."

"We're going to have to climb the wall, aren't we?" Grayson leaned over Reese to stare out at the massive barricade on our left, visible between the buildings.

Devi snorted. "Even if we could get that high with no footholds, the razor wire would shred us like paper."

"No one's ever gone over the wall, that I know of. No one human, anyway." Though that evening's televised massacre had proved that degenerates *could* get through our barrier en masse if they were motivated enough.

"We can't just drive through the gate!" Grayson whispered. "They'll shoot!"

"We'll be fine," Devi said, and I almost choked on shock when I realized she was truly trying to be nice. "Two lanes, one incoming, one outgoing. The guards are armed, but they won't be expecting us to try something so brash. All we have to do is make enough noise to bring everyone running, then head out into the badlands. Grace, you duck down on the floorboard and stay there."

"Don't worry, Nina." Maddock leaned past Devi so he could see me, his hands still clenching the wheel. "We got this. Go get your sister."

I stepped away from the vehicle, and he backed out of the parking space, then burned rubber on his way out of the lot, already drawing attention to give my sister her best shot at survival.

TWENTY

The streets were mostly dark and completely deserted, thanks to the lockdown, but I'd only run a couple of blocks before I heard the first sirens. A second after that, a pair of police cars raced toward me, red and blue lights flashing, and I ducked behind a parked car as they zoomed past, headed toward the town's south gate.

"This is too slow," I whispered, jogging through the shadows. "They'll already be through the gate or captured long before I get to the courthouse." I couldn't see or hear Finn, so I had no idea whether or not he'd heard me, and after spending the last couple of days with Anathema, being alone felt strange.

Lonely.

I'd gone four more blocks, avoiding both gravel and streetlights, when a soft whirring sound made me draw to a skittish stop. I twisted, looking for the source, and froze when a boy on a bicycle turned the corner I'd just passed, pedaling my way.

Heart thumping, I glanced around for somewhere to hide, praying he hadn't seen me. Then he rode through the light from a streetlamp and I realized his chest was bare. As were his feet. He was riding a bike in his pajamas, during a lockdown.

Wait a minute. . . .

"Nina!" the boy shout-whispered, and I exhaled in relief. I was starting to catch on to Finn's MO.

"Where did you get this?" I asked as he rolled the bike to a stop on the shadowed sidewalk next to me, and I wasn't sure if I was asking about the bike or the boy riding it.

"From a house a couple of blocks away. Here." He climbed down and leaned in for a quick kiss with unfamiliar, full lips that were cold from the night air. "Go. I'll catch up after I put him back to bed."

"Thanks. And hurry!" I climbed onto the bike as Finn jogged back the way he'd come, and then I took off on my new wheels.

I flew down darkened streets and through deserted shortcuts, while in the distance, wailing sirens were punctuated by gunshots and shouts. As grateful as I was for the distraction, fear for the other members of Anathema

311

lurked at the back of my mind, eclipsed only by the more immediate fear for my sister as I sped toward her.

The courthouse lawn and town square were abandoned, the building lit only by the normal floodlights, and as far as I could tell in the dark, all signs of the afternoon's massacre had been cleaned up. No blood, no ashes, no bodies. I stopped beneath the awning of a storefront across the street, shrouded in shadows, studying the front of the courthouse, trying to decide where they would keep a teenage prisoner.

The police department was headquartered on the first floor—Finn had been there that afternoon—but I wasn't sure which side of the building it was on. According to Adam's dad, there were additional cells in the basement. I'd always dismissed that claim as paranoia and the product of an active imagination, but considering that the Church was being run by demons, paranoia suddenly seemed like a reasonable state of mind.

I was about to head for the rear of the courthouse when headlights appeared at the end of the street and a car rumbled to a stop in front of the broad steps. A police officer got out of the driver's seat and opened the rear door for a passenger in pale blue fitted robes. Surprise quickened my pulse. Even from a distance, I recognized Anabelle's profile and her pale curls.

What was she doing there? Was she possessed?

No. She *couldn't* be. I'd known her all my life. I would

have noticed a change if she'd been possessed, no matter how skilled an actor the demon was.

They had to know she was my friend. Surely they'd brought her in to help deal with Melanie, or maybe to offer insight about me. Or both.

Or maybe they'd lured her in under some pretense, because Anabelle was to be my next warning—the next friend they'd burn on national television if I didn't turn myself in.

I watched until she and the cop disappeared into the building, and then I circled to the rear of the courthouse, sticking to the shadows, and parked my borrowed bike next to a large, rusted trash bin in the small, cracked parking lot. I'd quietly tried three of the four back exits—they were all locked—when the fourth opened and a police officer leaned out, lights from the parking lot glaring on his fitted navy cassock. He looked to his right, and I froze, certain that trying to open the locked doors had gotten me caught. Then he turned to the left and his eyes widened. "Nina!"

I couldn't see his irises, shaded as they were by the brim of his hat, but the familiarity and relief in the cop's voice told me his eyes were currently Finn-green.

He stepped onto the small concrete porch and wedged a thin pocket flashlight into place to hold the door open about an inch. "They're on high alert inside, thanks to the run on the gate," he whispered. "But almost none of those left in the courthouse are possessed. They're mostly low-level cops and a few clerks, and that's how I figured it out!"

"Figured what out?" I jogged up three short steps and suddenly we were face to face—my normal face to his newly dark, full features, yet another in an endless parade of faces that looked nothing like those that had come before, yet somehow looked exactly like Finn. Like the characteristics I was learning to identify with him specifically, regardless of the body he occupied.

"Only the consecrated Church members are possessed. The demons all wear embroidered robes!" He held out the plain navy sleeve of the cassock he wore, so I could see that it lacked the decorative thread pattern that a consecrated—high-ranking—Church member would have.

"Are you sure?" I ran my fingers over his unadorned sleeve as if touching it would confirm the humanity of the body beneath.

"I haven't seen anything yet to contradict the theory. All the consecrated Church members I saw in there—including several in the jail itself, unfortunately—are possessed."

Relief surged through me. That meant Anabelle was still human—for the next couple of days, at least. Which surely meant she didn't know about the Church elders. If Anabelle knew she was surrounded by demons, it would have taken more than one cop to get her into the courthouse.

"We may have an ally on the inside," I whispered,

and Finn's borrowed brows rose. "They just escorted my friend Anabelle inside. She's a teacher, but unconsecrated. I don't know how many of the lies about me she believes, but there's no way she could look into my sister's eyes and believe Mellie is possessed. If you can get to her, she may be able to help us."

"Okay. But even with your friend, we're short on manpower, so I suggest we proceed with stealth rather than brute force."

"We're not going to need either," I whispered, and his green eyes narrowed. "We're going to walk right in. Congratulations, Officer . . ."—I squinted at the name tag pinned over his chest—"Jennings. You've just captured public enemy number one."

Finn blinked. "You want me to turn you in?" His dark brows furrowed, and I could practically see the objection forming. "What's to keep them from shooting you on sight? They already tried that once."

"They were trying to shut me up. This time I won't give them a reason to. Even if they want me dead"—and I was far from sure about that—"they'll want a public execution, which they can't get until morning."

His jaw tightened. "And after they've interrogated you about the rest of Anathema."

"I suspect they'll call it an interview."

Finn's grim gaze held mine. "It won't be an interview."

"No." It would be torture. That's what demons do. "But

it won't last long. With me in custody, Melanie won't be so closely guarded. You can get her out. With any luck, Anabelle will help."

Finn's eyes narrowed. "I'm not leaving you here."

"Glad to hear it. Did the police costume come with handcuffs?"

Finn started patting down Officer Jennings's cassock. "Try the inside pockets," I said, and he reached into the front of his robe through a fold across his chest and pulled out a bundle of plastic zip ties.

"Even better. Got a knife?"

Another pocket search produced a small multi-tool. A minute later, he'd bound my wrists at my back with the doctored zip ties, and suddenly the reality of what we were about to do hit me. I choked back panic and turned to look up at him, steeling my spine with determination. Necessity. "Get Mellie. No matter what. Get her out, Finn."

"I'll do my best. But I won't leave you here."

"Finn—"

"No. I won't leave you," he said, and I could tell from the look in his eyes that he meant it. The only way for me to guarantee Melanie's survival was to fight for my own.

Committed to the course and running out of time before the fake-exorcist contingent returned from the town gate, we rounded the building again and I clenched my fists at my back to keep them from shaking as "Officer Jennings" marched me through the front door.

Two other cops stood guard just inside, and we'd made it fewer than ten feet across the marble floor of the large, open lobby before one of them shouted for us to halt. "Jennings!"

Finn turned with me slowly, cautiously, his hand on my arm more comfort than restraint, and I wasn't surprised to see both of the other officers aiming guns at me, feet spread in identical "on alert" stances.

"Where . . . ? How did you . . . ?" the older of the two said, and I swallowed my fear along with deep, slow, quiet sips of air. Both of the officers were unconsecrated. They were human. I didn't want to hurt them, but they were clearly willing to hurt me.

When Finn obviously didn't have answers to the questions they couldn't seem to complete, I opened my mouth. "I turned myself in," I said, and both guns swung upward, aiming at my head in sync. "He was the first officer I saw."

The one on the right—his name tag read "Lonnigan"—pulled a radio from the belt around the waist of his cassock and pressed a button. "This is Lonnigan, at the front door. Officer Jennings has just brought in the prime fugitive. Repeat, Jennings has brought in Nina Kane. Over," he added, almost as an afterthought.

The moment he let go of the button, a cacophony of shouts and orders erupted from the radio, and the other cop made some slight correction to his aim. At my head.

A door opened down the hall, and rapid, heavy footsteps clomped toward us. A second later, we were surrounded by armed men in navy cassocks, and my throat suddenly felt as tight as my chest.

"Thank you, Officer Jennings. We'll take her from here."

Finn's hand fell away from me, and another replaced it in a rough grip. Metal clicked all around me as more guns were cocked, and when the new hand turned me, I found myself looking into a face I knew from the news. "Chief Kaughman." My gaze traced the white embroidery climbing the center of his cassock and scrolling around his broad sleeves.

He was possessed.

"Nina Kane. I have to say, I'm surprised to see you here."

"She turned herself in," Officer Lonnigan said, and the chief nodded without even glancing at him.

"And why might she do that?" he said, looking at me even as he directed his question to Lonnigan.

"To give my friends a chance to get away," I said, and surprise flickered behind the chief's eyes. "Did it work?"

When he didn't answer, I knew it had. If the other members of Anathema had been captured or killed, he'd want me to know. He'd want to see my pain as the news sank in.

"Why would a demon protect her friends?" Lonnigan asked at my back, and the chief's eyes narrowed in irritation. "Why would a demon even *have* friends?"

"It wouldn't. It doesn't. Demons cannot feel camaraderie or affection." Chief Kaughman executed an abrupt about-face and made a stiff motion with one hand. "It's lying."

"Or I'm not a demon," I called after him. I turned to glance around at the other officers. "The chief's right about demons being unable to feel affection, so if I'm a demon, why would I voluntarily walk into the courthouse? It couldn't be to help my nonexistent friends escape, and it couldn't be to save a sister I can't possibly care about from purification by holy flames. So why *am* I here? Unless maybe I'm actually human, and the Church has been lying to you all along, about more than you can *possibly* imagine, and you all burned an innocent boy alive this afternoon!" My voice rose with each word until I was practically shouting, and fresh tears filled my eyes with the memory of Adam's merciless, senseless death.

"More demon theatrics. Actors, every one of them. Bring her this way," the chief called, without looking back. "And if she doesn't shut up on her own, shut her up."

A second officer took my other arm, and as I was dragged down the hall after the chief, I glanced around at the men aiming guns at me and was relieved to see that not one of the cops—other than the chief—wore embroidered robes. Anathema's distraction had done exactly what I'd hoped.

The courthouse was vastly understaffed, and almost all the Church members surrounding me were unconsecrated.

As I was hauled through an unmarked open doorway, blinking away my tears, I glanced down the hall toward the front of the courthouse, hoping for one more glance at Finn, but "Officer Jennings" was nowhere to be found.

* * *

The small interrogation room was cold and relentlessly bright, and I could see nothing but the white walls ahead and to my sides, and the white ceiling above me. A door opened at my back, then clicked shut, and the hiss of the heater vents from the hall gave way to stern silence. Footsteps came toward me from behind—two sets. One clicked like heels, and the other clomped like boots, but my ankles had been shackled, then secured to the floor beneath my chair, so I couldn't turn far enough to look.

"Nina Kane." The voice was familiar, but I couldn't place it until the owner stepped into sight on my right and pulled out the chair across the table, tugging down on one green-embroidered sleeve of her gray cassock.

"Deacon Bennett." Fear tightened my throat, and I fought the urge to swallow. I'd seen her face and heard her voice nearly every day of my life. She was a prominent figure at every official ceremony and civic function—the pinnacle of purity, devotion, and unwavering faith. Deacon Bennett was the public face of New Temperance and its highest authority. I'd been taught to respect her—or, at the very least, to fear her—by every news clip I'd ever seen and every word out of every one of my teachers' mouths.

Staring up at the deacon from across the table, even knowing that she was a demon and that she was willing to kill my sister to get to me, for just a second I had to fight an overwhelming urge to look down—or worse, to beg for her forgiveness.

"How thoughtful of you to turn yourself in, Nina," she said, the grave authority in her voice sharply edged with scorn. "I'm so glad for this chance to talk before officials from Umbra come to haul you off."

Officials? From the capitol? I tried to shield surprise and confusion from my expression. "You're not going to . . . deal with me here?" Fortunately, I planned to be long gone with my sister before anyone from Umbra could possibly make it to New Temperance.

"Are we sure she's secure?" Deacon Bennett asked, and whoever was behind me shuffled his feet against the floor.

"Her hands were bound when Jennings brought her in. We added leg shackles, bolted to the floor. Not even a demon in his prime could get out of that chair, Deacon."

Bennett's eyes narrowed. "That's exactly what she is, Officer. Leave us."

The cop's boots clomped behind me, and then the door closed. Deacon Bennett sank into the chair she'd pulled out, and suddenly I was at eye level with the woman—the demon—who ran New Temperance. Who represented my hometown on a national level. Who'd threatened to burn my sister alive.

"You've become a national vexation, Nina Kane. A cankerous sore on the face of this good town." Bennett leaned back in her chair, her embroidered bell sleeves hanging low as she crossed her arms over the front of her cassock. "Perhaps if your assassin playmates hadn't dragged New Temperance into the national spotlight, we could have kept you under wraps, but it's too late for that now, so no, we will not have the pleasure of 'dealing' with you here. Your sister, however . . . She remains under my sole authority."

"She has nothing to do with this. Would I be wasting my breath if I ask you to let her go?"

"Both your breath and my time." Deacon Bennett cleared her throat and sat straighter, as if for an official pronouncement. "After a thorough examination of your sister, the Church has determined that though she is guilty of several very egregious sins, she is not possessed. Naturally, she's eager to demonstrate the purity of her soul, so that there can be no doubt that she was neither involved with nor aware of your demonic exploits."

I understood from her tone and bearing that I was hearing the official statement of my sister's fate, almost exactly as it would be broadcast on the news the next morning.

"Melanie will be joining the Church to atone for her sins. She will make a public pledge in the morning, and we will expedite her ordination, for obvious reasons. She'll be branded before the sun goes down tomorrow night." Bennett's brows rose almost imperceptibly, and she leaned forward a little in her chair. "How soon she is consecrated, however, will depend on what you tell me in the next few minutes."

"And by consecrated, you mean possessed." Was the deacon saying I could delay, but not prevent, my sister's possession? If I stood no chance of protecting Mellie's soul, why on earth would Bennett expect me to cooperate? "We both know you're a demon." I studied her reaction for any sign of surprise. I found none.

"And we both know your mother was a breeder—the cockroach of our species, content to crawl around in the dark rather than commit to the cause and live in the light."

What cause? I frowned, searching for meaning in an unfamiliar phrase. Was she claiming the Church had some higher purpose? Had the demons begun to believe their own propaganda?

"So let's concentrate on what I *don't* know," she continued, while the gears in my head ground conjecture into mental sawdust. "Will your sister be an assassin?"

That was Bennett's second use of the term. "Is that what you call exorcists?"

Her brows rose over cold, dark eyes. "It's what you are."

"Why does it matter whether or not Melanie's an exorcist if you're going to possess her anyway?" Then, suddenly, I understood why my information would only affect *how soon* my sister was possessed.

I was bred to be my mother's next body. She'd specifically sought out an exorcist to be my father so that she would—she'd hoped—give birth to an exorcist, which implied that she'd wanted to possess an exorcist. Presumably because we were stronger and faster than the rest of our species. But only *after* we were triggered.

"If you possess her before she's triggered, she'll never be an exorcist." My guess held the confidence of certainty. "Whoever gets her won't get super speed or strength."

"Nor the ability to burn her enemies from their human husks." Bennett's eyes practically flashed with greed in anticipation of such a skill.

"You want her for yourself, don't you? And I'm guessing Umbra will let you have her if you hand me over peacefully?" Which would mean forgoing my public execution and her chance to show the world that a seventeen-year-old "demon" hadn't gotten the better of the deacon of New Temperance. "But you're only willing to make that deal if Mellie's body will be a step up from what you're wearing now." I glanced pointedly at her aging human shell.

Otherwise, the loss of her position and her power as a deacon would mean little.

"Will she?" The demon leaned forward to study me through narrowed eyes.

"How am I supposed to know that?"

Bennett frowned. "I saw your mother's body. It wouldn't have degenerated so quickly if your genetic gifts had come from her, so they must have come from your father. Your birth certificate names your mother's late husband." She opened the file on the table in front of her and glanced at the first page, then dropped the cover back into place. "Oliver Kane. Melanie's reads the same. But if the late Oliver Kane had been an exorcist, or even a healthy normal man, he probably wouldn't have died of . . ."—Bennett opened the file again, though that was probably just for show—"pneumonia, at the age of twenty-seven. The prevailing theory on your father's death is that your mother poisoned him."

I shrugged, trying to look like I was unaffected by hearing about the murder of one of the few people in the world who'd ever shown me kindness. "Sounds like he got off easy."

"Who was your real father, Nina?" She looked straight into my eyes, and I could practically feel her hunger—for both my soul and my information. "More important, was he Melanie's father as well?"

"Why should I answer that? What's in it for me? Or for Mellie?"

"Nothing." She leaned back in her chair and crossed her arms over her chest again. "Tomorrow you'll be on your way to Umbra, where the prelate will . . . well, he can't exactly *wear* you, after your picture has been all over the news and you've been declared possessed. But I have no doubt he'll find *some* use for you before he sees fit to turn on the camera and light a match. If you hadn't already been sterilized, you might have been able to prolong your life by around nine months so your genetic gift might be passed on. But my point is that your fate is sealed, as is your sister's. Her child, however . . ."

My voice came out low and more threatening than I'd ever heard it. "You're threatening to kill my sister's baby if I don't cooperate?"

"I'm promising to let it live if you do."

"Not good enough. I don't want him raised as a ward of the Church. I don't want him ordained or consecrated. Ever."

Bennett's eyes narrowed and her jaw tightened. "Fine. The baby will be sent to a children's home somewhere outside of New Temperance."

I studied her face for one long moment. Then I listened to my gut. "You're lying. If Melanie's an exorcist, her child might be too, and you won't lose him. Which means I have no reason to answer your question."

Bennett leaned back in her chair. Then she smiled slowly, an expression absent of warmth. "It was worth a shot." She shrugged, and the gesture looked foreign and careless on a body I'd never once seen cast off the restraints of authority and formality. "We are a patient species. We'll lock her in a cell for two years and see for ourselves."

"But you have to make a deal with Umbra *now,* don't you?" Long before she would know whether or not Melanie was an exorcist.

The demon's scowl was as good as an answer. "If you're not going to cooperate, I have only one more question: Why did you turn yourself in, Nina Kane?"

"I came for my sister." I gave her a shrug to hide the fact that I was twisting my hands behind my back, tugging on the restraints Finn had already weakened with his borrowed knife. "But before I go, I think I'll make time to kill you."

"Foolish child." The deacon shook her head slowly, like an instructor disappointed by ignorance. "I cannot die. With or without this body, and this world, and your arrogant ambition, I can never die, just as I was never born." She stood, her eyes glinting with demonic light, and I twisted my hands faster, harder, as her speech became more formal, her posture more dignified. "My native language has no word for youth, because in our native realm we have not your cycle of birth and death, nor the waxing and waning of seasons, nor even the concepts of growth and decline. There are no more and no fewer of us now than there have ever been or will ever be, and that unchanging number is sufficient to swallow your world whole, ten times over." The deacon glared down at me, and I made my hands go still so she could not notice my efforts. "We are both eternal and unchanging, and your simplistic human languages—all of them—lack the vocabulary necessary to express the tedium of millennia spent in stasis."

"Poetry, every word," I said, and her flashing eyes narrowed even further. "But even if I can't kill you, I can send you back to the hell you—"

A knock interrupted my threat, and I groaned when a door opened at my back, halting my progress on the zip ties. "Deacon, reports are coming in from the south gate."

Bennett circled me, headed for the hall. "Send Chief Kaughman in to watch her."

The door closed, and I had less than a minute to twist my plastic bindings before it opened again, and Chief Kaughman settled into the chair across from mine. "Well, well, little girl. Looks like you're in over your head." His eyes shone, and his lips turned up in a leering grin.

I gave my hands one last, fierce twist, and the plastic snapped. I lunged across the table, my left hand already ablaze. Shackles bit into my ankles. The table slid beneath my weight.

Kaughman's eyes widened. He stood and backed into his own chair. Then my glowing palm slammed into the police chief's chest.

TWENTY-ONE

Smoke curled from the smoldering cotton beneath my hand, and meaningless, pain-filled syllables dripped from the chief's lips as he hung from the bright force burning between us. His navy cap hit the table, then rolled onto the concrete. Seconds later, the light faded from my hand and I had to grab the front of his cassock to keep him from sliding to the floor. I laid Chief Kaughman across the table between us, facedown, then scrambled to search every pocket I could reach. The third held a set of keys.

My pounding heart counted the seconds ticking away while I squatted to try the keys in my shackles. When the fourth one slid home, I grabbed the chief's gun—careful to keep my hands off the trigger—and examined it, wishing

I knew how to check the clip. Or enable the safety. Or do anything with it other than aim and pull the trigger.

With my right hand wielding the gun and my left ready to ignite, I opened the door just enough to peek into the hall.

It was empty.

I tiptoed past several empty interrogation rooms, then peeked around a corner before silently searching another empty hallway. Anathema's run on the south gate had diverted most police and fake-exorcist manpower from the courthouse, but one corner and another hallway later, I heard the echo of voices headed toward me.

Panicked, I ducked into the nearest room—an office lit only by a desk lamp—and flattened my back against the wall by the door until the voices passed. When I was sure they were gone, I rounded the desk and rummaged through the drawers, hoping to find more bullets for my stolen gun, or some clue as to where they might be keeping my sister, but I came up empty. I was about to resume my search for Melanie when the title of a document lying open on the desk caught my attention: "Annual Loss Report."

"The insurrectionist Kastor continues to raid Church assets, leading to losses in excess of fifteen percent of the potential hosts. At the current rate of loss, Kastor's strength will exceed ours within the decade. The most vulnerable point of attack remains the consecration caravan. The most notable loss was the assassin Carey James. Recommendations for future confrontations include . . ."

Carey James. Grayson's brother.

If I understood what I'd read, the Church had taken Carey, but lost him in a caravan raid by an "insurrectionist" named Kastor.

Was Kastor an exorcist? Was he raising an army in opposition to the Church?

A bolt of excitement set my nerve endings on fire, but a second later logic doused the flames. If Kastor was an exorcist, why was he referred to as an insurrectionist rather than as an assassin? And if he *wasn't* an exorcist, why was he stealing "hosts" from the Church?

Armed with more questions than answers, I folded the paper and stuffed it into my back pocket, then grabbed the chief's gun and headed back into the hall. Three hallways and two hiding spots later, loud voices from the glass-walled office ahead and to my right told me I'd found the center of activity.

For a couple of minutes, I listened with my back pressed against a wall out of sight, trying to identify the speakers over the pounding of my own heart in my ears. But none of the voices was familiar, and their chatter was largely useless and self-congratulatory—as if they'd played some part in capturing me, when in truth, I'd surrendered.

Then someone asked for an update on the fight at the south gate, and my ears pricked up.

Two members of Anathema had been injured, another voice announced, but all had made it through the south gate and into the badlands, where they were currently being pursued by a full contingent of "exorcists."

I listened, hoping for more details about the injuries, but none came.

With a bolt of trepidation, I realized that my time was up. The police would resecure the gate, then head back to the courthouse, and they'd move quickly once they heard about the chief's death and my escape.

I peeked through the glass and counted the robed figures. Three gray. Four navy. One of each embroidered.

Four cops and three politicians, and all but two were human. Unfortunately, the demon in gray was Deacon Bennett.

Surely I could take on two demons by myself. But that left five humans, probably as dedicated to the Church as Anabelle was and as ignorant of its true nature as I'd been three days before. I'd never fired a gun and wasn't sure I actually knew how. But even if I figured it out, I wasn't willing to shoot a human unless he came between me and my sister.

Unfortunately, at the moment, that was exactly where the humans were standing, at least figuratively.

I sucked in a deep breath, steeling my nerves. Steadying my hands. I could think of only one way to avoid having to shoot anyone. One way that Melanie, Finn, and I could all emerge intact. So I double-checked the safety on the gun and slid it into my waistband, then waited until the consecrated cop stood with his back to the glass door.

When he was as close as I could expect him to come, I

shoved the door open and pressed my glowing left hand to the center of the possessed cop's back.

Air hissed as he inhaled sharply, and everyone turned to look.

The human politicians gasped, and all three of the human cops drew guns with barrels that looked stretched because of the built-in noise suppressors. But the demon that hung from the fire in my palm could only convulse as his life force was burned from his stolen body. In front of a live audience.

"Shoot to wound!" Deacon Bennett shouted, and as flames devoured my hand, I looked over the frying monster's shoulder to see the demonic politician staring at me in mounting fury.

The cops blinked, obviously unwilling to look away from the threat—me. "What's she doing? What's happening?" the one on the left demanded, and every human in the room looked tense and near panic while they waited for the answer. That was when I realized they could see the glow. The flames from my hand were shining *all the way through* the consecrated cop hanging from my palm.

"Aim for her leg!" Bennett ordered.

"I'm doing my job!" I had to shout to be heard as I answered the question the deacon had ignored. "He's possessed. I'm an exorcist. This is what a real exorcism looks like." I paused to let that sink in, hoping that seeing really was believing. "This is the *real* purifying flame!"

For a moment, silence reigned, except for the soft crackle

of the demon's skin and clothes. Then the glow began to fade from my hand, and the dead cop thunked to the floor at my feet. Everyone stared at me, guns raised, eyes wide. Two jaws hung open. I searched their expressions for disbelief, but found only utter shock—the inevitable result of a brutal awakening.

I kept my arm extended, fingers spread, so they could see the last of the light—the reflection of my soul—as it receded into me.

"Any questions?"

For a moment, no one spoke. No one moved. Then one of the cops cleared his throat. "Captain Mitchell was possessed?" His focus dropped to the body still smoking at my feet, then quickly found my face again.

"Yes. As is *every single consecrated member of the Unified Church.*"

"She's lying," Bennett said. "She's not an exorcist, she's a demon, and she just killed an innocent man with some kind of demonic power!"

"Deacon Bennett is possessed." I said it softly. Clearly. "Her sleeves are embroidered, her body is occupied, and her soul is being devoured as we speak. The demon inside her is scared, and it will say anything to protect itself."

"Lies!" Bennett hissed. "*She* is the only demon here. The Church has declared her anathema. Shoot her in the leg!" When no one obeyed, the deacon turned on them in fury. "It is your sacred duty to follow my orders!"

I spread my arms slowly to keep from startling the men

with guns, and my heart raced as I invited them to aim for my chest. "If you're going to shoot me, why not just kill me?"

Two of the three adjusted their aim, pointing their guns at my heart. The third aimed at my head, while my pulse pounded in my throat.

"No!" Bennett shouted. "Wait for the exorcists. If you kill her, you'll release the demon."

All three lowered their aim, and I swallowed a groan. She was using the facts against me, and suddenly I realized she'd probably been manipulating people with their own beliefs since long before my grandparents were even born. I couldn't convince my fellow humans that their revered leader was a demon. I would have to show them the truth—I would have to make *her* show them.

I took another deep breath and thought of Mellie, bound to the concrete on her knees, hungry and terrified. Then I lunged at the cop closest to the deacon.

His eyes went wide and he raised his aim. Bennett let loose an inhuman roar and sprang at him, blurring across my vision in order to protect me, because she couldn't deliver a dead exorcist to Umbra. I'd expected her to snatch his gun with demonic speed and strength, but the reality was much more violent.

Blood arced over the front of my coat, spraying my chin with warm droplets. My focus dulled beneath a red haze and I froze, stunned.

Gasps echoed all around me. I blinked blood from my

eyes, and Bennett's form came into focus, bent over a body on the ground. Blood pooled beneath her, flowing around the soles of her shoes, soaking into the tails of her cassock. She looked up at me and hissed like an angry cat, but I hardly saw the lips curled back from her teeth or the inhuman gleam in her eyes.

I could only look at the man I'd just sacrificed to expose the deacon. He lay dead on the ground, blood still pouring through the gaping hole in his throat. He'd died so fast he never had a chance to drop his gun.

I reached for Bennett, my hand already glowing, but before I could make contact, guns *thwuped* from my left—one, two, three, four shots—and I flinched with each one.

Bennett convulsed with the impacts, then fell over dead.

"No!" I shouted.

My ears rang with the echo of suppressed gunfire, and the bright light faded from my hand. I blinked again, trying to make sense of the past two minutes, but the only things I was sure of were that I was still breathing and that Deacon Bennett was dead.

Well, evicted from her body, at least. The demon itself could be anywhere, in search of a new host.

I stared at the corpse, horrified to realize I'd lost the chance to exorcise the highest-ranking demon in New Temperance. To send the biggest threat to my sister's safety back to the hell from which she'd sprung.

"She killed him," one of the politicians muttered, wiping

blood from the back of his hand onto his plain gray cassock, and I finally recognized him as one of Bennett's clerks—I'd seen him standing behind her during several recent press conferences.

"She wasn't a she." I grabbed a tissue from a box on the unmanned receptionist's desk to my right and finally realized I was in the front lobby of the police station. "She was a demon."

"And you're . . . ?" The third cop still had his gun aimed at Bennett's lifeless body, as if she might come back to life at any moment.

"An exorcist." I wiped my face with the tissue, and it came away smeared with blood. "A *real* exorcist. I'm human, and so is my sister. If you don't help me get her out of here, they'll kill her." That wasn't exactly true, but I didn't have time to explain the Church's entire nefarious plot to a bunch of traumatized civilians.

And that was when I realized I no longer thought of myself as one of them.

They were citizens.

I was a soldier.

I glanced around at the handful of survivors and finally settled on the second cop—the one who'd holstered his weapon. His name tag read "Flores," and he was the only one who didn't look ready to either vomit or cry. "Take me to her. Help me get her out. Please."

"I . . ." Flores blinked.

"Listen to me. My friends and I are the only things standing between you and a horde of demons hidden in plain sight." I pointed at Bennett's corpse for emphasis, acutely aware that I'd failed to vanquish that particular demon. "Do your part. Help me get my sister so I can go back to trying to save what's left of humanity."

He nodded once, hesitantly. Than again, more firmly.

"What about us? What about . . ." The other clerk hesitated, his focus skipping between the two dead demons. "What about *them*?" He turned to me, clutching the sides of his own plain cassock. "What about the rest of them? *All* the consecrated are possessed? How is that even possible? How do you know? How can you be *sure*?"

"I know it's a lot to take in, and I don't really know how to help you with that." I could only imagine how much worse the shock and betrayal must feel for someone who'd unknowingly committed his life—not to mention his soul—to a Church run by monsters. "What I *can* tell you is that if they find out what you know, they'll kill you. Or possess you. Your best bet is to pretend you don't know anything about the consecrated or about what happened here. And put off your own consecration as long as you can." I shrugged, already heading toward the hallway on the opposite side of the room. "If that doesn't work . . . run. At least in the badlands you know who the monsters are." Because they were rotting, drooling savages.

I turned back to Flores. "Let's go."

As he led me down deserted, labyrinthine halls, seemingly designed to confuse and disorient, Officer Flores pelted me with whispered questions about the secret demon occupation, and I answered as best I could.

"No, we don't think it's limited to New Temperance."

"Yes, we think they've been here all along."

"Yes, if you stay here, you will eventually be possessed. That's the only reason they've kept us alive this long."

When I got tired of answering and afraid of being caught, I grabbed his arm and pulled him to a halt. "The more you understand, the more danger you're in." I stared right into his eyes, letting him see the grave warning in mine. "You need to focus on feigning ignorance, or they will light you on fire on live television, just like they did to Adam Yung."

"He was innocent," Flores whispered, his voice half choked with horror.

I could only nod, my jaw clenched in some toxic combination of grief and rage. Then I waved toward the hallway, urging him on. "Do you have a car?"

He dug in an inner pocket of his cassock without slowing, then handed me a set of keys. "East parking lot, third row. I'll tell them you stole the keys." He stopped in front of an unmarked metal door and pulled another set of keys from another pocket. "Your sister's in here, but she has a visitor. Someone they brought in to get her to talk. They've had her on her knees for days, but she hasn't told them anything. She's in rough shape. Strong kid, though."

My heart ached. *Mellie shouldn't need to be that strong.*

Flores unlocked the door, then opened it, but he didn't put away his keys. The room beyond was actually two rows of steel-barred cells divided by a wide aisle. All the cells were empty except the one at the end on the left, outside of which stood a woman in a pale blue cassock and a cop frantically sorting through the keys on his metal ring.

"Anabelle!" I whispered, and she and the cop both turned. I couldn't see his eyes, but I recognized Officer Jennings, and the fact that he hadn't pulled his gun told me Finn was still in residence.

"Nina!" Anabelle's gaze slid from me to the cop behind me, and when she was sure he wasn't going to prevent our reunion, she raced down the aisle toward me and nearly bowled me over with her hug. "Officer Jennings said you're innocent."

Officer Jennings obviously hadn't mentioned that he wasn't himself at the moment—not that we had time for such a complicated explanation.

Anabelle pulled away from me and stared straight into my eyes as if she could verify my humanity at a glance. "You're still you, right?"

"Yes, and Mellie's still herself. It was all a lie, Anabelle. *So* many lies, the whole time, and we never saw it. My mom was a demon. She was never sick or high, she was *possessed*, right under our noses."

Anabelle's forehead furrowed. "Since when? How is that possible?"

"Since forever. Since before I was born." Seconds ticked away in my head, and I knew we were running out of time, but I needed Anabelle to understand, and I needed to keep her safe, somehow. I couldn't let the Church claim her soul. "I didn't know the truth about myself until I exorcised her—"

"You—" Her eyes widened.

"I'm an exorcist. The Church said I killed my mom because they can't afford for anyone to find out the truth, but I'm innocent, and Adam was innocent, and Melanie is damn well innocent." I glanced at Finn over her shoulder. "Speaking of which, where do we stand on the jailbreak?"

"I can't find the right key," he said, frustration echoing in his deep, borrowed voice.

"Let me." Officer Flores pushed past me, already flipping through the keys on his own ring as he marched down the aisle. Finn stepped aside to give him access to the cell door, and that was when I saw my sister. Melanie was lying facedown on the floor of her cell, her legs still pinned to the floor by steel bands bolted to the concrete just below her knees.

She wasn't moving.

TWENTY-TWO

"Melanie!" I raced down the aisle and gripped the bars of her cell with both hands while Flores unlocked the door. As soon as it swung open, I fell to my knees at her side and brushed limp, pale hair from her face. "Unlock her legs," I demanded, but Flores was already squatting next to me, searching for another key. "Mellie," I whispered into her ear. "Wake up. It's Nina. I came to rescue you, and that'll be a lot easier if you can walk."

Her eyes rolled behind their lids; then those lids fluttered open, and I exhaled.

"Nina?" My sister's voice was dry and hoarse, but she was awake and she recognized me.

"Yes. I'm here." I blinked away fresh tears. "Hold still for just a minute while we get you unlocked."

"Finn." I twisted to whisper into his ear while I smoothed Melanie's hair back. "Bennett was disembodied a few minutes ago."

His eyes widened and he glanced at my sister, then back at me. "You want me to make sure Mellie's . . . still in there?"

"Will you have to let go of Jennings to do that?"

"No, I should be able to sort of . . . push her, mentally. If there's give she's fine. If not, she's possessed," he whispered.

"Do it."

While Flores unlocked, then flipped back, the steel bands that had bound my sister into the posture of penitence until she'd lost consciousness, Finn closed his eyes. A second later, he opened them, and I saw his relief even before I heard it in his voice. "It's her. She's fine."

Tension eased within me—my unconscious sister would have been an easy and convenient target for the newly disembodied deacon. "Thanks," I said to Finn. Then I turned back to my sister. "Let's get you up slowly. Can you stand?"

"I think so," Mellie said. I helped her carefully to her feet and kept one arm around her while she stepped over the restraints bolted to the concrete floor. "Yeah. I'm tired, but I can walk."

Anabelle slid her arm around Melanie's other side and Mellie looked surprised to see her. "It was all a lie, Ana. Mom was the demon, not Nina, and—"

"I know." Anabelle smiled. "I'm not sure I understand it all yet, but I know," she said as we helped my sister out of the cell.

"You need to get going," Flores said. "Take a left into the hall, then two rights and another left. That'll put you in the parking lot. But you're on your own from there."

"Thank you, Officer Flores." I glanced back at him over my shoulder on our way down the aisle. "Be careful."

He nodded, and we left him in that room full of empty cells, clearly trying to decide how best to proceed, armed with knowledge that could get him killed.

We took a left turn and two rights and were halfway to that last hallway when a soft *thwup* from a room ahead and to my right drew me to a silent stop in the middle of the hall. Something growled—a thick, guttural sound—and then I heard the distinct, grisly tearing of flesh.

Chills shot up my spine.

"Shit," Finn whispered with Officer Jennings's voice as my heart began to pound deep within my chest.

I'd just recognized the room ahead as the police station lobby—where I'd exorcised a demon a quarter hour earlier—when a man in an unembroidered navy cassock stepped into the doorway, one hand pressed to a wound in his chest. Blood seeped between his fingers, and his face was already pale. His focus found me without even veering toward Finn, Melanie, or Anabelle.

"You killed them," the man said, and before I could

object or ask who I'd killed, he spoke again, a thin line of blood leaking from one corner of his mouth. "You killed them all with that little demonstration. You killed them the moment you opened your mouth."

And finally I understood. "Deacon Bennett?"

"Nina . . ." Terror and confusion rang in Melanie's voice.

"Deacon Bennett was a demon," I explained, without taking my eyes from the monster. "She lost her host, but now she's found a new one." And she'd slaughtered everyone I'd left alive in the lobby. Because I'd told them the truth.

Anabelle's breathing quickened and Finn tensed at my side. "Nina," he said. Time was running out. We needed to make a move. He was looking to me for a signal.

"Bennett is gone," the possessed cop said, still clutching his chest wound. "Half a human-lifetime spent elevating myself in her skin, campaigning for deacon, and some snot-nosed assassin *child* ends the whole thing in five minutes." He gasped, and when more blood dribbled down his chin, I realized Bennett's new body was dying. Soon the demon would be free to search for another host. And again, I would lose the opportunity to purge the monster from our world and send it back to hell.

My left hand began to tingle, and I slid it behind my thigh, letting the heat build, hidden by my body. I was about to lunge for Bennett's new host when the demon spoke again, and I froze, caught on his words like a fly in a web.

"I hope Kastor gets his hands on you."

I blinked, and my eyes narrowed at him in surprise. If Kastor was an enemy of the Church—a thief of hosts—why would she hope he got his hands on me?

"Kastor?" Finn said, and I thought I heard something strange in the question, but maybe I just wasn't used to his new voice yet.

"Who's Kastor?" Anabelle said, and the name trembled on her tongue.

The demon gave us a bloody smile, eyes glinting with an inhuman shine. "Kastor is the boogeyman. You think humanity has reason to fear the Church?" he demanded, his voice filled with pain, yet somehow still menacing.

We had *every* reason to fear the Church—the room full of bodies to Bennett's right was proof enough of that.

The demon read my reply in my expression, then snorted in derision. "Your fear is *wasted* on us, child. If Kastor rises, the Church will fall, and humanity will not be long for this world."

"You believe your own propaganda now? The Church isn't saving us—it's leading us to the slaughter."

Bennett's new pain-glazed, contemptuous stare focused on me. "A farmer slaughters his cattle because he must eat to survive, but he also protects the herd from thieves and predators. If you leave the pen, the wolves *will* find you, child."

"So Kastor is a wolf now? I thought he was the boogey-man." Was this a distraction? Was her plan to keep us talking until reinforcements arrived?

"Kastor is destruction beyond what you can imagine. He and his libertines will devour the human race whole, and our kind will be stuck in hell once again, crawling over one another in the dark for untold millennia, until the next species creeps from the primordial ooze and evolves into something we can work with." The demon's body seemed to deflate as blood continued to leak from it. "Have you *any* idea how many eons we've wasted in pre-vious cycles, thanks to gluttons like Kastor?"

Eons? Cycles?

"Yes, Kastor is the wolf," he continued. "And you are the sheep, and by the time he's done playing with his food, you'll wish you'd died alongside Adam Yung, devoured by merciful flames."

The jump in my pulse was part fury, part terror. I held up my glowing left hand and stepped forward. The demon pulled a gun from behind his back and aimed at Anabelle.

Before I could even process the threat or its purpose, Finn tackled Anabelle and Melanie, temporarily taking my sister and my friend out of the line of fire. "Get him!" Finn shouted.

I lunged for the former deacon, my left hand ablaze, but the demon was faster, even in the new, dying body. He pressed the barrel against his temple.

"No!" I shouted.

Bennett pulled the trigger. Blood and liquefied brains exploded into the lobby from the hallway, and I caught a brief glimpse of the carnage already laid out inside.

"Damn it!" I backed away from the body, turning to put the massacre in the lobby at my back, clutching my own stomach in horror as more tears filled my eyes.

Bennett was beyond my reach, no doubt already searching for a fresh body. I might never know whether she found one or got sucked back into hell for want of a host.

But there was no time to mourn the lost opportunity.

"Nina, we have to go," Finn said, and I turned to find him pulling my shocked sister to her feet. Anabelle sat blinking and stunned on the floor, leaning against the wall. "With any luck, the cops are headed back here from the gate."

And with that reversal in the concentration of security, we might just make it out of town alive.

"Come on!" I hauled Anabelle up with one hand, digging Flores's keys from my pocket with the other. "Are you okay?"

"I will be," Anabelle said, one hand on the wall for balance, while she avoided looking at all the blood. "I just can't believe she was a demon, hidden right in front of us."

"She's not the only one. Anyone wearing embroidered sleeves is possessed, Ana."

Anabelle blinked at me, visibly struggling to process

that new information—and the fact that she'd been days from consecration herself. But we were out of time. She'd have to process on the run.

"What about you?" I asked, turning to Melanie. "You okay?"

"I think so," she said, staring at the body on the floor. "Still tired and thirsty, though." And obviously in shock over everything she'd seen and heard in the past ten minutes.

"You can hydrate in the car. Let's go." We raced down the hall with Mellie half supported by Anabelle and Finn, and took the last corner so hard and fast I almost slammed into the wall. The parking lot was ahead, past a single glass door, and through the tall pane I saw red and blue lights flashing in the distance. In the direction of the south gate.

I pressed the bar on the door, and we burst out of the building, every breath puffing in front of our faces as we ran past the sparsely populated first and second rows, headed straight for the only car in the third. I shoved the key into its slot and twisted, and the car gave a soft thump as all four doors unlocked. We piled in, sirens growing louder in the distance as the colored lights flashed faster and brighter, and my heartbeat raced to match the pace.

Finn sat up front with me and I started the engine as Anabelle slammed her rear door. I shifted into reverse and backed out of the parking spot, thankful that it was too early in the season for snow and ice. Finn twisted to stare out the rear windshield as I pulled out of the lot and onto a back street, determined to take the longer but less visible path to the town gate.

"What's the plan?" Anabelle whispered, and in the rearview mirror, I saw her wrap one arm around Melanie.

"Some friends—fellow exorcists—are waiting for us between here and Solace." Assuming they'd shaken the fake exorcists pursuing them.

"You're an exorcist?" Mellie's eyes looked huge in the mirror. "You exorcised Mom?" she asked, obviously putting the pieces together, and I nodded. "Is Officer Jennings an exorcist too?"

"No." He twisted to look at her. "My real name is Finn, and I don't always look like this," he said, and when she started to ask another question, he shook his head. "It's complicated, but I promise I'll explain everything once we're out of town. For now, we need to be quiet."

We rolled down darkened streets with the headlights off, pulling into alleys and onto dark shoulders whenever another vehicle approached. I turned left a block from the wall so we could approach the gate head-on, and for several moments I let the car roll slowly forward, still unnoticed, while we evaluated the situation.

"I only see two guards," Finn said. "They must still think you're in custody at the courthouse."

"There will be more patrolling the perimeter," Anabelle said.

"We have to go now, before the patrol brings them close

to the gate." I slowed to a quiet stop in the middle of the dark street. "But Finn will have to drive, with Anabelle up front. They'll recognize me and Mellie."

After a moment of hesitation, Anabelle nodded. I put the car in park, then crawled into the backseat with Melanie while Finn slid into position behind the wheel and Anabelle buckled herself in next to him. He pushed back the sleeves of his police cassock, then shifted into drive and took his foot off the break. Mellie and I huddled on the rear floorboard, our heads pressed together, trying to see through the windshield between the front seats.

My heart thumped so hard my rib cage felt bruised as our stolen car slowly approached the wall I'd been trapped behind nearly every day of my life. The wheels rolled over the first speed bump, and Anabelle flinched. Her teeth chattered, a nervous habit certain to catch the guard's attention.

"Stop!" someone shouted, and I ducked even lower, fear crawling like tiny bugs beneath my skin. "Gate's closed," that same voice yelled. "Town's on lockdown. Don't you watch the news?"

We were completely shrouded in shadow, and I couldn't stand not knowing, so I peeked between the seats, nerves skittering along my spine. We were about twenty feet from the actual gate, a large steel panel mounted on wheels in a sunken track. Two police officers manned the gate itself, and four we hadn't seen—three men, one woman—were marching toward us in unembroidered navy cassocks, their cheeks red from the cold, their swaggers inflated by an uncommon measure of authority.

Yes, they'd just lost a confrontation with the rest of Anathema, but as far as they knew, the demon Nina Kane had been captured, and the guards obviously thought they were the only force standing between the good citizens of New Temperance and mass slaughter by degenerate hordes from the badlands.

I wanted to laugh at them. But I also pitied them. They were human, and they had no idea what was really going on. They looked simultaneously thrilled and terrified by the prospect of actually shooting a degenerate, and if they failed to stop me from leaving the town, they would likely pay with their lives.

Or at least with their bodies and souls.

There was a soft grinding sound as Finn cranked his window down, the car still rolling forward slowly, and then a frigid draft raised goose bumps all over me.

"Hey!" The guard's voice was sharper and louder with the window open. "Didn't you hear me? No one leaves tonight!" The shouter and his colleagues were almost to our car now, and if they shone a flashlight into the backseat, we were screwed. "Jennings, is that you?"

"Yeah." He stuck his head out the window. "Police business."

"Where's your car?" the guard asked, with another glance at the hood of our stolen vehicle.

Finn turned to Anabelle and whispered, "When I get out, slide behind the wheel and lock your door."

"What? Why?" she demanded in a fierce whisper, but he rolled up his window and got out of the car without answering. Anabelle slid into the driver's seat and locked the door as Finn waved the guard closer, as if for a private conversation. Then, suddenly, he went stiff, and I realized Finn had just abandoned Officer Jennings's body.

"Carter?" Jennings said, glancing around at the gate and the wall, and I could hear confusion in his voice, even through the glass.

"Oh shit, did you guys see that?" the guard to the right of the gate shouted, large automatic rifle aimed to his left along the wall. "Degenerates! Three of the bastards just jumped right over the barbed wire!"

My pulse raced.

Anabelle shifted into drive.

"Are you sure?" one of the other guards called. "I didn't see anything." No one was looking at us anymore. They were staring into the dark now, guns aimed at something they couldn't see.

That was when I realized Finn had stepped into the body of the guard who'd reported the wall breach. He was creating a distraction. Giving us a chance.

"Of course I'm sure! Go!" Finn-the-guard shouted. "We'll handle this," he added, and I peeked again in time to see him wave one hand at our car. The four guards closest to us hesitated for just a second, then took off into the dark after the imaginary monsters.

"What the hell is going on?" Jennings demanded, but there was no one left to answer.

"Nina . . . ?" Anabelle said, when he turned toward us with no sign of recognition.

"I'll explain in a minute. Drive. Slowly."

Finn waved us forward, and as our car rolled toward the gate, he ducked into the guard booth and pressed a button. Metal squealed, and the gate began rolling to the right.

The remaining guard glanced from Anabelle in the car to Finn in the guard booth. He lifted his gun—an unaimed precaution—and stepped into our path, still scowling at Finn. "What are you—"

"Get out of the way." Finn's borrowed voice was soft, but the command was strong.

"Turn off the engine and get out of the car!" The guard swung his huge gun toward our windshield. Jennings stared, still too confused to take action.

Anabelle stomped on the brakes hard enough to throw Melanie and me into the backs of the front seats, even at our low speed.

"Let her through!" Finn shouted as the gate rolled open slowly, like a huge metal snail in its track.

The guard's eyes widened, and we were close enough by then that I saw comprehension the moment it surfaced behind his eyes. He'd just spotted me between the seats, and even if he couldn't see my face, he knew we were hiding something.

The guard aimed. Anabelle ducked as light flashed and thunder exploded from the end of the rifle. A small hole appeared in the front windshield an instant before something thunked into the seat in front of me. Anabelle screamed. Melanie curled up on the floorboard, and I shielded as much of her as I could with my own body.

"Shhh," I whispered. "Be quiet and don't move." She tensed beneath me but didn't make a sound.

"Out, now!" the guard shouted, and I peeked again to find him still aiming at the windshield.

Finn fired his gun. "Go!" he yelled as the guard's body crumpled in front of our car.

Shouts came from our right as the rest of the cops were recalled from their wild goose chase by the gunfire. Anabelle sat up and stared at the hole in the windshield, and I noticed that the glass around it was cracked like a spiderweb. "What the *hell* is happening?" she demanded.

Jennings reached for his holster, and I realized that Finn had removed the gun before he'd given up the body.

"Anabelle, go!" I shouldered the back of her seat. "Drive!"

She stepped on the gas. The car bounced once, then twice, jarring us all as the wheels rolled over the fallen guard.

The gate was still moving, but it was too slow. It wouldn't

be open in time. Finn punched the button through the open window in the guard's shack, but the gate gained no speed.

"Who is that?" Anabelle asked, staring at him as she clutched the wheel.

"It's Finn," I told her. The explanation would have to wait.

"Go!" Finn shouted again, and Anabelle stomped on the gas again. The car lurched forward, and I fell against the rear bench seat. We flew past the guard shack as Finn took aim at another one of the guards. Light flashed from the barrel of his gun.

The gate knocked off the passenger's side-view mirror, then scraped the entire length of the vehicle on the right side as we breached the New Temperance town wall and shot out into the badlands.

Anabelle took a hard right just outside the gate, and I tumbled across the floorboard onto my sister. "Mellie, are you okay?" I asked, lifting myself off her with one hand on the seat.

"Fine," she said, as I crawled onto the backseat, trying to get a good look at her as the lights from the gate faded. "But totally lost. What happened to Finn?"

More gunfire rang out from behind the wall, and I caught my breath. Was Finn shooting, or being shot at?

"Finn's human, but he can possess people like a demon," I explained. Both Mellie and Anabelle started to throw questions at me, but I held up one hand to stop them. "For now, you'll have to trust me."

When the squeal of metal told me the gate was closing behind us, I stood on my knees to stare through the window. The gate was almost shut, trapping the guards inside until they could reverse the motor, and I still saw no sign of Finn.

"Anabelle, stop!" I shouted.

She slammed on the brakes. The car skidded on bare dirt and chunks of asphalt from the crumbling road. For several tense seconds, I stared at the gate as the opening narrowed, waiting for Finn even though I might not be able to see or hear him coming. I couldn't leave him. But we couldn't wait much longer without putting ourselves—and Melanie—in danger of being re-captured.

And finally, when my chest ached and my nerves were like live wires shooting sparks beneath the surface of my skin, a man slid through the gate just before it slammed shut. He raced toward us, arms and legs pumping, automatic rifle aimed at the ground.

"It's Finn!" I shouted, though I couldn't see the guard's eyes from that distance. "Unlock the doors!"

Anabelle hesitated for a second; then she punched a button in the driver's door and the locks thunked open. I got out, and Finn threw himself into my arms, gun still aimed at the dirt, new tall, firm body pressed against me as his borrowed heart thumped against my chest.

"Are you okay?" he whispered into my ear, and I nodded against his shirt.

"You?"

"Winded." He stepped back far enough that I could see moonlight shine in his bright green eyes. Then he kissed me.

"Get in the car!" Melanie snapped, and I pulled away enough to see her head sticking out of the rear driver's side window.

Finn pushed me toward the front seat, and while I climbed in, he sat next to Melanie, laying his gun across the rear floorboard while she stared at his new face. "We're in. Go!" he shouted, and Anabelle stomped on the gas again. The tires spun beneath us and gravel sprayed the ground. Finally rubber found purchase on what was left of the road, and our stolen car shot off into the dark, leaving the lights of New Temperance behind.

"Okay, Finn and I have a lot to tell you both," I said, twisting to stand on my knees in the front seat, facing backward. "And we have more friends for you to meet. But first, say goodbye to everything you've ever known." I pointed out the rear windshield.

Mellie turned to look, and Anabelle stared into the rearview mirror.

It took great effort for me to turn away from the glass.

Away from the ruin of my own past. But as Finn's hand settled over mine on the cracked upholstery of the seat back between us, I understood that my future lay ahead, as uncertain—and possibly as shrouded in darkness—as the black expanse of badlands spread out before us.

ACKNOWLEDGEMENTS

Thanks to my amazing agent, Merrilee Heifetz,
who makes things happen.

Thanks to my new editor, Wendy Loggia at Delacorte
Press, who championed this book all the
way into print.

Thanks, as always, to my critique partner,
Rinda Elliott, who saw several versions of the
beginning of this book, only a few passages of which
made it into the final text. Your input is invaluable.

Many thanks to the awesome Rachel Clarke
for a critical early read.

A big thank-you to Jennifer Lynn Barnes, for Panera
writing days, company and advice. There is no scene
that cannot be conquered with a little caffeine
and a bowl of soup.

And finally, thanks to everyone at Random House
who has worked on *The Stars Never Rise*. Your
dedication and experience are greatly appreciated.

And finally, thanks to everyone who has worked on
The Stars Never Rise. Your dedication and experience
are greatly appreciated. Thanks so much to Angharad
Kowal, my UK agent, and to Anna Baggaley and
Mira Ink, for making *The Stars Never Rise*
available in the UK.

BOOK 2
IN THE BRAND-NEW
TALON SAGA

Ember Hill left the dragon organisation Talon
to take her chances with rebel dragon Cobalt
and his crew of rogues.

But. with assassins after them and Ember's own
brother helping Talon with the hunt, a reckoning is
brewing…and the secrets hidden by both sides
are shocking and deadly. Soon Ember must
decide: should she retreat to fight another day…
or start an all-out war?

www.miraink.co.uk